SCANDAL
Of The
SEASON

D0057897

Christie Kelley

ZEBRA BOOKS
KENSINGTON PUBLISHING CORP.
http://www.kensingtonbooks.com

ZEBRA BOOKS are published by

Kensington Publishing Corp.
119 West 40th Street
New York, NY 10018

All Kensington titles, imprints, and distributed lines are available at special quantity discounts for bulk purchases for sales promotion, premiums, fund-raising, educational, or institutional use.

Special book excerpts or customized printings can also be created to fit specific needs. For details, write or phone the office of the Kensington Special Sales Manager: Attn.: Special Sales Department. Kensington Publishing Corp., 119 West 40th Street, New York, NY 10018. Phone: 1-800-221-2647.

Zebra and the Z logo Reg. U.S. Pat. & TM Off.

ISBN-13: 978-1-4201-0877-4
ISBN-10: 1-4201-0877-8

First Printing: October 2010

10 9 8 7 6 5 4 3 2 1

Printed in the United States of America

ACKNOWLEDGMENTS

I want to thank my sister, Louise Kelley, RN, FNP, for her assistance with my questions regarding infections and fevers. You're the best! Oh, and I'm sure I'll be calling on your expertise again.

A big thank you to my critique partner and friend, Kathy Love, for reading through this book at lightning speed and helping me sort out my plot. I think I still owe you a glass (maybe a bottle) of wine for that.

Another thank you to my critique partners, The Tarts. Kate Dolan, Kathy Love, Janet Mullany, and Kate Poole thanks for reading what I could get to you and for helping me plot this thing out.

And my heartfelt thanks to Peter Senftleben, my editor, for giving me the extra time needed to get Somerton in line.

Last but certainly not least, thanks to my husband Mike and my sons Stephen and Tommy. Thanks for understanding when I had to shut myself in my office to finish this book. I love you all!

Chapter One

London, 1807

Her smile attracted him like a beacon on that damp, cold night, drawing Anthony nearer to her warmth. But his friends yanked him away from the beautiful woman selling oranges. The force propelled him into the cobbled street. A hackney veered to the left just in time, preventing Anthony Westfield, Viscount Somerton from obliteration before ever giving his father the one thing he wanted—a proper heir.

Anthony stood and then stumbled back over the cobbles, landing at the woman's worn brown boots. Perhaps he shouldn't have had that third, or was it fourth?, glass of brandy. Trey and Nicholas pulled him to his feet.

"Are you all right, sir?" she asked in a small voice.

She couldn't have been more than eighteen. Her big eyes looked light, possibly blue, in the pale illumination of the moon. It wasn't the first time he'd seen her. Whenever he passed this street, she was there with her basket of oranges and a shy smile for him. Every time he saw her, he felt this pull of attraction to her.

She had always favored him with a bright smile, but now her face appeared lined with concern. For him.

"Fine," he mumbled. "Just a bit too much brandy tonight."

Her blond eyebrows lowered in what could only be condemnation. She wasn't the only one who would disapprove of his behavior tonight. Unless he completely sobered up by the time he arrived home, he would catch a severe dressing-down by his father. First gambling, then drinking, and he had an idea of what his friends had in mind next, not exactly proper behavior for the son of an earl. At least in his father's opinion.

Anthony continued to stare at the woman. He wanted to know her name, discover if the scent of oranges was purely from the fruit she sold or if it permeated her skin. Yet once again, his friends pulled him away from her, this time more gently.

"Good night, fair lady," he said as they dragged him away from her.

"Good night, sir." The light sound of her musical voice carried to his ears.

"No more drooling over a woman who isn't about to give you what you want," Nicholas said with a slight slur to his voice. "And we're not about to let you swive some poor innocent." He turned his head and smirked at them both. "One of you should have some experience."

Trey and Nicholas led him around the corner to a house on Maddox Street. After a very successful evening of gambling, his two friends had accomplished the not so difficult task of getting Anthony foxed. Perhaps they knew it was the only way to convince him to come with them. He looked up at the house and shook his head. As a man entered the building, the sound of merriment filled the air.

"Where are we?" Anthony asked, knowing their likely location.

"Lady Whitely has the cleanest girls in town," Trey replied.

The women might claim to be clean, but the last thing Anthony needed was a woman to give him a disease, or worse, a bastard. His father would never forgive him for that dishonor.

"I should be getting home."

Nicholas only laughed. "Don't be nervous, Anthony. We all have to have our first time."

Trey joined in the chortling. "I can't believe you still haven't . . ."

But Anthony hadn't. His father had warned him about the unclean prostitutes around Eton and in town. As the heir to the earldom, Anthony had a responsibility to lead a clean life, marry when the time was right, and have his own heir. Besides, Father had been through enough with Mother dying in a carriage accident when Anthony was only ten and his sister only two. Attempting to live up to his father's wishes was the least he could do. Or at least try to.

"I really need to go," Anthony tried again. But his friends wouldn't release their tight grip on his forearms.

"Not this time," Trey said. "Lady Whitely will find you the perfect girl."

"I don't need to pay for a woman," Anthony grumbled.

"You're not," Nicholas said. "It's your birthday and almost Christmas. Think of it as a gift from two old friends."

Paying for a woman seemed completely wicked and

morally wrong. Women like that only went down the wrong path because they had nothing else. They had no one else.

"I just don't think this is a good—"

"This *is* a good idea. *A very good idea*," Nicholas interrupted. "One of Lady Whitely's ladies will teach you exactly what a man needs to know before he takes a wife."

Anthony frowned. He knew the rudiments of the act; how much more was there to it? "I'm not planning on taking a wife for a few years. And I still—"

"Too late, we're already here," Trey said with a laugh.

They pulled Anthony up the steps, opened the black lacquer door and pushed him into the front hallway. He almost tripped and fell onto the black and white checkered marble floor. Luckily, Nicholas caught him.

"Be a man and do this," Nicholas whispered in his ear. "Your future wife will thank you."

Now his friend sounded like his father. Anthony didn't want a wife yet. He was only eighteen. As he walked into the salon and glanced around, he suddenly realized he did want to learn more about the relations between a man and a woman. Several women strolled around in gowns designed to show off all their assets. Lady Whitely offered an excellent selection of women—redheads, blondes, several brunettes, too. Small-breasted women, large-breasted women, and a few in between.

Their arrival brought whispers and giggles from some of the younger ladies, and leering glances from the older ones. Trey leaned over and spoke softly to one of the women while Anthony continued to gawk. His breeches felt confining against his unruly erection. After blinking to clear his vision, he walked over to the servant selling drinks in the corner and ordered a brandy.

"I haven't seen you here before," a husky voice sounded behind him.

Anthony turned and stared at the woman. Her dress was cut almost to her belly, giving him a splendid view of the valley of her abundant breasts. He picked up his brandy and gulped it down.

"First time?" she asked with a knowing smile. "Well, I do hope you will pick me. My name is Giselle, and I love teaching a man what he needs to know."

"Thank you, Giselle. I'll remember that." Anthony quickly ordered another drink and moved away from the strumpet. There had to be a better way to learn about sex than to lie with a woman who'd been with numerous men.

"Come on, Somerton," Nicholas called to him from the doorway. "We have everything arranged."

Anthony cringed with the thought. But he couldn't back down now, could he? What would his friends think of him? He knew exactly what they would think, that he was a coward. A boy too scared to become a man.

He had to do this at least this once. Then he would do something to help these poor women. He'd find a way of reforming them so they didn't have to work on their backs for a few pounds.

Following Nicholas up the stairs, Anthony took in his surroundings for the first time. When his friends implied they were taking him to a brothel, he'd expected a poorhouse with naked women prancing about. He had never thought that the staircase would be marble, the railing a burled walnut, that a fine crystal chandelier would hang from the two story ceiling, and there would be beautiful—and completely erotic—paintings on the burgundy walls.

Nicholas dragged him down the long corridor. Murmurs and moans filled the cavernous walkway. Hearing the excited voices and the groans of pleasure sent blood racing to Anthony's stiff cock. Perhaps his body wanted this night more than his mind.

"Yes, Dickie. Oh, yes!"

Anthony could only imagine what Dickie was doing to that woman to elicit such a passionate response. Maybe learning a few things before marriage would help him and his future wife—whoever she might be.

"Come along, Anthony. You'll get yours soon enough." Nicholas stopped before the last room on the left and then opened the door.

Anthony followed him inside a small room painted a dark red and filled with all things feminine. A large four-poster bed with a white, Belgian lace coverlet took up most of the room. The table nearest the bed contained a variety of lotions and oils, which permeated the room with exotic scents of the Far East.

"Lady Whitely is assisting another patron but will be here in a few minutes to help you decide on your best choice of woman," Nicholas said by the doorway. "Have fun and stop listening to your father's voice in your head. I'm quite certain even he has been known to visit a brothel."

Anthony almost laughed as Nicholas shut the door behind him. His father would never call on a strumpet. He was the one who always told Anthony to control his base urges and save himself for marriage. After all, Mother had been dead for eight years and his father had never remarried or kept a mistress, at least as far as Anthony knew.

He sat down on the edge of the bed and thought

about what kind of woman he wanted for his first time. Closing his eyes, visions of his little orange blossom, as he liked to think of her, came to his head. Perhaps if he asked for a young woman with blond hair, blue eyes, and a smile like an angel, Lady Whitely could provide him with his fantasy. Opening his eyes, reality sank in. Even if she did find him a woman who looked like his orange blossom, she wouldn't smell fresh and clean with a hint of spicy orange to her.

A quick knock scraped across the door. This was it. Time to face Lady Whitely, choose a lady, and become a man. He rose unsteadily and cleared his throat. "Come in."

The door opened and a woman in her mid-thirties walked into the room. Her dark blond hair had been lavishly swept back, except the few curls artfully left to frame her oval face. As she stared at him, her perfect smile seemed frozen in place.

And he stared back, wondering why she looked slightly familiar to him. Neither moved. They only gazed at each other as if trying to decide how they knew each other. A small clock on the nightstand ticked away the minutes.

"Anthony?" she finally whispered.

That voice! He knew that voice. He'd heard it so many times when he'd been scared at night or when she sang him to sleep.

No!

It could not be her. She was dead. It must be the brandy addling his mind tonight.

"Anthony, is that really you?" Slowly she approached him. She reached her hand out to cup his cheek.

He reeled away from her as if her light touch had burned his skin. Turning back to face her, he said in the most damning tone he'd ever used, "Mother?"

She blinked away tears and pressed her lips tightly together. She acknowledged his condemnation by taking a step away from him.

"It is you, isn't it?" he asked.

"Of course."

He grabbed the post of the bed and hung onto it like a lifeline. Hundreds of questions bounced in his head but only one came out. "Why?"

"Why what?" She moved to the end of the bed, sat on the edge and looked up at him. "Why did I leave you and your sister? Why did I leave your father? Why did I come here and set up such a house?"

There was only one more important question. "Does Father know?"

A delicate shudder visibly rolled through her body. "Yes," she whispered.

Anthony clung tighter to the bedpost. It was one thing for one parent to lie and deceive her child, but quite another when both parents were in collusion to betray their children. But his father would never do such an underhanded thing. He must have only recently discovered the truth of her deception.

"How long has he known?"

"Almost from the day I left."

Anger broke through his drunken haze. "He's known you were alive and did nothing to save you from this life?"

His mother laughed softly. "I know you may find this difficult to believe, but my life has been far better away from your father than with him."

"How can you say that?" He finally released the bedpost, stood in front of her, and hoped the world would stop spinning soon. "Why didn't you let *me* know you were alive?"

"I couldn't, Anthony. I was trying to protect you."

"Protect me?" he all but yelled. "You're the one who needs protecting."

"Why is that?" She swept her arm around the room. "Look around, I am quite safe here."

"You make your living by . . . by . . ."

"By what, Anthony?"

"Lying with any man who would pay you."

She reached out to clasp his hand but he pulled it away. Her dainty shoulders drooped. "I only lie with the men I wish to be with."

"And that is supposed to make me feel better?"

She shrugged. "I suppose not." Slowly she stood before him, barely reaching his shoulders. He had not realized just how small she was . . . petite, with dark blue eyes that flashed in anger at him. "You have no idea what I've been through with your father. When the time is right, I shall be happy to tell you."

"Then tell me now," he growled.

"No. This is not the time. You're intoxicated, and you've had far too much of a shock. You need to go home and think about what you discovered tonight. And when you are ready, I shall explain everything to you."

"I'm supposed to just leave here and accept the fact that my dead mother is actually alive and well, living as a prostitute?"

Her face whitened. "I am not a—"

"Oh? You run this house. You already said that you lie with whomever you please. You are a strumpet."

Before she could try to deny her profession again, he strode to the door and then down the stairs. He passed a footman on his way up the steps with a bottle of fine brandy on a silver salver. Anthony grabbed the bottle and ran from the house of horrors.

He raced down Maddox Street until he nearly

collapsed at the side entrance to St. George's Church. After sitting down on the brick step, he opened the bottle of brandy and gulped a large amount down.

She was alive.

After almost eight years to the day, she was alive.

How?

How had his mother kept herself from them all these years? Hadn't she cared about her children, if not her husband? She was alive. The past eight years had been a complete farce, which made him nothing but a fool for believing everything Father had ever told him.

A prostitute.

A common strumpet.

His mother was no better than a lightskirt. And even worse, his father had known all along. His father had lied to him . . . and his sister. Genna didn't even remember her mother. His sister had been only two when the whore had left two days before Christmas. If it ever came out that their mother was alive and living as a prostitute, his sister would be ruined.

Genna must never discover the truth.

A cold December rain dampened his breeches. He pulled his legs in under the archway of the stoop and took another long draught of the stolen brandy to chase the chill away. He couldn't go home drunk and furious. First, he had to determine exactly what he would say to his lying father when he confronted him.

He'd never felt so lost and alone in all his life. Not even when his mother had died. He shook his head. But she wasn't dead. She left them to go sell herself to anyone who would have her. He dropped his head to his knees.

How could she have left her children? Left him?

The rain turned to a steady downpour as he sat

there drinking the brandy. His mind turned hazy as he watched the carriages drive by his spot. Suddenly something, or rather someone, stumbled over his feet in an effort to be out of the rain.

"Bloody hell," he mumbled. "You almost spilled my brandy."

Blinking, he tried to get his eyes to focus on the small body huddled in the opposite corner. The fresh scent of oranges washed over him. It was her. His orange blossom. The woman he'd truly wanted tonight.

"Doesn't appear to be much left in the bottle," she replied, holding it up.

"Help yourself."

"I intend to." She held the bottle up to her lips and drank some down.

Fascinated, Anthony stared at her slender neck as she tilted her head back and drank from the bottle. "Who are you?"

"No one." She handed the bottle back to him. "Thank you."

"Why are you here?"

She laughed softly. "The same reason as you, to get out of the rain." She shivered and her teeth chattered.

He pushed the bottle back toward her. "Drink."

She accepted it back greedily. "Th—thank you again. It's helpin' me get warmer." She sipped some more before asking, "What's yer name?"

He hesitated just a moment. "Tony," he said, although only Genna called him that. "Why were you out selling oranges so late tonight?"

"I was trying to sell all the oranges. Today wasn't a good day."

"No. Definitely not a good day," he agreed, staring at the basket half full of fruit. The Christmas season was never good. Everything bad seemed to happen then, at least to him.

"Did you lose too much gamblin' tonight?"

"How did you know I'd been gaming?" he asked.

She shrugged. "Isn't that what most young bucks do? It's either gamblin' or whorin'."

Maybe she wasn't the innocent she pretended to be, he thought. "Actually, I won a substantial sum tonight," he said, pride lacing his voice. "What do you do with your money?"

"You mean the measly amount I get by sellin' oranges?" She pressed her lips together. "I just try to get ahead."

He shifted and his shoulder collided with hers. A jingle of coins rang from the pocket in his coat. "What if I offered to buy the rest of your lot?"

"I don't take charity. I work for the extra money I need."

"Hmm, a woman with scruples." He inched closer to her warmth. "I like that."

"I should get home," she whispered.

"Don't."

She turned her head toward his. Mere inches separated them. The urge to move slightly until his lips touched hers was almost too much to resist. Would she taste sweet like the oranges she sold?

"Have another sip." He shifted away and handed her the bottle.

"I have to go." She scrambled to her feet and picked up her basket. "I—"

He stood up quickly. "I want to kiss you," he whispered, trapping her between the stone and his body.

"No," she whispered.

"I need a woman who isn't like her," he muttered.

Anthony brought his lips to hers. Pulling her to

him, he slid his tongue across her lips until she opened for him. Drowning in a desire he'd never felt before, he knew he had to have her. He needed her comfort, her softness. As he brought his hand to cup her breast, he heard her gasp.

"No," she cried softly. "Not like this."

Only Anthony was far too gone to understand her meaning.

Chapter Two

London, 1817

Anthony slammed the door behind him and hurled his hat across the room. Why did this bother him so much tonight? It wasn't as if something similar hadn't happened on several occasions during the past eight years. He crossed the room to the fireplace and held out his hands for some warmth. There certainly hadn't been any warmth from that damned ballroom tonight.

Still, he'd never been specifically asked to leave a party.

Until tonight.

He walked over to the small decanter and poured a glass of whisky. He drank it all down and refilled his glass before heading to a chair. As he took a sip, he heard the door open and wondered at his choice for a place of refuge.

"I rather doubt that will help your problem," the feminine voice said as she strolled closer. She tousled his hair as she walked past his seat and took the chair across from him.

Anthony held up the glass in salute then drank down the rest. "This is helping immensely."

"I just cannot believe Lord Eastleigh made such a spectacle of asking you to leave in front of everyone," Lady Whitely commented.

He grimaced. "Well, if *you* know about it already, I am quite certain the entire *ton* has heard of it by now."

His mother laughed softly. "Now that is an exaggeration by far. Most of the *ton* are snug in their ancestral estates far from London."

"Not all of them," he whispered, thinking of his newly married friends. Perhaps it was what he deserved after all. He gave up being the respectable young gentleman ten years ago.

"You can easily solve this problem," his mother said, staring at him.

"How am I supposed to fix my reputation at this point? My dead mother is alive and the owner of the most popular brothel in London, my father has told everyone that my mother is dead, and the last I've heard, I have killed over twenty people and will seduce innocent virgins in their own beds."

"No one knows about me except you and your father. Besides," she said with a little laugh, "I thought it was only one virgin and not in her bed."

"Exactly. And the last time I checked, I had only killed five people, all of whom had attempted to kill me first."

His mother leaned back against her blue velvet chair and sighed. She scarcely looked like a prostitute in her fine silk gown. Even ten years after discovering her, he still had no idea if she even took men to her bedroom. Not that it mattered. She owned the house and took her cut from the girls.

"Anthony, setting your reputation to rights is not

that difficult. You are the son of an earl. You are wealthy in your own right."

Anthony slammed down the whisky glass on the table. "I am not interested in marriage."

"Why not?"

"You of all people have to ask that question?" He spun the empty glass on the table until he finally slammed his hand down on it. "Perhaps, I am too much like my mother."

She released a long sigh. "Do not let my mistakes taint your future."

"It's far too late for that, Mother."

"Anthony, I know you think I was selfish," she said softly. "If I had known the outcome of leaving you and Genna, I never would have done it."

"I know." He closed his eyes against the painful subject. It wasn't the first time she had tried to explain her actions of eighteen years ago. His father had just as much blame to account for as she did. Perhaps even more. He was the one who declared she'd died. He was the one who told her never to return to the estate or attempt to see her children. He was the one who left her destitute, forcing her to turn to prostitution.

"You will need an heir someday," his mother said, reverting the subject back to his respectability issue. "And marriage to the right woman would solve your problems. All you need is a father who might want a title for his daughter. I believe Miss Susan Coddington would be a good choice. Her father is a baron and I have heard he might like to see her become a viscountess."

He closed his eyes and considered her words. His mother made sense, but he never wanted to marry. Marriage meant trust and honesty. Not something he could ever give to a woman. Then again, if he were only marrying for respectability, it would not matter. As long as she gave him an heir and put him back in the *ton,* he could keep his secrets.

"Anthony, a good woman can greatly improve your reputation. The right one can make you respectable just with a ring on her finger. But only if . . ." her voice trailed off as she stared into the fireplace.

"If what?"

"Only if you stop working for Mr. Ainsworth. As long as you continue doing jobs for him, your reputation will continue to suffer."

He blew out a breath and wondered if her comments stemmed from the desire to see his reputation corrected or her need to keep him out of harm's way. Not that it mattered either way. As long as he worked for Ainsworth, he put both his life and reputation at risk.

"Anthony, I have something for you to give to your sister." She walked over to a small chest on her desk and pulled out a pendant. Rubies sparkled in the light of the fire as she held it out for him.

"You want me to give this to Genna?"

"Yes, as a Christmas gift."

"Christmas isn't for three weeks," Anthony commented with a scowl. Christmas always reminded him of the dreadful times in his life.

"I want to make sure she receives it before her wedding. Tell her I wore it on my wedding day and you thought she would like to wear it on hers."

Anthony reached for the rubies and studied them. They were a fine quality, but he wondered at their origins. "Am I supposed to tell her you gave them to her?"

"Oh, Anthony," she clutched her hands over his, "please, just do this for me."

Unable to resist tears in her eyes, he nodded. "I will tell her that Father found them with your things."

"Tell her *you* found them in the attic, please."

He had learned so little of what had made his mother leave his father. When he had finally made his return to this house a year after that fateful night, she had told him of his father's infidelities. He knew the reason for her leaving involved several mistresses and a bastard daughter.

"As you wish," he said.

She released his hands. "Promise me you shall at least think about what I've said concerning your reputation, Anthony."

He stood up to leave and looked back at her. Before he even thought of marriage he had one wrong that he had to make right. Finding that woman had been the one thing he had never been able to do . . . until now.

"I will consider what you said carefully."

Anthony quietly walked into Lord Selby's house. While he had been invited to join the festivities celebrating the christening of Selby's daughter, there was only one reason to be here. The cold December air had chilled him to the bone but the house was warm. He handed his greatcoat to the butler and walked into the salon.

After a journey that took him to France for five months, he was exhausted and done playing the dual roles thrust upon him. He searched for the only reason he had attended tonight. Sophie Reynard arched a brow at him and then inclined her head toward the hall. He waited while she walked out of the room before joining her in Selby's study.

"Welcome back, Anthony. How was your trip? Successful?"

The last thing he wanted to talk about was chasing

all over France for an English spy. "Enough, Sophie. I have waited an additional five months to get her name. I want it now."

Sophie laughed softly. "Very well, I shall keep my promise. The woman you are searching for is Anne Smith."

Anthony waited for some sign of recognition but her name was as common as she had been. Just an orange seller. "Do you know if she is still alive? It's been ten years."

"She is definitely alive."

Anthony frowned seeing the way Sophie looked down when she answered. "What are you keeping from me?"

Sophie smiled and patted his cheek. "Why would I keep anything from you, my dearest brother? The woman you are searching for was in the room you just left."

"She's here? In Selby's salon?"

"Yes," Sophie replied with a smile.

"Dammit, Sophie," he almost shouted. "Why didn't you tell me in there?"

"Because of just that reaction." She stared at him for a moment.

Anthony glared back at his half sister. With her raven hair and gray eyes, she looked nothing like him but there was a slight resemblance to his sister, Genna. And Sophie seemed to have inherited the same stubborn attitude he had from their father.

After learning about Sophie's existence, he had sought her out, assuming he would find her living in squalor. Instead, he'd discovered a beautiful seventeen-year-old living in Mayfair with an aunt who acted as her guardian. He then discovered that his father paid all of her expenses as long as she never revealed his name as her father.

Finding Sophie nine years ago had been one of the few positive outcomes of his family disaster. Even if sometimes he wanted to throttle her, such as now.

"The timing must be perfect," Sophie said quietly.

"The timing of what?"

"When you meet her again."

"You are not matching us. The only thing that matters is I meet her and apologize for my actions." Sophie's medium skills had made her the eminent matchmaker amongst the *ton*. But only a few people knew how she had coerced him into assisting her with three of the matches.

"I agree," Sophie said, then walked toward him. "You two would make a disastrous pair."

Anthony ignored her remark and reached into his jacket pocket. Pulling out the ruby necklace, he dangled it from his hand until she grabbed it from him. He had only brought it with him so she could tell him more about it.

"It is beautiful," Sophie said with awe.

"Yes, it is. Genna will love it."

Sophie held the necklace tightly between both hands. "It is from Lady Whitely, is it not?"

"Yes, a Christmas gift for Genna to wear on her wedding day," he replied.

"It is very old. I believe it might have belonged to your grandmother, too."

"I had hoped it might be a family heirloom and not some bauble bought from the revenues of the brothel."

Sophie opened her hands and looked at it with a touch of sadness in her eyes. "But she will never know it was from her mother so it doesn't have the sentimental value it should."

"I will tell her Mother wore it on her wedding day. That will be enough for her."

"If you say so." She handed him the ruby necklace. "Don't lose that before Christmas."

Anthony tilted his head and looked at his sister. "Do you really think I would let anything happen to this?"

"Of course not."

"I must go find Anne Smith," he said, walking toward the door.

"Anthony, be kind to her," Sophie said quietly. "She has been through much in her life."

Anthony blew out a breath. Knowing he'd caused some of that pain, he nodded to his sister. "Very well."

He strolled out of the study and back to the salon. Since she had been an orange seller, he assumed she must have gone into service. Footmen lined the room, but no female servants were present. Perhaps he had just missed her.

As the moments passed, he made conversation with Selby, but his gaze watched every servant who entered the room. None fit the vague description that had stayed with him for ten long years of a petite blonde with blue eyes.

Frustration grew as he realized Sophie must have lied to him again. He eased away from the conversation to speak with Lady Selby. He found her sitting on the sofa, holding her infant daughter, Isabel.

"Somerton, come sit with me," she said with a kind smile.

Marriage and motherhood suited her, he decided. "How are you, Lady Selby?"

"Very well. Would you like to hold her?"

He was not the type of man to fawn over children, especially infants, but something made him agree. She placed the squirming little girl in his arms and showed him how to support her neck. As he looked down at her, she gurgled and gave him a toothless smile.

"You are a natural," she commented. "It took Banning several days to feel comfortable holding her."

Anthony smirked. "Selby never learned how to treat a lady."

"Oh?" a deep voice replied.

Anthony glanced up to see Selby glaring down at him. "It is true."

Selby reached down and plucked his daughter out of Anthony's arms. "I think I should warn you to keep your hands off my daughter."

Lady Selby laughed softly. "I think even Somerton likes them a little older than Isabel, Banning."

"I do prefer that they can walk," Anthony said with a note of sarcasm. "Have you seen Miss Reynard?"

"Sophie?" Lady Selby asked. "Why, no. I noticed she left the room and never returned. Unlike you. Is there something you need from her?"

"No." Anthony resisted the urge to roll his eyes at his friend's wife. Her tone inferred a sensual meaning. Obviously, Sophie had never told a soul about their relationship. Just the way his father wanted it.

Sophie must have sneaked out without him seeing her. And with no other hints as to whom this Anne Smith might be, he should leave. His stomach decided to rumble. Perhaps he didn't have to leave just yet.

He found Lord Blackburn at the refreshment table. "Good evening, Blackburn."

"You missed a beautiful christening, Somerton."

"Well, I didn't think the church could survive me walking inside."

Blackburn chuckled. "Most likely not. I heard about the incident at Lord Eastleigh's ball last night. I certainly hope his boorish actions won't stop you from getting back into Society."

"Why should they?" he asked with more carelessness than he felt.

"Exactly. Marrying Jennette and returning to Society was the best thing I could have done."

Anthony preferred to ignore Blackburn's comment and selected a few items from the refreshment table. Seeing the eggnog in a large crystal bowl, his stomach roiled. He needed no reminders of the upcoming season. "Eggnog, already?"

Blackburn chuckled. "It was my wife's idea. She had Lady Selby's cook make some to get us thinking about Christmas. Personally, I think it was Jennette's way of reminding me I had better find her something nice for Christmas."

Blackburn had done exactly what Anthony's mother had recommended and it worked out perfectly for him. Blackburn not only had his reputation on the mend but a loving wife, too.

Anthony speared a piece of ham and dropped it on his plate. Reaching for another piece, he stopped when he felt a slight nudge near his side.

"Oh, excuse me."

Anthony smiled down at the petite woman. She pushed her spectacles up her nose and glanced at him. Something about her seemed slightly familiar, but he could not place her. With her high-neck gray dress, tight chignon and spectacles, he assumed she must be one of Lady Selby's bluestocking friends.

"Have we met?"

"I do not believe so." She tried to step back but Lady Blackburn was directly behind her.

"Somerton," Lady Blackburn said with a nod. "I must apologize. I bumped into Victoria who must have nudged you." She took a step back allowing her friend a small bit of space. "This is a dear friend of mine, Miss Seaton. She runs—"

"The home for orphans on Maddox," Anthony finished for her. That was why she looked familiar. He must have seen her coming in or out of the house next to Lady Whitely's.

Lady Blackburn smiled. "I might have known you would be aware of her."

"Only her work." Anthony glanced over at Miss Seaton who looked as if she would like the floor to swallow her. She continued to stare at the toes of her shoes barely visible from the bottom of her muslin skirts. The poor woman looked so completely out of place here. He wondered how the daughter of a vicar had become such good friends with these highborn ladies.

"Victoria, this is Viscount Somerton," Lady Blackburn said with a smile.

"It is a pleasure to meet you, Miss Seaton."

"Thank you, my lord," she replied meekly with a quick curtsy. "Jennette, I must take my leave now."

"Of course," Lady Blackburn replied. "Come say your farewells to Avis and Elizabeth."

Anthony watched as the ladies walked toward Lady Selby and Lady Kendal. What was it about Miss Seaton that made him unable to look away? He shook his head. Lust. Though there was no real reason for that either. He'd taken advantage of his time in France to avail himself of too many women.

Watching Miss Seaton made no sense. She was an innocent, barely able to maintain eye contact with him. And that was the last thing he needed or wanted in a woman. He wanted willing and experienced without the artifice of a prostitute. Miss Seaton was none of those things.

Chapter Three

Victoria relaxed against the comfort of her bed and breathed in deeply. Even now, an hour later, her hands still trembled. How could she have done that? In front of her friends!

Even worse, at her friend's home and to a viscount!

A very handsome viscount.

There was something about Lord Somerton. His lips, she thought with a smile. They were the most perfect lips she had ever seen on a man. She grimaced. There had been one other man with lips so perfect. Victoria shook her head. That man had not been a viscount.

He'd only been a drunken young buck with sandy brown hair and green eyes. Viscount Somerton's eyes were hazel. Which, her mind countered, could sometimes be considered a shade of green. It could not be him. He would have said something, or given her some indication that he knew of her. Unless he had been so foxed that night, he didn't remember her.

No, it was definitely not him, she decided.

Slowly, she reached into her skirt pocket and withdrew today's catch. The rubies sparkled in the dim candlelight. Staring at the pendant, fear turned to frustration. The intricate gold design formed a crest over the largest ruby in the center.

"Dammit!"

She threw the necklace on the bed. What was she to do now? That pendant was too unique to take to a pawnshop. The broker might recognize the crest and turn her into the constable. How could she have been so stupid?

A small knock on her door sounded and then an older woman entered without waiting for a reply. "Did you get anythin' good?"

Maggie sat down on the bed and stared at the rubies spreading across the coverlet like spilled blood.

"Too good," Victoria replied.

"How did you get somethin' like that?" Maggie's voice raised an octave.

Victoria covered her face with her hands. "I had no luck on Bond Street this afternoon. So I picked a man's pocket at the christening party. I thought I might find some spare coins. I never thought I would find that. I was so nervous I just dropped it into my pocket. Jennette bumped into me, and I'm quite certain he felt me reaching in his pocket."

"What are you goin' to do?"

Slowly, she removed her hands from her face and shook her head. "I have no idea. Look at the crest. I can't pawn this."

Maggie stared at the pendant. "I have a brother who might give you some money for it."

"I cannot take the risk." Victoria picked up the necklace and put it around her neck. She grabbed her hand mirror and gasped at her reflection. "Could you imagine wearing something so fine?"

"Not me. Maybe you with those fine manners."

Fine manners, she scoffed. If Maggie knew the truth, she wouldn't be so impressed. Anyone can learn manners. Victoria removed the necklace and stared at it once again. Suddenly, the door to her room hurtled open and a little girl raced inside.

"Miss Torie," she screamed and threw her small body into Victoria's arms. "I had a bad dream."

Victoria wrapped the little girl into a tight embrace. "Shh, Bronwyn. Everything is all right now."

"It's not," she sobbed. "The man was after me again. He wanted to take me away from here."

"That's not going to happen," Victoria whispered. Of all the children in her care, Bronwyn was special. She had been her first. Without Bronwyn, there was no telling how different her life would be now. The little girl had saved her from the inevitable course her life had been heading toward—prostitution.

Victoria smoothed the girl's curly black hair and whispered soothing words to her. Feeling her rhythmic breathing, Victoria knew the girl had fallen back to sleep.

"That's the second time this week," Victoria whispered to Maggie. "It's not like her."

"And it's always the same dream about a man tryin' to take her away from here."

"Do you think I should be worried?" Victoria asked.

"It's just a phase. I'll take her back," Maggie whispered.

Victoria released her embrace and let Maggie lift Bronwyn from her arms. She stared down at the necklace again and knew what she would do with it. Little Bronwyn might only be nine, but someday, she would wear fine things like silk gowns and ruby necklaces. And if not, maybe by then she could pawn it for the girl.

Standing up, Victoria moved to her linen press

and the box with Bronwyn's name on it. She placed the pendant in the box. When Bronwyn was older and the necklace forgotten about, then Victoria could give it to the child.

Now her only concern was finding something else to pawn before they ran out of food and coal. She knew she could go next door and ask Lady Whitely for money, but she hated that idea.

It was Victoria's fault that they were low on funds. She had brought two new children in last month who were not like the others. Then there were the few trinkets she had bought the children to give them on Christmas morning. And she never should have bought presents for Avis's and Jennette's babies. She should have said she could not attend the christening party. But she wanted to see her friends.

She wanted to be one of them instead of always on the fringe.

It mattered not, she told herself for the millionth time. She would never truly be one of them. And today's actions proved that. What would they think if they discovered she was nothing more than a petty thief?

Anthony walked up the steps of his home on Duke Street. He loved the small home that his grandmother's inheritance had afforded him. It had allowed him to leave his father's house of lies. For almost ten years Anthony had lived here . . . alone.

Why was that suddenly rubbing him wrong? He loved his life. With plenty of cousins, he had no reason to marry just to give his father an heir. But the past few months something felt off in his life, and Lord Eastleigh's actions at that party last night had only made it worse. Maybe being away for five months had made him forget how much he loved his unfettered life.

Nevertheless, even that notion didn't sit well with him. After watching three friends fall madly in love and marry, he could not possibly think he wanted that too. He didn't. He could have any woman he wanted, whenever he wanted. What man would want more than that? So what could be bothering him?

Perhaps it was his need to apologize to that woman. *Anne Smith.*

She was the only regret he had in his life. He'd been so damned drunk that night her words never reached his brandy soaked brain. Taking that poor girl up against the wall of the church had been more than bad form. It had been rape. And at the very least, he owed her an apology and probably much more than that.

For years, he had been trying to find her. But without a name, he'd had no luck. He finally went to Sophie for advice two years ago, and she promised to help him find the girl's name with her abilities as a medium. But before she had given him Anne Smith's name, she'd required his assistance with matching her friends.

Tomorrow, he would return to Sophie's and demand an explanation. He wanted more than a name now. He wanted to know everything about the woman.

Reese opened the door as Anthony reached the top step.

"Good evening, sir."

"Good evening, Reese." Anthony shook the light snow off his greatcoat and handed it to his butler. "I believe I shall retire."

Reese glanced over at the clock in the parlor. "It is only ten."

Anthony chuckled. "I am tired tonight. After all the traveling, I want an early night in my bed."

"Are you expecting someone?"

Anthony smirked at Reese's knowing remark. "Believe it or not, I just want some sleep tonight."

"As you wish, my lord."

Anthony trudged up the stairs eager for the comforts of his bed. He could hear the sound of his valet's footsteps following him up the stairs. "Evening, Huntley."

"Evening, my lord. Did you have an enjoyable time?"

"Hardly."

Walking into his room, Huntley trailed behind. "I can manage my clothing tonight, Huntley. You may retire."

"Yes, my lord. If you are certain?"

"I promise not to leave my trousers and jacket in a rumpled heap."

"Very well." Huntley left the room with one glance back as if expecting to catch Anthony tossing his jacket on the floor.

As the door shut, Anthony fell onto the bed. Exhaustion had settled into his bones. Slowly, he untied his cravat and then unraveled it from his neck. He thought about tossing it on the floor but folded it neatly and then placed the cloth on his bureau.

Remembering the necklace in his jacket pocket, he reached down to pull it out.

"Bloody hell!"

There was nothing in his pocket but a piece of lint. He mentally traced his tracks throughout the day. After picking up the necklace from Lady Whitely yesterday, he'd placed it on his nightstand. This evening, he had dropped it into his jacket pocket and then went directly to Selby's home for the christening party. Then he'd shown the piece to Sophie and replaced it in his pocket. Perhaps it had fallen out during the ride home.

He strode down the stairs. "Reese, I need the carriage

checked for a ruby necklace I lost. And send a footman to Lord Selby."

Anthony continued to walk toward his study. He wrote a quick note to Banning explaining what he had lost. "This must be given directly to Lord Selby and wait for a reply."

"Yes, sir." Reese took the missive and walked away.

With nothing left to do but wait, Anthony paced the small confines of his study. There had to be something he was missing. He walked to the decanter of whisky and poured himself a large glass. The liquid washed over his tongue and warmed him.

What had he missed?

He drank down the rest of his whisky and then he poured another glass. Lifting the glass to his lips, he stopped and frowned. Miss Seaton had bumped him near the refreshment table. He shook his head. The woman took in orphans to keep them from turning to crime. He'd met plenty of pickpockets in his line of work. She was no pickpocket.

Who else could it have been? No one had come close enough to him to reach into his pocket. Besides, there was not a person at that party who needed the money the necklace could bring.

"Sir, the groomsmen checked the carriage thoroughly and found nothing."

Anthony turned toward Reese. "Any word from Lord Selby?"

"Not yet, sir."

"Very well."

He moved his attention back to the glass of whisky in his hand and slowly sipped it. There was no hole in his pocket and no one at the party who would have pinched the necklace from him. His mind returned to Miss Seaton. She reminded him slightly of the woman he searched for but, again, she was no orange seller. He'd heard enough about her to know she was the daughter of a vicar. And yet, she matched the vague description he remembered from ten years ago.

He tried to think back to the other times he'd seen the woman selling oranges. The only thing that came to mind was her blond hair, blue eyes, and a smile that brightened her face and creased two dimples in her cheeks. He'd never seen Miss Seaton smile but doubted the timid woman had such a sweet smile.

Damn. If only he hadn't been so damn foxed that night.

None of this would have happened.

"Sir, a note from Lord Selby," Reese said, walking into the room.

Anthony grabbed the note and read it quickly. Selby had found nothing but promised to continue searching. He crumpled the paper and threw it into the small fire burning in the fireplace. "Damn."

"Do you need anything else, sir?"

"No." Just answers. Tomorrow morning he would make another call on Sophie and then he might even pay a visit to the angelic Miss Seaton at her home for orphans.

Angelic?

"Oh hell," he muttered, disgusted with himself.

He'd been deceived by the oldest ruse. Send in the angelic woman whom no one would suspect and have her perform the crime. Well Miss Seaton had no idea that she had just cheated the devil.

And the devil always wins.

Chapter Four

Victoria walked to Sophie's house hoping her friend could give her a little advice. After spending most of the night brooding over her meeting with Lord Somerton, Victoria prayed Sophie would tell her everything would be all right. Perhaps Sophie could use her skills as a medium to let her know Somerton wasn't the man from her past.

Although, Victoria was beginning to think he was the man.

"Good afternoon, Miss Seaton," Sophie's butler said as he opened the door for her.

"Good afternoon, Hendricks. Is Miss Reynard home?"

"I believe she has a caller, but let me see if she would like you to wait."

"Thank you." Victoria sat in the velvet-padded chair in the hall.

Hendricks returned quickly with a smile. "She asked you to wait in the salon."

As she started up the stairs to the salon, she heard a commotion from the back corridor. Loud footsteps stomped forward. She backed herself against the wall as if to disappear.

"Anthony, wait," Sophie called to the man.

Victoria watched as Lord Somerton halted and turned toward Sophie. Anthony . . . Tony? Her breath caught. Oh, dear Lord, it must be him.

"I have nothing to wait for except more lies from you."

"I told you the truth yesterday. She was there," Sophie said.

"Sophie, if you know her name then you can tell me if she is in service to the Selbys or not."

Sophie sighed. "No, she is not."

Somerton grimaced. "Then it is as I thought."

"What will you do?"

"I do not have any ideas just yet. But friend or not, she will pay for what she did."

Sophie straightened. "Just as you shall pay for what you did."

"Fair enough." Somerton walked toward the door. Hendricks opened the door, and Somerton started out. He turned as if to say one last thing to Sophie when he caught sight of her.

Sophie glanced up and noticed her standing on the staircase. Her eyes rounded in surprise.

He started to step back into the house, but Sophie was there with a hand to his chest.

"Sophie," he said in a low voice.

"Not now. You know nothing yet, and you know better than to make assumptions."

"Good afternoon, Miss Seaton." He stared up at her with cold eyes.

"Good afternoon, Lord Somerton." Fear made her tremble. He knew nothing, she told herself again. If he knew she'd taken the necklace, he would say or do something.

"Have a pleasant afternoon, Miss Seaton. Be warned,

I hear the evening may turn nasty." He turned and left without another word.

Victoria wondered about his words. His ominous tone sent a trickle of apprehension through her. Did he suspect she was the thief?

Sophie walked quickly to her. "I had no idea you were there, Victoria."

"I am sorry. I didn't mean to overhear you. I didn't know you knew Lord Somerton. Is he a client?"

Sophie had become quite the thing as a matchmaker among the *ton*. Perhaps Somerton was looking for a wife.

"No, he is not a client," Sophie replied flatly. "We met many years ago."

Victoria walked into the salon expecting Sophie would continue, but she did not.

"Now, what brings you here today?" Sophie asked as she sat in the brocade wingback chair.

"I need some assistance," Victoria started slowly. She had to know if the handsome man making veiled threats was whom she thought he was. "There is a man in my past."

"And he wasn't exactly a gentleman, was he?"

Victoria frowned and looked over at her friend. How much could Sophie know about this? "No, he was a gentleman but did not act as such. I fear he may be returning to my life, and I was hoping you might tell me if that is true."

Sophie bit down on her lower lip. She reached over and clasped Victoria's hand. "Yes, it is true. I think in your heart, you already knew this, didn't you."

Victoria trembled again. "Does he know who I am? *Do you?*"

Sophie nodded. "I know you are not Victoria Seaton."

Victoria slapped her hand over her mouth. Everything

she had spent the last ten years trying to forget came crashing back to her. She had to determine a way out of this mess.

"Does he know who I am?"

"Yes," Sophie whispered. "I don't believe he means to harm you, Victoria. I think he wishes to apologize for his actions."

"What do you know about this?"

Sophie sat back, and said, "I believe you and this man had a brief relationship. After which, you somehow came into some money, changed your name, and opened your home to several orphans."

"That is all you know?" Victoria asked.

"I know your real name was Anne Smith. And I know who the man was who treated you so poorly."

Victoria stared at the floral design on the rug. "It's him, isn't it?"

"You don't remember?"

"He only told me his name was Tony. And he was different then. Younger. His hair was longer and lighter. His nature softer and sweeter—"

"Somerton sweet?" Sophie asked incredulously. "In my nine years of knowing him, I would never have called him that. He is one of the hardest men I have ever met. He seems to care about nothing and will do whatever it takes to get what he wants or needs."

Sophie's perception of Somerton didn't match up with the young man Victoria remembered. He had been the only gentleman who actually said hello to her when she sold oranges. He would smile at her and not in a leering manner. He could not have changed so drastically.

"What do I do now, Sophie?"

"You will return home, and hopefully, if he comes

to pay you a visit, it will be to apologize for his actions. Accept his apology and he will leave."

"He can expose me for the fraud I am," Victoria cried. "Everything I have spent the last ten years building will be for naught. If Avis, Jennette, or Elizabeth discovers the truth, they will hate me for lying to them."

"Your friends will not desert you. But if you are that concerned, then you must make that part of the apology. You only accept it as long as he promises to keep your identity secret."

Victoria nodded. Deep inside her was still the fearless girl she had been. The girl who at nine could pick a man's pocket without being caught. She had known every street and alley in Whitechapel. She only hoped her last ten years of playing the timid mouse hadn't destroyed her.

"I am finished with this business," Anthony said, glancing around the room at White's. To anyone who might see them, they appeared to be two friends settling in for a drink.

Roger Ainsworth sat back against his chair and smiled. "You do not mean it. You love the excitement of it all. Travel and intrigue, you live for it."

Anthony raked his fingers through his short hair. He'd considered his mother's words with extreme care for the past day and she was right. In order to get his respectability back, he had to stop performing jobs for Ainsworth. He lowered his voice to a whisper. "I am tired, Ainsworth. I've been doing this for almost ten years. I have caught your spies and other assorted criminals. I am done."

"You cannot be."

Anthony raised an eyebrow at him in question. "I can."

"Do not make me beg, Somerton. There is no one else I can turn to for this. It's quite a simple case and you do not even have to leave the country."

"No."

"Please, hear me out before you say no again." Ainsworth reached for the bottle of whisky and poured two glasses.

"Drinking on the job?"

"If that is what I must do to get you to agree, the prince won't mind."

Anthony wondered how much information the prince even had of these jobs.

"All I need you to do is collect a missive. Marcus Hardy will be at Lord Farleigh's house party starting on the twelfth of December. My source said Hardy will be given information regarding a plot to kill the prince regent. All you have to do is collect the note and bring it to me as quickly as possible."

"Farleigh?"

Ainsworth nodded and then sipped his drink.

Anthony wondered exactly how Ainsworth would get him invited to that party. Farleigh's jealousy of his wife was renowned, especially with Anthony.

He sipped his whisky and tilted his head back. This was the last thing he wanted to do. Until the note came requesting his presence here, he had planned to watch the sneaky little Miss Seaton. But the royal family was in an uproar since Princess Charlotte's untimely death only weeks ago. With the question of succession still in doubt, if anyone managed to kill the prince regent it would produce turmoil.

"And?" Anthony prodded.

"That is it. The information will be in a missive that someone will give to Hardy."

"So all I have to do is steal it away from him. Why not get Roberts for the job?"

Ainsworth glanced down at the papers on the table. "Roberts was killed trying to get this information three days ago. Besides, I need your ears there listening in case anything is mentioned. And I need someone who can steal into a room to find this note if needed."

Anthony muttered a curse. "All right. I will do this as long as you realize that this is my last case. Forever."

Ainsworth stood and held out his hand. "I do understand. Thank you."

As Ainsworth left, Anthony sat back in his chair in thought. Somehow, he would need to allay Farleigh's jealousy. A smile lifted his lips upward. All he needed was a mistress to bring with him. No one of any social importance attended Farleigh's parties because of Lady Farleigh. Therefore, no one would mind him bringing a woman with him. But who?

He had plenty of women he could ask, but he knew they would all want a commitment to become his real mistress, or worse, his wife. He had no real interest in any of them other than an occasional night of pleasure. There had to be someone.

He downed his whisky and checked the time. Damn. It was already almost two in the afternoon. He'd promised the boy watching Miss Seaton that he would not be gone long.

After nodding to a few acquaintances, he walked out of the men's club and found his carriage. He rode to Sophie's house to see if Miss Seaton was still speaking with his half sister. Anthony found the boy standing by a lamppost watching Sophie's home.

"Anyone left the house, lad?" he asked, as he approached the boy.

"She's still in there."

Anthony pulled a few coins from his pocket and handed them to him. "Thank you, but I shall take over now."

"Yes, sir," the boy said and then ran down the street with a smile.

Anthony waited in his carriage for almost an hour before she finally departed. Foolish woman had no maid trailing behind. He stepped out of the carriage just as she was walking toward it.

She stopped and gaped at him with wide eyes. As she started to turn the opposite direction, he clasped her elbow and steered her toward the waiting carriage.

"Lord Somerton!" she gasped.

"Miss Seaton, it is a fine afternoon, is it not?"

"You must let go of me," she whispered as if trying not to make a scene.

"Get in the carriage, Miss Seaton. We have much to discuss."

She attempted to twist out of his grip once more. Realizing her defeat, she entered the carriage. She sat back against the velvet squabs and crossed her arms over her chest.

Anthony climbed inside and sat across from the defiant lady. Her quiet beauty surprised him. She had put her hair up into a loose chignon and several blond tendrils fell across her pale cheeks. Seeing her again, he noticed just how petite she was and far too thin.

And this time, he had no doubt she was the woman he'd been searching for these past ten years.

"You are very good," he said quietly.

Her blue eyes widened slightly. "At what, my lord?"

"At your chosen profession."

"I take care of eight children. Nothing more," she said in a tight voice.

"Indeed."

She glanced out the window. "Where are you taking me and why?"

"We shall be there soon." He wondered at her calm demeanor. Most women forced into a carriage would be close to hysterics by now. Something told him instead of panic, she was plotting her escape.

Victoria sat across from the demon lord trying to determine the best course of action. Even if she managed to escape his clutches, he knew where she lived. He knew who her friends were. He would find her.

It appeared there was nothing more to do but wait and discover his intentions. As she watched the shadows fall over his handsome face, she didn't believe his intentions were respectable.

Seeing him in the light of day, she wondered how she could have imagined it wasn't him. The man from her past. Somerton had changed the direction of her life whether he realized it or not. And she preferred he never know how much what happened that night affected her life.

The carriage finally slowed to a stop. Somerton quickly scrambled to get down before she could make a move. Her lips turned upward. She could never outrun the man.

"I am not sure what you are smiling about, but if I were you, I would be worried," he warned.

"About what?" she answered in defiance.

"About what I might have planned for you."

She climbed down and attempted to pass him only to find her elbow back in his strong grip. "I doubt it could be any worse than what you have already done to me."

His jaw tightened until a little tic started beating near his chin. "Let's go."

Victoria smiled fully. She had found her weapon against him. He led her up the steps of a small townhome only a few blocks from her own house. Well, her home in principle. She certainly could never afford such a place.

The door opened and a gape-mouthed butler stood silent as his employer forced a woman into the house.

"She is not to leave without my permission, Reese."

"Y—yes, sir."

He guided her up the stairs to the second floor and then flung open a door. After pushing her into the room, he blocked the door with his large body. A sliver of fear swept down her back. His face had darkened, and his eyes turned from a lovely shade of hazel to a dark green.

"What do you plan to do now?" she asked insolently. There was nothing he could do to her that he hadn't done in the past.

"Get to the truth."

"Truth about what?"

"Everything," he answered ominously.

He walked toward her slowly. Victoria glanced around for an alternate means of escape. Being two stories up, with the door blocked by an angry man, she could only retreat. She continued to step backwards until her legs hit the large bed. Why had it taken her this long to realize he had her in a bedroom? His bedchamber from the looks of it.

"What do you want from me, Somerton?"

A small half smile lifted his lips upward. "What's mine."

Victoria swallowed the lump in her throat. He could not possibly know about the necklace. Oh God, what if he did? She was never one to let panic overtake her but suddenly her world spun around her. He must never discover where she'd put the necklace.

"I have no idea what you mean," she said evenly.

He stepped close enough that she could inhale the scent of his sandalwood soap. "It was gold with rubies."

She pushed away all her anxieties. She could lie her way out of this situation. "And why would I have such a thing? I am a poor woman who cares for orphans, nothing more."

Why couldn't she take her gaze off his lips?

"Indeed? So if I were to rummage through your home, I would find nothing that matched the item that I am looking for?"

She stared at him. "Go ahead and check my home, I do not have your necklace."

Suddenly, he pushed her back against the bed and confined her with his body. She thrust at his shoulders until he seized her wrists and pinned them over her head with his hand. She felt his other hand reach down to her reticule and grab the contents.

She twisted under him trying to break free only to feel his erection pressing into her thigh. "Let me up!"

He chuckled softly near her ear. "Are you certain? There are just so many possible things we could do."

"I do not have your necklace."

"I never said it was a necklace."

Chapter Five

Anthony watched the play of emotions on her face and tried not to laugh. She was, without a doubt, attempting to formulate a believable lie. He'd promised his mother that Genna would receive the necklace on Christmas morning so she could wear it on her wedding day planned for New Year's Eve. That only gave him a few weeks to find it or have her return it to him.

"All right," she said with a shrug. "You caught me. Now what?"

He blinked and shook his head slightly. Had she really just admitted her guilt that easily? He rolled off her to sit on the bed. "I beg your pardon?"

"Perhaps I did take a necklace from you. Do you plan on telling the constable?"

How had this slip of a woman turned the tables on him? He'd expected pleading, crying, perhaps even a suggestive bribe to keep him quiet. Not the goddamned truth.

"Should I?" he finally replied.

"Not if you want your necklace returned," she said with a hint of a smile.

"You are holding my necklace for ransom?"

She slowly stood and walked a step away from him. "It's a rather brilliant plan, don't you think? After all, you have no idea where the necklace is. For all you know, I might have pawned it."

Somehow, the chit had read him that quickly. She knew the necklace was important to him. Damn her. There was only one thing to do—bluff.

"The necklace is not that important. Still, you did commit a crime, so I think I shall take your advice and call a constable."

She eyed him carefully with one blond eyebrow arched. "Then do it. And you will never find out where the necklace is because I would never be so foolish as to keep it in my home. Only I know who is storing it for me."

He rose and took a step closer. "And what about your friends? What will they say when they discover you are a pickpocket? And that they don't even know your real name, Anne Smith."

She visibly swallowed and then retreated a step. "If they are truly my friends, they will understand."

Anthony shook his head. "They are ladies of quality. Their husbands would never allow them to come near you or associate with you ever again."

"Then it appears we are at an impasse."

"I really don't see it that way," he commented.

"What do you really want, Lord Somerton? There is more here than just a necklace." She crossed her slim arms over her chest.

Anthony sighed. If he ever wanted a mistress, she would be exactly his type. Shrewd, beautiful, and with the ability to keep him guessing. She was the perfect woman to take on this assignment with him. Except, the only way he could have her accompany him was as his mistress.

And that was a dangerous proposition.

Still, short of absconding with one of his mother's ladies, he knew of no one who wouldn't be looking for something more out of the situation. He only needed a woman to pretend to be his mistress. This little charlatan might be just the thing. She obviously needed money or she wouldn't have pinched the pendant from him. Paying her would also absolve some of his guilt for what he'd done to her.

"Very well, take a seat." He pointed to a chair near the window. For once, she did as he asked without a fight.

Once she sat, he started, "I have a proposition for you, Miss Seaton."

"Oh, I'm sure you do," she said softly.

"Not in that manner. Well, in a way it is in the manner you believe."

She stood up as if thinking about walking out of the room.

"Sit down, Miss Seaton," he ordered gruffly.

"What do you want from me?"

"I need some assistance with a slight problem I have. And I believe you are the solution to my issue."

She tilted her head and a blond tendril fell across her face. She blew the hair out of her eyes. "What is your problem?"

"I need a mistress," he admitted quietly.

She smirked. "Oh? And you think I will just fall into bed with you because you are a viscount and you made me an offer?"

A part of him wanted to throttle her while another part wanted to reach over and kiss her smart mouth. He did his best to ignore both urges. "In order for me to attend a party in the country, I need a mistress."

"Well, I have to admit, I have never heard this excuse before."

"I would like you to assist me."

"And what do I get out of this?" she asked, staring over at him.

He arched a brow at her.

"Do not even think I will be your mistress in truth. What do I get out of this?"

"If you perform this job with me and return my necklace, I will give you my word not to speak of your criminal activity. Nor will I tell your friends your true identity." As she started to object, he added, "And I shall give you five thousand pounds."

Victoria's mouth dropped. His offer was more than generous, it bordered on madness. She would have done this job for one hundred pounds. After being raised on the streets of London, she knew there was more to this than he presented. Five thousand pounds was a bloody fortune!

"Why so much money?" she demanded. "What else do you expect of me?"

"Think of it as an apology for my previous actions toward you," he muttered.

Guilt. She might be able to use that if needed. "Very well. I would still like to know what you expect of me."

He sat on the end of the bed. "All right, as I said, you would need to attend a week long party with me."

"As your mistress?"

"Yes, but you may use an assumed name. I doubt very many people amongst the *ton* know you."

"A few but not many," she admitted. "Still, I do not like the idea of people assuming I am your mistress. If word of this gets out to my friends . . ."

"You mean the ladies Selby, Blackburn, and Kendal?"

After all her words discouraging them from taking

a man to their bed, they would be horrified. "They must not discover what I am doing."

"There is no other way." He glanced away from her. "None of your friends would associate with anyone attending this party."

"Are you certain?"

"Yes."

"I see. If you think I will allow you any advances, you are mistaken."

His face tinged slightly. "I would not expect that of you. This would be strictly a business arrangement. But realize that we will share a room and likely a bed."

Victoria closed her eyes. Sharing a bed with him would be a difficult task. Just being in the same room with him had her heart beating erratically. But five thousand pounds would keep the children clothed, fed, and warm for a very long time.

"I will do it."

"We will need to leave on Thursday." He perused her from head to toe. "I shall pick you up tomorrow for a day of shopping."

Victoria looked down at the rug. Until she had that money, she could not afford to spend a farthing. "I cannot—"

"I will pay for the dresses."

She nodded slowly. "I will need to hire someone to help out with the children while I'm gone."

"Whatever expenses you incur because of this, I will pay for them."

"Very well, then." Victoria needed to leave this room. The overpowering essence of him was driving her mad. Seeing him again after all these years served to remind her of her initial feelings for him. She would have done anything for him then. And had.

Even today, she could have rejected his proposal.

He had no proof that she stole the necklace. While most people didn't know her personally, her works of charity stood out in this sordid town. No one would believe the rake. But instead of standing her ground, she gave into him like a weak coward.

She had to remember that her true reason for doing this had nothing to do with him. Only the children mattered. She would be able to give them a true Christmas with a few gifts and a large holiday meal. She could even bring in some sprigs of holly on Christmas Eve to make the house look more festive. All things she never had the money to do before now. But more importantly, the money from this would keep them in coal and food for a very long time.

"I should take my leave now," she finally said. She rose and walked toward the door.

He caught her wrist before she could reach for the knob. "Victoria, there is one more thing."

She inhaled sharply and turned to face him. His blasted grip was so tight she couldn't get him to release her.

"Oh?" she replied.

"While in private, I promise not to touch you. Nonetheless, during the public aspect of this party you may need to get used to me touching you to make this believable." He dragged her closer. "I might even have need to do this."

He closed the distance between them and lowered his mouth so quickly she had no time to fight him. And the hot sensation of his mouth on hers made her realize that she didn't want to fight him. She had to resist him no matter how much she wanted to wrap her arms around his neck and press her body closer to his.

His tongue slipped across her lips as if searching

for a sign of surrender. She could not give in to the desire seeping into her veins. Victoria moaned slightly. This is how everything started the last time, one simple kiss. Remembering that painful scene forced Victoria away from him.

"As I said," he muttered in a husky voice. "You shall have to get used to it."

"I do not think that is possible."

"You will pretend you enjoy my kisses or no one will believe us."

He tilted her chin up. In the pale light, his eyes were almost dark green, with no sign of hazel. And he was too handsome by far. She would need to shore up her defenses if she was to be that close to him again.

Victoria twisted her chin out of his grip and took a step toward the door. "Don't worry. I'm certain I can act the part of the doting mistress."

"Well, seeing your proficiency at lying, I wasn't too concerned." He moved and placed his hand on the door. Then he reached for her spectacles and removed them. Holding them up to his eyes, he laughed scornfully. "Just as I thought. Another lie."

She grabbed them out of his hand and placed them firmly on her nose.

"You will leave them home. No mistress of mine is going to look like a bloody bluestocking."

"As you wish." She reached for the doorknob only to have his large hand cover hers.

"There is just one more thing," he whispered harshly. "I despise liars. From this point on, you will only speak the truth to me."

She smiled. "You ask me to pretend to be your mistress yet you believe I should always tell you the truth."

"No, I insist on it."

Victoria stared down at his hand. "As you wish, my lord. But I demand the same respect."

"Of course." He turned the knob and opened the door. "I shall pick you up at noon for shopping."

Slowly, Anthony walked to his study, wondering at his sense of melancholy. Perhaps it was the usual feeling that came over him every December. He couldn't remember anything good ever happening in this month.

Still, his meeting with Miss Seaton went better than expected. Although, had she given him the necklace, he would have been happier. He understood her reasoning and most likely would have done the same thing in her situation. Now she knew she had something to hold over him.

He just prayed she didn't realize the other thing she could use against him. If she knew the guilt he felt for his actions of ten years ago, she could use it to her advantage. He would be unable to refuse her anything. She must never discover the extent of his guilt.

He sat down at his desk and perused the stack of unopened mail. A few invitations he might reply to but most of it was nothing he could be bothered with. He put the notes into a pile and wrote "no" on top. Huntley also served as his secretary and could respond to the invitations for him.

"Sir," Reese said from the doorway. "Your sister is here."

"Genna?"

Reese smiled. "She is your only sister, sir."

Well, not quite but no one else knew about Sophie. "Send her in."

He stood knowing his sister would come straight

into his arms. The sound of light footsteps preceded her entry.

"Tony!" And as expected, she threw herself into his waiting arms. "I cannot believe it's been five months. And why didn't you come by the house to see me?"

He detached himself from her clinging arms. "Come have a seat on the sofa."

"I already told Reese to bring us some tea." Genna sat on the sofa and waited for him. "You must tell me all about your trip. How was Florence?"

As much as he hated liars, in his position it was sometimes necessary to be one. Soon he would be done with this business and the only lies would be the secrets of his family. "It was lovely. In addition to meeting with a business partner, I was able to see a wonderful museum."

Genna laughed softly. "You, in a museum? Come now, Tony, you must do better than that."

"Well, if I did anything else it would be rude to speak of it in polite company."

Genna reached over and squeezed his hand. "I've missed you, brother."

"And I you. How is your betrothed?" He waited for Reese to set the tea on the table. "Will you pour?"

"Of course." She reached for the teapot and poured two steaming cups.

He watched, proud that his sister had become such a gentile lady. With her oval face, black curls, and big blue eyes, she was quite the thing during her Seasons. Until Lindal caught her.

After handing a cup to him, she continued, "Lindal is well but distant lately. I fear he may be getting nervous with less than a month left to his bachelorhood."

"Lindal is a good man from an excellent family. I'm sure you are right about his nerves but he won't do anything foolish." Anthony sipped his tea and felt a sense of comfort. His sister was here and they had good English tea, everything was right with the world.

Genna chewed on her lower lip. He knew that look. There was more to this than Lindal. "What is really wrong, Genna?"

"I am feeling nervous, too." She looked up at him with her blue eyes. "What if I am making a huge mistake? I tried to speak with Father about my concerns, but he just brushed them aside."

Of course, their father would do that. He wanted Genna married off. Lindal was an earl so more than suitable for his daughter. "Why do you think it might be a mistake?"

"I cannot put my finger on it. Lately, I am just not excited to see him. I find myself relieved if he sends a note telling me he cannot call. Shouldn't I feel happy to see the man I love?"

Anthony blew out a breath. How was he to give love advice when he had never been in love? "Genna, I wish I could tell you what you need to hear."

"But you have never been in love, have you?"

He shrugged. Infatuation with an orange seller scarcely counted as love. "Have you talked to your friends?"

"I tried, but they all thought I was being silly. All they can say is what a catch Lindal is, and how proud I should feel that he picked me."

He wanted to tell her how wrong her friends were. She was the catch, not Lindal. "You are not being silly. Perhaps you should take the next week to really examine your feelings for him before it's too late." And if she delayed the wedding, then he would have more time to retrieve the necklace should Miss Seaton not return it.

"Perhaps you are right. It's just his family is so maddening sometimes. His mother pulled me aside at the Houghton's dinner party to tell me the dress I wore was inappropriate." Genna breathed in as if to calm herself then sipped her tea.

"What was so wrong with your dress?"

"It was a shade too dark for an unmarried woman," she said in an angry tone. "It was not, Tony. Aunt Westfield would never allow me to wear something unacceptable."

Anthony smothered a smile. "I am sure if you and Aunt Westfield picked it out, the dress was perfect." The poor girl looked terribly distressed, and Anthony didn't believe it all had to do with a gown. "What other things are they driving you mad about?"

She glanced away. "You. His mother has made a few comments under her breath about Lindal marrying *Somerton's* sister. I think she wonders if it will look bad on them."

He fisted his hands wanting to throw something across the room. What he did should have no impact on Genna. Although, he knew it always would. More and more, the respectable wife idea was seeping into his brain.

"Do you love him, Genna? And I mean truly deep down in your heart?"

Genna stared at her jonquil gown.

"Can you imagine your life without him?" he whispered.

She nodded slightly. "I can. And sometimes I think it might be better."

Anthony closed his eyes and leaned his head back against the sofa. His father would be furious and probably blame her backing out of the wedding on him.

According to his father, everything was his fault. Why should this be any different?

"Genna, if you honestly believe that then you need to put a stop to this wedding before the plans go any further."

"I know," she whispered. "I just don't know how to tell him."

Anthony didn't need to ask to which "him" she referred. Lindal would take her rejection with a stiff upper lip. Her father, however, would not.

"If you would like to tell him before Thursday, I will stand with you. But I leave for a country party on Thursday and won't return until the following week."

"Thank you, Tony. I shall let you know what I decide. I believe I may take the weekend to think about my feelings for Lindal. Aunt Westfield and I are also attending a party with Lindal's family."

"Enjoy yourself, then."

"And you, brother."

Anthony knew he would not be able to enjoy himself this week. Along with getting this job done, he would also be fighting a damning attraction to a petite blonde.

Chapter Six

Victoria stared at the blue velvet material and sighed. She had never felt any fabric this fine. Somerton insisted that the dressmaker create a gown out of the velvet. While she would have the week to wear it, after she returned home, she would have to either give back the dress to him, or perhaps sell it. Of all the material chosen so far, this was her favorite. Maybe he would not mind if she kept just this one dress.

"It will look beautiful on you," he whispered near her ear.

She started.

"Are you all right?"

"I did not realize you were so close," she replied.

"As I told you before, you must become used to it."

She would never grow accustomed to having him so near. His presence overwhelmed her senses and created unruly sensations in the pit of her stomach. Somehow, she had to keep their relationship on a professional level. Nothing personal.

She almost laughed aloud at the thought. With Somerton, it was all too personal.

"Come and see the other fabrics I have chosen for

you," he said, taking her elbow. "You will need two more silk gowns for the evenings and a riding habit if the weather is fair enough for riding."

"Somerton," she said, coming to a stop. "This is all too much. Surely, I don't need all these gowns for a simple house party."

He squeezed her elbow in warning and drew her nearer to him. "You need all this and more. Do not argue with me about it."

The dark sound of his voice made her realize that arguing would be futile. "Very well."

He brought her over to a table where the shopkeeper draped two silk fabrics. Victoria could not take her eyes off the deep red material. She wanted to reach out and stroke the fabric to see if it was as luxurious as she imagined. The dressmaker insisted on green trimming to make the gown look more festive since the theme of the ball was Christmas.

"This is too much," she whispered.

"It is perfect and will look beautiful on you." He picked up the cloth and draped it over her shoulder. His lips turned upward.

"Somerton," she hissed as the shopkeeper turned away. "I cannot wear something as decadent as this. What will people think?"

He arched an eyebrow at her.

She knew what they would think. That she was his mistress and as such could wear a sensual gown. Before that fateful night, she'd tried so hard not to fall into the trap that most in her situation had already done. But it hadn't been easy. She had known the money those women made for letting a man have sex with them. Had she agreed, she might have even found a position as a mistress of a wealthy man. Nevertheless, she hadn't wanted that for herself. Yet now, she found herself in the same position, even if it was pretence.

As always, she wondered what her mother would think of her. Victoria barely remembered the woman who died when she was only seven. After Father died when Victoria was three, her mother went to the tavern and served ale. If Victoria was truthful with herself, her mother most likely served more than ale to the customers.

"What are you thinking about?" he asked.

"Nothing important."

She wandered the store again while Somerton gave the instructions to the woman. She wondered what it would be like if this wasn't pretend. If she had the money to shop at a place like this. She had to stop dreaming. Only the daughters and wives of lords shopped here.

She walked back toward a bolt of plaid wool and stared at it. Lost in thought of what it would be like to be a real lady again, Somerton suddenly dragged her away and into the back of the store behind a curtain. Before she could sputter a word, he backed himself against the wall with her in front of him. His hand covered her mouth. Her heart pounded against her chest.

"Shh, or we will have something to explain," he whispered sharply in her ear.

Victoria heard the bell on the shopkeeper's door and then some ladies chattering as they entered. The ladies' voices came closer as they examined bolts of fabric. Oh, dear God, he had saved her after all. Jennette and Avis had entered the shop. If they had discovered her with Somerton . . . she shuddered to think about the consequences.

Instead, her mind wandered to the hard chest she found herself pressed against, the calloused hand covering her mouth and the scent of sandalwood permeating the air around them.

"Do you understand?" he whispered so quietly she barely heard him.

She nodded.

He slowly removed his hand and slipped it around her waist. She prayed Avis and Jennette would finish quickly. Being this close to him caused her heart to beat erratically and warmth to spread throughout her body. How could he expect her to sleep next to him all week?

They stood there a few minutes more before she finally heard her friends leaving the store. She exhaled a long held breath and moved away from him.

"We need to leave before someone else walks in," she said.

"I agree, but we are not done shopping yet." He walked away to speak with the shopkeeper again.

Victoria clenched her fists. Never had she met such an exasperating man. She could not walk into another shop with him!

"All right, everything is set. The gowns will be finished by Wednesday afternoon. That should give you time to pack them." He paused for a moment. "You do have a trunk, don't you?"

"Yes, I have a trunk," she retorted. There was no need to tell him it would be a borrowed trunk.

"Good, now you need new undergarments, bonnets, gloves—"

She crossed her arms over her chest and stared at him. "You will not assist me in buying undergarments. Besides no one will see them so what I have is serviceable enough."

"Oh?" He cocked a brow at her. "Is that not what a man does for a mistress?"

"No."

"I believe it is. And do not forget that I shall see you in your undergarments and will not be pleased to find you wearing 'serviceable' things."

"Bastard," she hissed as she walked out the door. He grabbed her arm and swung her toward him. His hazel eyes had turned green with anger.

"I am the man who can rip your world apart. Don't ever forget that."

She yanked her arm out of his grip. "I am quite certain you will never let me forget it."

"I won't," he whispered.

Anthony opened the door to Lady Whitely's brothel and walked upstairs after a few nods to the ladies. Several of them looked disappointed that he was heading toward his mother's private rooms. After a quick knock, he entered the empty room. His mother would hear about his entrance from one of the ladies and follow him quickly.

He wandered the suite of rooms, admiring her style of decorating. While she had most of the house decorated in gaudy reds and burgundies, this room had pale blue wall coverings with white and gold accents. It hardly looked like the bedroom of a brothel owner.

Ten years ago, he had run from this place as if the devil had been chasing him. Now, he found it, and her, far less unpleasant than visiting his childhood home. He only called there to see his sister. His father could rot in hell for all he cared.

"Anthony."

He turned his head at the soothing sound of his mother's voice. "Good afternoon, Mother."

"This is a pleasant surprise."

"I happened to be near and thought I would call on you." He sat in the gold velvet chair.

"What is really wrong, Anthony?"

He should have known she would immediately realize he was worrying about something.

He told her about Genna's visit and lack of enthusiasm toward her upcoming nuptials. "I'm not certain she even loves the man," he added.

His mother's brows drew downward into a pained frown. "I wish I could give her some advice."

"You gave up that right almost twenty years ago," he said harshly. Sometimes when he least expected it, the anger at her surfaced. While he understood it wasn't all her fault, it never stopped the resentment from returning.

"I understand that, Anthony. However, it doesn't mean I can't yearn for something I will never have."

She stared down at her silk skirts. At forty-five, she was still a beautiful woman. A few gray strands sprinkled her blond hair and several lines around her eyes were now apparent. But she radiated beauty.

"So why else did you call on me today, Anthony?"

"I will be leaving on Thursday for a house party. So I won't be able to call for a fortnight."

She nodded. "Farleigh's party, no doubt."

"How did you know . . . ? Never mind, I'm sure I do not want to know how you learned about the party." Whom his mother slept with was none of his business. He had decided that years ago.

"I hear everything in here," she said with a small laugh.

Anthony looked around the room and then stood to glance out the window. His gaze slid to Victoria's home. Was she there now?

"What is really bothering you, my dear?" she asked softly. "Have you thought about what I said?"

"Yes."

"Excellent. I have been thinking that Lord Farber's oldest might be another option for you. She's been out for three Seasons and has not taken an interest in anyone."

"Mother, I will think about Miss Farber and Miss Coddington when I return from the party."

She frowned and crossed her arms over her chest. "You are doing another job for Ainsworth."

"Yes, but I have decided this is my last. But that is not what is bothering me."

"Then what is it?"

"What do you know of Miss Seaton?" He needed to find out all he could before he depended on her for such an important assignment.

"Miss Seaton?"

"Your neighbor, next door," he replied.

"Yes, I know of her," she answered stiffly. "Of course, we don't socialize. I believe she is the daughter of a vicar. She takes in orphans. She appears pleasant enough."

Anthony turned and stared at his mother for a long moment. There was an odd tone to her voice as if she wasn't telling him everything. But what more could she know about Victoria? That was the impression Victoria gave to the world. The quiet mouse who brought orphans into her house to save them from a life of crime. He wondered if anyone, save him, knew she was really a thief.

"My mind wonders what *you* know of her . . . and why." His mother rose and crossed her arms over her chest. "Miss Seaton is not a woman for the likes of you."

Anthony blinked. "The likes of me? *Your* son."

"Exactly. A man who uses women for his pleasure—"

"And their pleasure, too."

She continued as if she hadn't heard him, "A man who has just decided that respectability is important. A man who has no real desire for marriage. A man who doesn't seem to even respect women."

"Now, I really must protest that last statement. I fully respect women," he said solemnly.

"No, you do not. They are nothing but playthings to you. And I will not stand for you treating Miss Seaton poorly." She sounded like a protective mother lioness. "Besides, Miss Seaton will not correct your position in Society. You need the daughter of a peer."

"You have nothing to worry about, Mother. I have no intention of treating Miss Seaton with anything but respect." And with their history, he could never do more than give her a kiss. Touching her in any other manner was out of the question. She must hate him for what he'd done to her.

"You had best not, Anthony. That young woman is a sweet, innocent lady."

Anthony smothered a laugh. He wondered how his mother would feel about the sweet, innocent lady if she knew Victoria had stolen her daughter's necklace.

"Victoria, *she's* here," Maggie said from the threshold of Victoria's small office.

"Are the children all upstairs?" Victoria asked as she placed her quill in its holder.

"Yes."

"Very well, then." Victoria straightened her hair. "Send her in."

She took a sip of her tepid tea and swallowed down

her trepidation. Listening to the soft footfalls, her nerves tightened and her stomach clenched.

"Good afternoon, Victoria."

"Good afternoon, Lady Whitely. Shall we sit at the sofa?" God, she hated the way her voice quivered whenever she talked to the woman.

"Yes." Lady Whitely moved gracefully toward the worn sofa. After sitting, she patted the cushion next to her. "Join me."

Victoria stood and slowly walked to the sofa. This woman could take everything away from her if she desired it. But not for long. Once she made it through next week, she would have enough money that Lady Whitely could do nothing to her. Somerton's money would give her the safety and security she'd been searching for all her life.

"Sit," she ordered.

Victoria promptly sat on the sofa. She folded her trembling hands together on her lap.

"How do you know Lord Somerton?" Lady Whitely asked directly.

Victoria frowned. Ten years ago, she had admitted to Lady Whitely that she had given her innocence to a man. But she had never told Lady Whitely the man's name so why was she questioning her about him? Could she have seen them shopping?

"I met him a few days ago at Lady Selby's party. It was the first time I had met him, though he is friends with Lord Selby."

"Damn him." Lady Whitely stared at Victoria. "You need to stay away from him."

"Why?" she asked in an innocent tone.

"The man is a hardened rake. He will use you more so than any other man." Lady Whitely looked away. "And do not think for a moment that he will ask for your hand in marriage. He wants nothing to do with that. He has no respect for women."

"Of course," Victoria murmured demurely. Just the interactions she had with him the past two days had shown her how much he'd changed in ten years.

Lady Whitely's face was pinched and pained as if Somerton had hurt her in some manner. Perhaps Lady Whitely had an infatuation with him. It wasn't that odd, she might be older but Somerton had his charms. Victoria knew that far too well.

"Victoria, I am not certain you recognize the significance of what I am saying. You must not under any circumstances encourage even a friendship with Lord Somerton."

"As you wish." And it wasn't a lie. Victoria had no intention of encouraging a friendship or any other relationship with the man. All she had to do was tolerate him for a week. She could feign indifference around him, and hopefully he would believe she had no interest in him. Once their week passed, she would only see him at a few functions.

"I'm sorry, Victoria," Lady Whitely murmured. "I would tell you more if I could but I cannot. Please just take my advice with this man."

"Lady Whitely, I owe you everything and more. If you ask me not to see Lord Somerton, then I shall do my best not to. I cannot help if he is at a function of one of my friends. But I will not encourage him."

Lady Whitely rose and walked toward the small fireplace. "If only that would stop him. Once he decides on a woman, he will do everything in his power to have her. I should hate to see you become his mistress, Victoria."

She hated lying to her but had no choice in the

matter. Lady Whitely must not discover her plans for next week.

"Lady Whitely, I will never be Lord Somerton's mistress. Or any other man's for that matter. I have eight children to care for. When would I find the time?" she said with a laugh.

Lady Whitely laughed softly. "Very true, my dear. They keep you very busy." She sat back down on the sofa and finally smiled at Victoria. "How is she?"

"She is very well."

Lady Whitely looked toward the door wistfully. "I saw her a week ago from my window. She is becoming so grown-up."

"And more beautiful every day. When the time is right, I will find a sponsor for her. She deserves a Season and a man who will treat her well." Victoria hoped Avis or Jennette would sponsor the child when the time came. If not, she had no idea how to accomplish such a thing. But it did not matter right now. She had to get everyone ready for her week away.

And pray Lady Whitely didn't discover with whom she was going.

Chapter Seven

Victoria sat back against the comfortable carriage seat and sighed. She'd never been away from the children and would miss them terribly. Leaving them this morning had been one of the hardest things she'd ever done. All of them had tears in their eyes and made her promise she would return before Christmas.

Thankfully, Somerton had found a very suitable woman to come in and assist Maggie to keep the children under control. They could survive one week without her. Or at least Victoria tried to tell herself that.

They had driven for about an hour and other than a brief comment, the man across from her was silent. Perhaps he had many things on his mind. Although, as she looked over at him, his eyes were shuttered tight and his breathing even as if he slept. She had no idea how he could sleep in a moving carriage.

Then again, Somerton had probably left London before, unlike her. Victoria tucked the fur robe over her shoulder and glanced out the window. The buildings of London were now in the distance and ahead lay fields of white from the light falling snow. A few small houses and inns were coming into sight but mostly the scenery held her captive.

Excitement filled her as they drove farther away from the only place she had ever known. Her mind bounced with curiosity about the estate to which they traveled. She had heard some descriptions of Lord Selby's estates from Avis, but Victoria could never imagine the enormity of it all. Having grown up in squalor, her very modest home on Maddox Street seemed huge.

"What are you thinking about?" Somerton's voice sounded gravelly as if he had just awakened.

She turned her head and glanced over at him. His sleepy eyes had opened slightly as he stared at her. Her heart raced at the sight of the handsome man. "I was only looking outside."

"Why?"

She broke away from his stare and looked out the window again. "I have never been this far from London."

"Never?" he asked in an incredulous tone.

"No," she replied with a shrug.

"But we are barely out of town."

"Still, farther than I have been."

He chuckled softly. "I am truly amazed. I have traveled all my life so I must admit I assumed everyone did the same."

"You think my life is funny?" Indignation rose up in her. How dare the man laugh at her life?

"No," he said quietly. "I think it's rather sad."

"Lovely," she said, looking over at him again. "Now, I'm just the object of your pity."

"The only thing you are the object of in my mind is . . ."

"Is?" she pressed when he left the sentence unfinished.

"Nothing," he said roughly. "The only thing you are here for is to pretend to be my mistress."

"Why a pretend mistress, Somerton?" She tilted her head and pursed her lips. "I find it difficult to believe that you would have any issues finding a real one."

"I do not need the complications of a real mistress this week. I need a woman who will play her part and not get some foolish notion in her head that I will change for her." His intense gaze burned through her. "I will not. Do we understand each other?"

"Perfectly. You want no commitment or attachments of a sensual nature." And if she believed that to be true, why was there such tension in the carriage? Why when he looked over at her did her heart race?

The next few minutes passed slowly. She returned to viewing the scenery and attempting to ignore him, while Somerton sat across from her with a scowl.

"How did you go from selling oranges to taking in children?" he asked, breaking the stifling silence. "The amount you stole from me wouldn't have given you enough to lease a home for more than a few months."

Victoria shook her head in confusion. "What are you talking about? I never stole any money from you."

"The money I won gambling that night. It was gone and so were you."

She crossed her arms over her chest as disappointment filled her. "So you just assumed I took it."

"You knew I had won some money. It was in my pocket when we were talking. Later it was gone. Why would I think otherwise? I never faulted you. After what had happened, I assumed you took your due."

He thought she was nothing more than a whore. "You were drunk that night. You were asleep when I left you *and* the money at the church. Someone probably came by and stole it from you after I left."

He looked away from her as he tightened his jaw. "Perhaps," he admitted softly.

"Why would you believe me?" she mumbled, shaking her head. Why would he? She'd been nothing but an orange seller who gave herself to a man on the street like a prostitute. And of course, she had pinched a necklace from his pocket. She wouldn't have believed her either.

"I said, perhaps. But even you would have to admit that I have just cause in believing you stole the money."

"It really does not matter." Although, it did matter to her. Most of her life she'd done the wrong thing, but that time, she hadn't. And it mattered to her.

She turned away and stared out the window knowing she would never be the type of woman whom he could trust. And she wondered why she should care what he thought of her. Her position here was only to play a part, like an actress on a stage.

"You never did answer my question," he said in a quiet tone.

Frowning, she glanced back at him. "What question was that?"

"How did you go from selling oranges to taking in children?"

She closed her eyes and fought back the tears. The promise she had made ten years ago had never been difficult to keep . . . until now.

"How do you think I did it?" she asked, staring at him until he looked away.

"The easy way," he muttered with a sound of disgust.

Victoria bit down on her tongue to hold in the truth until she felt the metallic taste of blood. She wished she could tell him the truth. After living a lie for ten years, it would be nice to unburden herself to another person. The urge to tell him overwhelmed her, but she could not give into it. What he thought of her could not matter.

"A true lady would deny it," he whispered.

"I'm not a true lady and never will be," she retorted.

Anthony fisted his hands and fought back the anger at what she had become. Quite possibly, what he had made her become. Perhaps if he had never touched her, she would have continued to sell oranges until she could have gone into service for a reputable family. Where the master of the house would have taken her, he thought with disgust.

Instead, she'd sold her luscious body to any man who would have her. And worse, he would have been the first in line had he known where she'd stayed. He blamed himself for her misfortune, although he knew it wasn't entirely his fault. She could have asked him to help her.

But after what he'd been through that night, he doubted he would have done anything for her. His trust of women had been shattered. They were all out for themselves.

So why did it matter what had happened to this slip of a girl?

Because what he had done linked them for the rest of their lives. He owed her a debt he could never repay with money. And as much as he desired forgiveness, he would never have it. Nor did he deserve it.

If only he could understand why he craved to know more about her. He desired to understand her more, to get to know her better. And worse, he wanted her. The one woman he could never have again was the one he wanted unlike any other. The silence in the carriage was causing him to think about dangerous things.

"Victoria," he said to break the silence, "tell me about your parents."

She whipped her head toward him with a scowl. "There is nothing to tell. My father worked as a baker until he died when I was three. My mother did what she had to until an illness took her when I was seven."

"Who took you in after that?"

"The woman upstairs." She glanced down at her shoes peeking out from the blanket.

"And she was the person who made you sell oranges?"

"Mrs. Perkins did what she had to."

"Which was?"

"She taught me to pick pockets to bring enough money in to support her," she whispered. "I had to do it or she would have forced me to leave."

"What kind of heartless woman would let a young girl out on the streets to make money for her?" The desire to kick something surged in him.

Victoria laughed scornfully. "You are not that innocent, Somerton. You know what happens to young girls who are left on the streets. Picking pockets was my salvation. And I was good at it. I had a warm place to stay and food to eat. Most of the boys and girls who picked pockets would have killed for what I had."

He knew too well what became of most of those young girls because his mother exploited them. "Why didn't you come to me for assistance after . . . ?"

She folded her arms over her chest. "After? The only thing I knew about you was that your name was Tony. How exactly was I supposed to seek you out?"

"I don't know," he whispered. He could remember so little of that night. After his mother's return from death, he'd been blinded by anger and then brandy. Even after nine years of knowing why she'd done it, the frustration surged within him for the deception.

"Why is my life so important to you?"

"It most certainly is not. I am merely curious about what you have been doing the past ten years and making conversation to pass the time."

"I have been taking care of orphaned children. Nothing more."

"And picking pockets when the mood strikes you," he added.

"No, only when money is short," she retorted.

"So what will you do with the money you get from this little job?"

She glanced out the window with a wistful look on her face. "Give the children a proper Christmas with gifts and a large meal and nice clothes to wear for church."

The woman was nothing but contradictions. She stole from people but apparently only to help the children in her care. Now when given the chance to walk away from her responsibilities, she only wanted to give more to the children.

Anthony turned his attention to the window and the passing scenery. Something about this nagged at his brain. How did a woman with no means keep a home for orphans based solely on her pickpocket abilities? She *was* good. Nonetheless, the odds of being caught were always high, and pawned goods never paid near what they were worth.

So where did the money come from? The only way he knew for a woman to make the amount of money she would need to keep that house was prostitution. Not just prostitution but being some wealthy man's mistress. Was that possible? Could Victoria have a man who supported her?

He couldn't very well ask her that question. And who was he to judge her? His life had hardly been perfect. Women had a much harder lot in life especially if they didn't have a man to support them. Career options were rather limited.

Still, the idea that she let any man with the blunt have her made his stomach roil. She deserved far better than that. Perhaps the money he paid her would help her become free of her latest protector. If she even wanted that freedom, his mind countered.

She appeared to be a mass of contradictions. He couldn't help his curiosity about her. If she truly had a protector, they must be very secretive; otherwise, her friends might discover the matter. Perhaps her friends assisted her with money for the orphans.

"Victoria, how did you come to be associated with your friends?"

She glanced over at him coldly, and for a moment, he thought she would refuse to answer. Looking down her hands, a small smile lifted her lips and creased small dimples in her cheeks.

"I met Avis at the lending library."

"You can read, then."

"Yes, I learned when I was eighteen," she replied in a proud tone.

He stored that information away for later. While she seemed happy to know how to read, the fact that she was that age meant something.

"Avis and I wanted to read the same book." She turned her head toward him. "We ended up talking and then she invited me to her home for a literary salon to discuss the book."

"Indeed?"

She laughed softly. "I never felt so out of place in my life. But Avis, Jennette, and Elizabeth engaged me in the conversation and invited me back the next month. When they discovered I ran the home for orphans and, like them, had no desire for marriage, they started to invite me for tea. Before long, we all became fast friends."

"But the three of them are married now," he reminded her.

"True, but only after they found their perfect match."

Or the person Sophie thought was their perfect match, he thought. "I am glad you found such good friends."

She smiled at him fully, causing his heart to increase its beat.

"Thank you," she said in a shy tone.

The carriage slowed to a stop and Victoria looked at him with a frown. "Why are we stopping now? It's far too soon to be at Farleigh's home."

A groomsman knocked on the carriage door. "My lord, a moment if you please?"

"Of course," Anthony answered.

The groomsman opened the door and snow swirled about him. "The driver says the weather is getting worse. He recommends we stop a few miles up the road at an inn."

"No," Victoria whispered. "We must get to Farleigh's home."

"The party does not really begin until tomorrow night. I would much prefer we make it in one piece." Anthony turned to the groomsman. "Tell Mr. Chester to do what he believes is best."

"Yes, my lord."

Anthony sat back against the squabs and glanced

over at her worried face. "Why the sudden hurry to be at Farleigh's?"

"I have a job to do. I would prefer to do it and be finished," she retorted.

"And receive your payment."

She smiled tightly at him. "Exactly. I'm glad to see we understand our positions. I am here only to pretend to be your mistress. Just remember it is nothing more than an act. When we are alone together, our relationship is . . . is nothing more than employer and employee."

"I understand perfectly, Miss Seaton. You are my employee and nothing more."

Victoria took Somerton's hand and climbed down from the carriage. She had to admit that after four hours in the coach, she needed a break away from him. His presence overwhelmed her in the confining space. And his questions intimidated her.

At least now she would have peace for a night. The idea of spending a night alone sounded heavenly. No children waking her at all hours of the night. She couldn't remember the last time she had a full nights sleep.

"Let's go," he said, holding his arm out to her.

"Yes."

As they reached the door to the inn, it swung open. A large man with brown hair and a wide smile greeted them. "Somerton! Are you on your way to Farleigh's?"

"Ancroft, I haven't seen you in months," Somerton replied with a slight grimace.

Ancroft looked over at her and smiled, revealing deep dimples in his cheeks. "I can see why. You must be keeping yourself very busy."

Heat flashed across her cheeks with his implied meaning. She hoped Somerton would set the man straight but then realized he could not do that. She was here to play a part.

There was something familiar sounding about his name but she couldn't place him. Had one of the women next door mentioned him? She didn't think that was it because they were usually discreet. Why did she know that name?

Somerton pulled her closer. "Very busy, indeed, Nicholas."

"Are you staying the night too, then? The weather has taken a nasty turn," Ancroft said, looking up at the snow falling from the clouds.

"Yes. Hopefully, we shall be able to make it the rest of the way tomorrow. And speaking of the nasty weather, I need to get this lovely woman out of it." Anthony moved forward.

"We should dine together tonight, Somerton. The three of us."

"Nicholas."

Victoria sensed the warning Anthony gave the other man but didn't understand why.

"I already procured a private dining room and would prefer the company of an old friend and per- haps, a new one." Ancroft winked at her.

"Very well, dinner at seven," Somerton replied. He stepped forward dragging her along with him.

"Good day, sir."

As the door shut behind them, Somerton said, "It's 'my lord' to him."

She stopped and pulled her arm out of his grip. "And exactly how would I know that since you never introduced us?"

"We will discuss this upstairs."

Irritation at his manners washed over her. "Since I shall be in my room with the door securely locked, I doubt that conversation will take place."

He pulled her close enough that she could feel his hot breath on her cheek. "But you are mistaken because I would never let my mistress sleep alone."

Her heart pounded in her chest. He couldn't possibly mean what he said. This was all an act. She wasn't, couldn't, wouldn't be his mistress. She couldn't look away from his intense stare.

"B—but we are at an inn, not the party," she stuttered.

"And yet, already the Lord Ancroft knows we are together. So together, we shall stay . . . all night."

Chapter Eight

Anthony walked up the creaking staircase with Victoria trailing behind him. Damn Nicholas for being here. With him here, Anthony had no choice but to keep her in the same room. As he opened the door to their room, he confirmed his suspicion. The one bed in the center of the room would barely fit two people unless they were snuggled close.

And he could never sleep that close to her.

The time he had spent alone with her in the carriage had almost done him in. He constantly let his gaze slide to her sweet face. His thoughts had stayed on her lips until he finally decided making conversation would eliminate the temptation. Not that their discussion helped, either.

How could a woman who had gone through so much still look so innocent?

"This will never do," she said as she followed him into the room.

"You have no say in the matter," he replied a little too harshly. He understood her reason, but he would not sleep on a floor again. After spending five months without a decent bed most nights, he would sleep where he damn well pleased.

"I have no choice?"

"None at all. The bed is small but we shall manage."

"A gentleman would offer to sleep on the floor," she said, placing her portmanteau on the floor. Folding her arms across her chest, she tapped her foot impatiently.

He laughed softly. "Sweetheart, I am no gentleman."

"I learned that ten years ago," she retorted with one brow arched.

Anthony removed his greatcoat and then poked at the fire sending embers up the chimney. Resting his arm on the mantel, he stared at the fire. No woman had ever affected him so thoroughly and in so many different ways. He wanted to protect her and yet wanted to ravish her at the same time. Nevertheless, he had no right to do either.

He wondered how she could stand to be in the same room with the man who raped her. Perhaps her hard life had taught her to forget the past—something he could not seem to do.

As she moved in the room, he heard every intake of her breath, every swish of her petticoats. *Damn it!* Why her? Why couldn't he control his damned attraction to her? This was a mistake. If he had any sense, he would return her to London and face Farleigh's jealousy alone.

She sat on the small chair close to the fireplace and far too near him. "Perhaps now you will tell me why you did not see fit to introduce me to Lord Ancroft?"

He pushed away from the fireplace and walked to the window. "We have not developed our story."

"Our story?"

"Who you are, when and how we met." Anthony

stared out at the falling snow, praying it would stop soon so they wouldn't be stuck here another night.

"Oh," she replied softly. "I had not considered that."

He turned and faced her. "I know. Perhaps now is a good time for that discussion."

"I agree. So who am I?" she said with a smile.

"I think it's best if we say you are a widow from the country."

"Mrs. Smith, perhaps?"

Anthony took the seat across from her and said, "Perfect. Now how exactly did I meet a widow in the country?"

She tapped her finger against her full lips. Her blue eyes sparkled in the waning light. A slow smile lifted her full lips upward. "But you did not meet me in the country. I came to town to visit my aunt."

"And while visiting . . ." He had no idea where they might have met.

"The British Museum?"

He shook his head. "Highly unlikely I would be there."

"The opera?"

"No."

"A bookstore?" she suggested.

"Very well, then. We met at a bookstore. You could not reach a volume of poetry, so I pulled it down for you. From there we spoke at length before you decided you wished to take a lover. Your first since your husband died two years ago."

"What did he die of?" she asked.

"What does it matter?"

"Someone might ask. I need to know that we would say the same thing."

"Consumption," he said, knowing it was a common enough malady.

"Really?"

Impatient with the conversation, he raked his hands through his short hair. "Why not?"

"I was rather hoping for something far more exciting than dull consumption," she replied with a shrug.

"Kill him off any way you deem fit."

She smiled and her eyes widened with amusement. "Very well, then. It was a dreadful scandal, you know. His best friend took an improper interest in me. Poor Harry had no choice but to call the man out. Can you imagine, his best friend? And when it was over, both men were dead because of me." She shook her head with tears in her eyes. "Tragic."

Anthony burst out laughing. He couldn't remember the last time anything or anyone had made him laugh, really laugh. "Well played, Mrs. Smith."

"Were the tears too much?"

"Absolutely perfect." He suddenly had no fear of her performance this week. She would play the part as if she'd been born on the stage. And it would be best for him to remember that her being here was nothing but a job.

Victoria watched the serving maid close the door behind her, leaving Victoria in the company of two men with no chaperone. If any of her friends saw her now, she would be mortified. Thankfully, no one would ever discover the truth. Once this week was over, she would return to being Victoria Seaton, the pious woman who took in orphans. And she would have an extra amount of money to allow her a little freedom and security.

Lady Whitely would not have much say in what Victoria did or with whom she interacted. As much as she owed the lady everything, Victoria had always known Lady Whitely could take it away in an instant, leaving her back on the streets with nothing.

"Do I now get to meet this beautiful woman?" Lord Ancroft asked with a smile as he walked up to them.

"Nicholas, this is Mrs. Smith," Somerton said slowly. "Anne, this is Nicholas, Marquess of Ancroft."

Victoria curtsied and hoped she did it properly. Lady Whitely had taught her the correct way to curtsy but it wasn't a common thing for her. "My lord," she whispered.

Ancroft lifted her hand to his lips and kissed the top. "It is a pleasure to meet you, Mrs. Smith."

"And you, my lord." She stood up fully and took the man in as any mistress would. His brown eyes sparkled as he sent her an easy smile. The unease that had consumed her all day in the carriage and then in the room with Somerton finally dissipated. Lord Ancroft seemed to know how to make a woman feel comfortable.

"Shall we sit down?" Ancroft asked, pointing to the table set for three.

"Mrs. Mayweather did not join you?" Somerton asked as he walked to the table.

"She was looking for a little more than I could give her."

"Ahh, marriage," Somerton said with a smug grin.

"That is what most women want, is it not, Mrs. Smith?"

Victoria sat in the seat Somerton held out for her. "For some women, I suppose that is true."

Somerton took his seat with a frown. "But not you?"

She shook her head and rolled her eyes. "You forget I have been married, darling. Why would I want to lock myself into that institution again? It is only made so men can control us."

Ancroft laughed. "I like her, Somerton. It is refreshing to hear a woman speak so candidly."

"Yes," he answered but gave her a curious look as if he didn't believe her.

The innkeeper knocked and then entered with two servants trailing behind him. One maid placed a bottle of wine on the table while the other held a loaf of warm bread in a basket. Instantly, Victoria heard her stomach rumble.

The maid poured wine for everyone as the innkeeper told them the menu for the evening. Victoria picked up her wineglass and took a sip of the dry fruity beverage. The warmth soothed her tired body. If only she were in her own room where she could order a bath.

"Vi—Anne," Somerton started and looked over at her. "Did you want the fish or the roast beef?"

"The beef, please."

"Are you all right?" he asked, leaning in closer to her. "You look a little dazed."

"Excuse me, my lords. I am just a little weary from the trip."

Ancroft nodded. "I understand completely. At least you are better off than my cousin's friend."

"Oh?" she muttered.

"Poor Avis cannot bear the motion of a carriage for long without . . . well, you do understand I'm certain."

Victoria looked over at Somerton in shock. She suddenly could not catch her breath. Ancroft . . . now she remembered! Of course, he knew Avis because he was Elizabeth's cousin, and Lord Selby's friend and Jennette's friend, too. While Victoria had never met him, she had heard several conversations regarding him.

He knew her friends.

She would be ruined.

And it was all Somerton's fault.

Seeing Somerton's gaze grow cold, she understood he wanted her to continue the conversation. "Who is your cousin, my lord? Perhaps I know of her."

"Lady Elizabeth. She recently married and is now the Duchess of Kendal."

"Do you know of her, Anne?" Somerton said as he stared at her. The warning in his eyes was not needed.

Victoria shook her head slowly as if mulling over the question. She turned toward Ancroft. "I don't believe I do. I am certain they must be lovely ladies if they are friends of yours, my lord."

Thankfully, the servers returned with food. Victoria picked up her wine and drank down deeply. This act might be far harder than she ever expected. Somerton had told her that no one of her acquaintance would be at the party. This was a dreadful situation and she was in far too deep to halt it.

As the evening wore on, Victoria realized several things. Ancroft and Somerton had known each other for many years, but still there was a certain distance as if Somerton wouldn't let anyone get too close to him. But more importantly, she felt quite certain that the only reason they were dining together was to test her. Somerton must have wanted to gauge her reaction to Ancroft's relationship with her friends. That only served to increase her anger at the man sitting next to her, which in turn caused her to drink more than she ever had in her life.

"Do you remember the night of your eighteenth birthday, Somerton?" Ancroft smiled. "We thought you'd never get the nerve up to walk into Lady Whitely's."

"Lady Whitely? Who is she?" Victoria asked in an

innocent tone. He'd gone to Lady Whitely's before they'd had sexual congress on the side step of St. George's Church. Her ire surged again.

"Perhaps this is a topic for just the two of us to reminisce upon, Nicholas." Somerton sat back against his chair and sipped his wine.

Ancroft shrugged. "Somerton, do not be such a prude. The woman is your mistress for godsakes."

"True, but it still is in bad form to speak of such things in front of her."

"Nonetheless," Victoria interjected. "As I am sitting right here and asked a question which no one has deemed necessary to answer, I think we should speak of it."

"I do like her, Somerton," Ancroft said with a chuckle. He leaned over closer to her and said, "If he should ever bore you, I would be happy to be your protector."

Victoria smiled at him and then glanced over at Somerton. She reached over and stroked Somerton's cheek relishing the hard feel of his jaw, hoping to unnerve him as much as meeting Ancroft had unsettled her.

"I highly doubt he could ever bore me. And I intend to make certain he never becomes bored with me."

Somerton clasped her hand and kissed it softly. Sparks traveled up her arm as she attempted to pull away. His hand held her tight. He stared at her as his eyes turned greener.

So much for unnerving *him*.

"Sweetheart," he whispered, "you have nothing to worry about there."

Anthony watched as Victoria endeavored to maintain her stability while she walked up the uneven steps. He opened the door, and she tripped over the threshold. Catching her close, he whispered, "Just how much wine did you have?"

"Three glasses."

"If you are to maintain your pretense as my mistress you must learn to hold your drink better." He shut the door with his foot and walked her over to the chair by the fireplace.

She put a hand to her forehead. "Why is the room moving?"

"It is not." He placed more coal on the brazier to last the night. "You are drunk."

"No, I am *mot*. Did I say *mot*?"

"Yes, I believe you did, which only proves my point. You've had far too much to drink."

She stood up unsteadily. "Well, I am not drunk. And why didn't you tell me Ancroft is Elizabeth's cousin?"

"If I had believed it might come up, then I would have informed you."

"No, you wouldn't have. It was a test, wasn't it? You wanted to discover if I could handle an introduction to a man who knew my friends." She crossed her arms over her chest. "Did I pass?"

"No. You looked at me as if seeking an answer when your eyes should only have been on Ancroft." How did the woman know he had been testing her? Once he'd seen Ancroft in the courtyard, and she did not comment on his name, Anthony seized the opportunity to determine how she would react to a man that was not only acquainted but also related to one of her friends. Had Nicholas not brought up Avis's name, Anthony would have mentioned Elizabeth's name.

"Well, perhaps I should keep my eyes on Ancroft all the time. After all, he did infer he was looking for a new mistress."

A flash of anger surged in him. He crossed the distance and pulled her close to him. "You shall do no such thing. As long as I am paying you the only person you will look at is me."

He stared down at the fire in her blue eyes and started. The urge to kiss her lips again filled him with unwanted desire. He couldn't have her after what he did to her. But nothing his brain told him stopped his head from inclining toward hers. Her eyes widened as she realized his intention. Her beautiful lips parted with anticipation that his lips would touch hers.

Just as he started to pull her closer and let his eyes shut, she pushed him away.

"Just exactly what do you think you're doing?" she exclaimed. "I am certainly not *that* drunk."

"Of course not," he muttered. Because in order for him to touch her she would need to be completely foxed. He turned away from the scent of her alluring perfume.

"I need to change my clothing," she said with a sigh.

"Go behind the screen."

"I cannot get out of my stays without assistance. You told me Lady Farleigh would supply a lady's maid."

Oh, dear God, he was going to have to untie her stays, watch as her pearly white skin was bared for his lecherous gaze. Being this close to her was going to be the death of him. He'd been a fool not to quench his blatant desires with one of Lady Whitely's girls last night. Then he might be able to survive this trial.

"I will unlace your stays," he finally managed to get out.

She glared back at him. "I'm sure you have had much practice."

"As a matter of fact, I have." He pointed to the screen. "Now get your night clothes."

She removed a heavy flannel nightgown and glanced back at him.

"Where is the nightgown I bought for you?"

"It is in my trunk. Not that I will ever wear that in front of you."

With the wary look she leveled him, he understood her nervousness. "Wear what you want to bed. I will do nothing more than unlace your stays," he said softly. "You have my word."

"Excellent. I have the word of a rake, whoremonger, and gambler. I'm certain to have no worries." She stomped behind the screen and added, "I also need your assistance with the buttons on my gown."

He groaned softly.

Anthony walked behind the screen and raised his hands to the back of her gown. He slipped the buttons through their holes one at a time. Slowly the pearly skin of her back was exposed to his hungry gaze until he reached the last button. His hands shook as he slid the fabric off her shoulders.

"I can remove my dress," she whispered in a hoarse voice.

If only she was as affected by this as he. Blood pounded in his veins as he waited for her to remove her dress. Bloody hell, this was madness, he thought.

"Can you unlace the stays now?"

He could, and he could remove them along with her shift, then lay her on the bed, and make love to her all night. Only he could do none of those things. Quickly, he unlaced her stays.

"There," he said and walked back by the bed. He grabbed the bedpost and sighed.

"Thank you."

The sound of clothes rustling forced his imagination into erotic dreams of her naked body. He heard her footsteps come nearer. He didn't want to see her in her nightgown. It was wrong. Even if it was flannel.

"Are you all right?" she asked. "You're holding on to the post like you're about to topple over."

"I'm perfectly well," he managed to say. Finally, he peaked around to see her body covered in flannel from neck to toe.

She laughed. "I thought for a moment you were going to tell me this nightgown would never do for a mistress."

She just had to put the idea of her in a sensual nightgown back into his head.

"You are right. That gown would never do for a real mistress. But you are only an imitation so that nightgown is more than appropriate."

"And an imitation mistress is all I will ever be," she whispered.

Chapter Nine

Victoria awoke slowly, trying to determine where she was laying. She blinked her eyes again and noticed Somerton in the chair by the fireplace with his eyes closed. Sitting up, the pounding in her head increased. Why had she thought three glasses of wine would help things yesterday?

With a groan, she tossed the covers off her and quietly picked out her clothing for the day. If she worked with haste, she might be dressed before he woke. She glanced over at Somerton again and sighed. His rumpled clothes told her that he'd slept in the chair rather than in the bed with her. She longed to reach over and touch the dark hairs covering his jaw. But she wasn't his lover or mistress and had no right. Instead, she marched behind the screen to dress.

"What time is it?" his sleepy voice asked.

"Just after seven," Victoria replied as she tied her front lacing stays.

After foolishly wearing back-lacing stays yesterday, she'd learned her lesson. Having Somerton that close and touching her bare skin was not something she could repeat. It had taken every ounce of control not to turn around and kiss him last night. She was only here to do a job. Her lustful emotions would have to subside.

She heard Somerton rustling around the room. His footsteps seemed to stop. Unable to contain her curiosity, she glanced around the screen to see him staring out the window.

"Please tell me the snow stopped," she said.

"It did. We should be all right this morning but we'll have to go slowly."

"Why did Lord Farleigh decide to have a party in the winter?"

Somerton shook his head. "He has this romanticized idea that the Christmas season should be celebrated throughout the month of December."

"Well, that is odd indeed."

"Wait until you see his home," Somerton added with a shake of his head.

"Why?"

"Have you ever heard of the German custom of bringing an evergreen into the home and placing candles on it?"

Fully dressed, Victoria walked from behind the screen. "A tree covered with candles, inside the house? How odd! And sounds particularly dangerous if you ask me."

"I agree." Somerton rummaged through his bag for a clean shirt. "I don't think that custom will ever be embraced by sensible people."

Victoria waited while Somerton washed and changed his clothes. She didn't want to think about him being possibly naked with only a fabric screen between them. Yet, her mind couldn't stop thinking about it. The dratted man was far too handsome for her senses.

She closed her eyes and thought about what her

friends would say if they knew she was in a room alone with Somerton. Smiling, she could hear Jennette tell her to seduce the man. Avis would agree. Elizabeth might be more cautious but would most likely tell her the same thing.

But what would Sophie think? Of all her friends, Victoria had always felt the closest to Sophie. Perhaps it was the fact that Sophie's upbringing was only slightly better than hers. And not as good as Victoria's pretend upbringing, which all her friends believed was true.

"Everything all right?"

Victoria blinked her eyes open and then repressed a sigh. Dressed in his black jacket and trousers, the man looked dark and entirely too handsome. "Why do you ask?"

He smirked like only Somerton could. "You had your eyes closed."

"I was thinking of my friends, nothing more."

"Ah, I thought you might be regretting the three glasses of wine."

She couldn't help but smile. "I already did that."

Somerton chuckled softly. "Then I believe the rest of the trip shall be a nice quiet ride."

"That it shall." Now she just had to figure out how to resist the man when they actually had to sleep together.

Anthony tapped his foot impatiently as he waited for the groomsman to open the carriage door. After another six hours closely enclosed with Victoria, he needed room to breathe without the tempting scent of her filling his nostrils. Finally, the door opened and he clamored out. He held out his hand and steeled himself for the shock of excitement that skipped up his arm every time he touched her.

She placed her hand in his and there it was again.

After stepping down, she gasped. "That can't really be Farleigh's home," she turned to stare at him, "is it?"

Anthony glanced at the light brown granite home and then back to her. "Of course, this is his home."

She tilted her head. "I mean, someone actually lives in this place?"

"Well, yes," his patience getting the best of him, "Farleigh."

Victoria only shook her head.

He started to take a step but stopped when she didn't move with him. "What is wrong?"

"Look at the size of this place," she whispered. "It's as big as a castle."

Anthony glanced back at the house again and shrugged. "It's truly not that big. My father's home in Dorset is larger than this."

Her mouth gaped. "Your father's house is larger? What does he do with all the space?"

"Mostly he keeps the place closed up."

"What an incredible waste," she mumbled. She took a step forward and sighed.

He finally understood why she was acting this way. "You have never been inside a home like this, have you?"

"Never. The closest thing I have ever been in is Elizabeth's home in London."

While the ducal townhome was large for London, it was insignificant when compared to most of the country estates of the *ton*. "Victoria, you must not appear in awe of this place. Everyone would expect that as my mistress you are a woman of some means."

Her face reddened slightly but she nodded her agreement.

"If you would like, once we get to our room, you can gush about the place to me."

"Thank you, Somerton."

He smiled down at her. "Very well then, Mrs. Smith. Are you ready?"

"Yes."

The snow covered gravel crunched under their boots as they walked toward the door. A butler opened the door and ushered them into the warm house. Anthony glanced down at Victoria and suppressed a smile. Her look of awe outside had turned to ennui as they entered the hall.

"Good afternoon, my lord," the butler said and bowed to Victoria. "Good afternoon, ma'am. The footman will take you to your room. Dinner is at seven but sherry will be served in the salon at six."

"Thank you," Anthony replied and then followed a footman upstairs.

The footman opened the door and allowed them to enter the suite of rooms. A small salon, with a sofa and two chairs, preceded the large room with an enormous mahogany bed taking up most of the space. At least that bed was large enough for them both to sleep in without touching each other.

"Your trunks will be brought up presently, my lord."

"Thank you."

Victoria walked to the window and looked out at the large expanse of grounds. As the door closed behind the footman, Anthony expected her to start talking about the house. Instead, she remained quiet.

Slowly, he walked closer to her. "Is everything all right?"

She shook her head. "No."

"What is wrong?"

"Everything! I don't belong here. This place is for ladies and I am not one."

He turned her to face him. "Maybe Victoria Seaton is not a lady, but Mrs. Anne Smith is. Do not forget that."

She closed her eyes and nodded. "I shall do my best."

Grabbing her shoulders, he gave a little shake until she opened her eyes. "You shall do much better than that. You will make everyone in the rooms downstairs believe you are Mrs. Smith, and Mrs. Smith is the widow of a squire."

"I know my job," she retorted, pulling out of his grip. "That doesn't mean I have to feel comfortable with it."

"Exactly what are you not comfortable with?" he demanded.

She turned away and mumbled, "Pretending to be your mistress."

"And why is that?" She'd all but admitted to having been a prostitute. Why would pretending to be his mistress be all that difficult?

"It matters not. I will do my job, and you will pay me my wages when we are finished."

Anthony released a frustrated sigh. "Victoria, just for once, could you be truthful with me?"

"Very well." She walked back to the window and glanced out. "Because I cannot abide being in the same room as you."

Why did this surprise him? He'd wondered how the woman could stand to be near him after what happened ten years ago. Now at least, she'd admitted the truth.

"You have nothing to fear from me, Victoria. I shall

do nothing to cause you any pain. In fact, I will do my best not to come into the room until you are asleep."

Turning back toward him, she grimaced. "We both know that will only cause talk. I will get over my abhorrence of the situation and make the best of it."

"How will you do that?"

"I shall endeavor to enjoy the company and the food."

He stepped closer. "And if I am forced to touch you in front of others?"

One blond eyebrow arched at him. "I shall do my best to act as if I am enjoying it."

It suddenly struck him that she was lying. Perhaps it was his gambler's intuition, but he knew a bluff when he saw one. And Victoria Seaton was bluffing.

"And if I'm forced to kiss you?" The soft tone of his voice underlied the anger he felt at her lying to him again.

"I shall be forced to endure it."

"Shall we see just how you do at enduring my kisses?"

Before she could back away, he pulled her close and brought his lips down on hers. The anger that he felt at her lying softened as her lips opened slightly. Taking advantage, he deepened the kiss, savored the tentative touch of her tongue against his.

She pressed her body to his and lifted her arms to wrap around his neck. He still had some lingering doubts about her bluffing. For some reason she acted as if she wanted to push him away, but her kiss told him the opposite. But was her reaction a learned response from her profession? Did she like to play the innocent prostitute?

As she responded to him, his body begged him to walk her to the bed. He couldn't do that while there was still the incident of ten years ago between them.

She would hate him forever if he did. And for some odd reason, he didn't want that.

Slowly he lifted away from her and smiled down at her bemused face. The look on her face was not the look of a woman enduring his kiss.

He lifted her chin upward. "If you keep kissing me like that, *I* might even believe you want me."

At precisely six o'clock, they closed the door to their room and walked silently down the steps. The past three hours had been awash with tension for Victoria. After a kiss that nearly made her knees give out, she had attempted to stay away from him. But in such close quarters, there wasn't much she could do.

He had stretched across the bed in a wholly inappropriate manner and napped for an hour. She watched the rise and fall of his chest as he slept. With his eyes closed, his face relaxed and he looked even more handsome. She had to get that image out of her head. The man was a rake. And her employer for the moment, nothing else.

"You look quite beautiful this evening," he said as they reached the grand staircase.

"Thank you."

"Do not show your nervousness, Victoria," he whispered in her ear.

The heat of his breath sent shivers down her back. "I will not forget what I'm here to do."

"Then show me."

Victoria plastered a smile on her face and gave him a loving look. She reached over and touched his jaw with her gloved hand. His hazel eyes darkened to an emerald green.

"You have nothing to worry about, Somerton. I know my part."

"Too well," he muttered.

Stupid man thought she was some kind of strumpet. Perhaps she should tell him the truth, but for the moment, she wouldn't. She needed the little distance they had between each other for her own sanity. Although after that kiss, she had almost told him everything. She didn't understand his reaction to her. He wasn't the type of man who should care if she'd been with several men. From what she'd heard, he frequented Lady Whitely's house regularly.

"Let's go," he said and held out his arm to her.

She looped her arm with his and ignored the sensual awareness running up her arm. As they walked down the stairs, she kept the smile on her face and tried to pretend he really was her protector.

They entered the room together and heads turned to look at the woman on Somerton's arm. The men smiled back at her appreciatively while some of the women glared in jealousy at her.

One man approached them slowly. With her arm linked with Somerton's, she felt him tense as the man came closer.

"Somerton, interesting to see you here. I can only assume you could not resist Hannah's invitation?"

"Farleigh, some day perhaps you will get over your jealousy." Somerton led her away without even an introduction.

"That was rather rude," she commented. "Especially to our host."

"Leave it be, Mrs. Smith."

He moved them off to the edge of the room. Victoria scanned the room for anyone she might know.

Thankfully, Somerton seemed to be correct in his assumption that no one would know her.

Lord Farleigh approached them again, only this time with a beautiful woman with auburn hair leading him to them. The woman smiled at Somerton in an entirely inappropriate manner. Victoria glanced up to see a smile of appreciation on Somerton's face.

She tried to ignore the stab of envy that attacked her. This woman was one of the most beautiful that Victoria had ever seen. The lady carried herself in a way that showed her confidence to everyone in the room.

"Somerton," she said in a breathy tone.

"Lady Farleigh, it is a pleasure to see you again."

Lady Farleigh looked down at Victoria. "And who is this little gem?"

"Lord and Lady Farleigh, this is Mrs. Anne Smith." He pulled her slightly closer. "Anne, Lord and Lady Farleigh."

Victoria curtsied with her eyes locked on the earl's. She knew enough that mistresses were always looking for their next protector, and she could act no differently. Besides, after the interaction between Lady Farleigh and Somerton, she wanted a little retribution. Lord Farleigh took her hand and kissed it.

"It is a pleasure to meet you, Mrs. Smith. I do hope you and Lord Somerton will enjoy my little party."

Little party? Victoria glanced around the room and counted at least fifty people. "Thank you, my lord. I am certain Somerton and I will enjoy ourselves." She hoped the tone of her voice sounded flirtatious to the earl and told Lady Farleigh that Somerton was taken.

Somerton leveled her a swift glare. "Come along, Mrs. Smith. We have many more people to meet."

As he dragged her away from the earl, he whispered

in her ear, "Well done, Victoria. Just don't overplay your hand."

"What do you mean?"

"Your flirtatious manner might appear as encouragement to most men. They might even think you are looking for a new protector."

Victoria laughed softly. "That is what a mistress does, my lord."

He stopped and clasped her arm tightly. "Perhaps it is. But I would like everyone to believe you are my mistress only. You are not looking for another man. Do you understand?"

She attempted to pull her arm away to no avail. "Perfectly," she bit out. "As long as you are not looking for another woman."

"What do you mean by that?"

She rolled her eyes. "It wasn't difficult to determine that Lady Farleigh had her eyes on you."

"Perhaps she did," he replied with a smirk.

Two younger men approached them with wary smiles on their faces.

"Somerton, how are you?" one of the men said.

"Very well, Singleton."

Singleton looked down at Victoria with a leer. "Farleigh has outdone himself this time."

"And who is this beauty?" a younger man asked, staring at Victoria's breasts.

"Mrs. Smith, this is Lord Brentwood and Mr. Singleton."

"Lovely to meet you, Mrs. Smith," Lord Brentwood said in an overly enthusiastic manner.

Victoria muttered a reply, suddenly eager to be away from this group. Their leering glances sent an odd sensation down her back.

"Are you all right?" Somerton queried. "You have

become quite pensive since meeting the last group of people."

"Those two men did nothing but stare at me in a totally lurid manner."

His left brow rose. "And that comes as a surprise? You are a mistress and as such, fair game."

"Well, I do not like it."

He pulled out her chair for her. He took the seat next to her and leaned close to her ear again. "Then put all of your attention on me. I should be the only one you think of during dinner."

"Why?"

"Then everyone understands you are only here for my pleasure."

She sent him a feigned smile. "Of course, I am."

During dinner, she watched him and spent most of her time making conversation with him and the couple across the table from them. She noticed the way he watched everyone at dinner, analyzing them. What was his reason for being here? He'd never told her anything, but she didn't believe he would be here without a valid reason.

Even though the tone of the party was more casual and less reputable than she imagined the usual *ton* party was, the women were still expected to gather in the salon while the men had their brandy and cigars.

"Mrs. Smith," a cultured voice called to her. "Might I have a word?"

"Yes, ma'am." A sense of trepidation filled her as she strolled toward Lady Farleigh.

Lady Farleigh clasped Victoria's arm and led her to the salon. "I could not help but notice the way you looked at that devil Somerton. He will not be an easy man to catch. But then again, neither was Farleigh."

She didn't want to say this as Lady Farleigh appeared to be such a friendly woman, but Victoria had no choice. "Lady Farleigh, I am nothing to him but a mistress."

The woman laughed softly as they entered the salon. "As was I to Farleigh. You must make yourself something more than a mistress to catch him."

Victoria stopped and looked at the woman. "You were his . . . ?"

"Yes, my dear. Going from mistress to countess is no easy task. But it can be done. Should you need any assistance in this matter, please know you can come to me."

"Thank you, Lady Farleigh."

"Please call me Hannah."

Victoria smiled at the woman. She had no desire to become Somerton's mistress or wife but Lady Farleigh did not need to know that. "Thank you, Hannah."

Chapter Ten

As the evening progressed with no sign of Marcus Hardy, Anthony's frustration grew. How was he to watch Hardy when the man was not in attendance? What if Ainsworth's information was incorrect? Anthony had been doing these "odd" jobs for Ainsworth for almost ten years. It would not be the first time some piece of misinformation had been given to him.

But after ten years, he was tired of the game playing, lying, and secrets. The first few years had helped take his mind off the reality of his family situation. After discovering his dead mother was a brothel owner, he had almost gone mad. And then what he'd done to Victoria had only made things worse.

He could not stand to be in the same house as his lying father and had taken every job Ainsworth had given him. When Anthony finally made amends with his mother, he had slowly realized running from his problems would not work. Six years ago, he decided he had to find Victoria and at least apologize for his actions. He had only planned to apologize and assist her monetarily. Instead, he'd dragged her down into his life of lies.

Glancing over at her, he smiled. She appeared in deep conversation with Farleigh's wife, Hannah.

"Can't keep your eyes off of her, can you?"

Anthony blinked and looked over at Nicholas. Now he had to make conversation about her. "Can you blame me?"

Nicholas laughed soundly. "Not at all. I wouldn't let her out of my sight."

"Exactly."

Nicholas lowered his voice, "So what is the real reason you chose to come here this week?"

Anthony clenched his jaw. "I have been out of the country for several months. I thought this might be a nice time to relax with Mrs. Smith."

"Right. So instead of ensconcing her in a lovely little cottage, you take her to a party where you know there will be nothing but degenerate men." Nicholas laughed again. "Yes, it makes perfect sense to me."

"Stay out of my life," Anthony replied. Sometimes he wondered how different his life would have been if Nicholas and Trey hadn't dragged him to the brothel.

"Absolutely." Nicholas glared at him then stood and walked out of the room.

Instead of partaking in any of the gaming that occupied the back room, Anthony walked around the rooms looking once more for Hardy. The man still had not made an appearance. Asking Farleigh might bring suspicion upon Anthony should Farleigh be involved in the plot.

He walked back into the salon and toward Victoria. He desperately needed a good night's sleep and doubted he would get that with her next to him. Holding out his hand to her, he said, "I believe it's time to retire, Mrs. Smith."

"So formal, Somerton," Hannah said with a sensual smile. "I believe it is acceptable for you to call her Anne."

"Yes, I suppose it is."

Victoria accepted his hand and stood. "I don't mind at all." She glanced back at Hannah and said with a smile, "It only matters what he calls me in private."

Hannah raised her brown brows. "I suppose you are right. Good night."

If only it would be a good night, Anthony thought. He held out his arm for Victoria and led her upstairs. "You did very well tonight."

"Thank you," she replied stiffly. "I thought I should come speak with you after the gentlemen returned from their brandies, but Hannah wanted me to stay and talk with her."

"You did the right thing. What did you two talk about?"

"She would like my help with some decorating. She wants greens brought in and placed on the mantels, mistletoe bunches hung, and big Yule logs in the fire-places. I have never heard of doing all this, especially with Christmas still two weeks away."

Anthony chuckled. "They want everyone to enjoy themselves and they feel Christmas fills people with goodwill. Just enjoy it."

"I did like speaking with Lady Farleigh," she commented.

"Hannah is a lovely woman. I've known her a long time." Anthony opened the door to their room.

"I'm sure you have," she retorted.

Hearing the bitter tone in her voice made him wonder what exactly she and Hannah had discussed. He closed the door behind them. "What do you want to know, Victoria?"

She crossed the thick carpet and sank into a brocade chair. "Were you intimate with her?"

He leaned against the door and folded his arms over his chest. "I don't believe that is any of your business."

"Indeed? You wanted to know all about my past. I think I have a right to ask the same questions." She stood and crossed her arms over her chest. "So how many women have you bedded?"

"You sound like a jealous wife, not a mistress who should be doing everything she can to make me happy."

"Make you happy? I am only a pretend mistress, remember?"

"You don't have to be," he whispered. The way her arms were over her chest only pronounced the soft curves of her breasts.

She smirked at him. "You cannot change the rules now."

"I can do anything I want," he said in a soft voice.

"Not without my permission."

Her words were like a bucket of cold water dumped on him. "You are right, of course."

"Why don't you go back to Lady Farleigh? I am certain she would be happy to see you again."

He stared at her until she looked away. "Perhaps I will. At least with her, I would have a nice warm body next to me."

Her eyes widened as she comprehended the insult he'd given her. "You may take the bed tonight. I shall take my cold body and sleep out here."

He walked to the door, furious that this slip of a woman could heighten his anger so quickly. All he wanted was a good night's sleep. He would not get that until the wench went to sleep.

"I might be more comfortable in another bed." He strode to the door and slammed it behind him.

The soft pink rays of morning streamed in through a small slit in the draperies. Victoria closed her eyes tighter. It could not be morning yet. Seeing the pale sunlight, she realized that she had slept longer this morning than in years. Every morning she was up by six, usually because several of the children were awake by then. Knowing it was futile to try to get back to sleep, she opened her eyes.

She was not on the sofa as she had been when she went to sleep last night. Lying still, she heard his rhythmic breathing next to her. Had she been sleepwalking last night? No, she never did that.

He must have carried her here once she had fallen asleep. Why would he have done that? When would he have done it? After he slammed the door shut, she'd had no idea if he would return or not. Unwilling to take a chance that he would come back, she had decided to sleep on the sofa.

She wondered if he had slept with Hannah. Or one of the other loose ladies staying at the party. It certainly would not surprise her. The man was nothing but a hardened rake. Even Lady Whitely had told her that. So why did she feel a sense of disappointment? She did not want to become involved with a man like Somerton again.

Once was enough.

She silently moved the coverlet off and lowered her feet to the floor. Tiptoeing to the linen press, she prayed it wouldn't squeak as she opened it. After pulling out a day gown of green wool, she walked to the screen and dressed quickly. Thankfully, she could reach the buttons on this dress.

Once dressed, she pulled her hair into a loose chignon. As she walked across the room, she paused and stared at the man in the bed. Somerton looked relaxed. She had never seen him like that. In the few short days that she had known him, he always held himself rigid and had laughed only once. She wondered what demons the man held so tight inside of him.

Shaking her head, she continued to the door. It mattered not what demons were at work in him. He had coerced her into this job. Once they were done with the week, they would only see each other at functions held by their mutual friends. And she doubted he attended many of those.

She quietly departed the room and walked to the stairs. For the first time, she gawked at her surroundings. The white marble steps led to a huge entranceway for guests. Massive portraits in gilded frames hung from the silk covered walls. As she walked down the stairs to the breakfast room, the extravagance of the rooms continued to amaze her.

"Well, you are up quite early," a male voice drawled.

Victoria turned her head and smiled at Lord Ancroft. "I am used to being up early. And it is almost eight."

He shrugged. "I would have thought Somerton would try to keep you in bed all day."

Heat scaled her cheeks. What would a mistress say to that? "Perhaps he needed his sleep."

"I am certain after being with you, he would," Ancroft muttered.

Victoria stood there mouth agape. She had no idea how to reply to such a comment.

"I apologize, Mrs. Smith," Ancroft said softly. "I have been rather out of sorts lately."

"Apology accepted." She moved toward the table and sat down across from him. "Why have you been so out of sorts?"

"I am not certain. Perhaps I should get out of England for a time. Maybe travel to Italy. A dear friend of mine always wanted to visit Florence and Venice."

"Then maybe you should go together," she suggested.

Ancroft's lips tilted upward. "I believe her husband might object. And of course, her infant son."

He was speaking of Jennette, of course. "You might consider going alone," Victoria offered.

He leaned across the table and clasped her hand. "I might. Or perhaps you would consider traveling with me."

"I rather doubt she will do that, Nicholas," Somerton's cold voice sounded from the threshold.

Ancroft instantly released her hand and sat back against his chair. "You can't fault me for trying, Somerton. At some point, she is bound to see that you never commit to anything. In fact, I have never heard of you having a mistress at all. Women, yes. But never a mistress."

Somerton crossed the room like a panther. "But now I have."

Victoria tensed as he drew nearer. The air grew thick as the two men stared at each other. She felt like the female lion caught between two rival males. There had to be something she could say to relieve the tension.

She laughed softly until both men looked at her. "I think you both may have forgotten that I have the say in who I take to my bed. If I wish, I could take Ancroft." She glanced up to see Somerton glaring at her. "But I prefer my current arrangement."

Somerton sat in the chair next to her. "As do I," he replied in a muffled tone.

Ancroft frowned as he stared at them. "Forgive me, Mrs. Smith. I meant no disrespect."

"I do understand," Victoria said. "Perhaps all you need to do is find another mistress to keep you entertained."

Ancroft glanced toward the window with a faraway look in his eyes. "I rather doubt that will satisfy my current condition."

A tall man with light brown hair entered the room and glanced at the group sitting at the small round table. "Ancroft," he said with a nod.

Ancroft nodded. "Hardy, what brings you here?"

"I arrived a few minutes ago. I have some business with Lord Farleigh, but I won't be staying for more than a few days." Hardy looked over at Somerton with a slight frown. "Somerton?"

"I don't believe we have actually met," Somerton said as he stood to shake the man's hand. "And this is a friend of mine, Mrs. Smith."

After shaking Somerton's hand, Mr. Hardy bowed over her hand. "It is a pleasure, Mrs. Smith."

Somerton's hand clasped down on her shoulder with a biting pain. "Darling, I need a moment of your time before you dine."

"Of course, dear." Victoria stood up and glared at him.

"In the salon." He took her hand and led her out of the room while Ancroft's gaze burned into her back.

Hearing people in the salon, Somerton continued on to the empty library. The click of the lock told her of the importance of this meeting.

"Is there a problem?" she asked softly. She had never seen the full brunt of his anger but had a feeling it would not be pleasant.

"Yes, there are several." He paced the room. "First, why did you leave our room without informing me?"

She sat on the brocade chair and watched him walk the room. "You were still asleep. I did not believe I should wake you just so I could get a bite of breakfast."

He stopped in front of her chair and stared down at her. His hazel eyes turned a brilliant green. "Do not leave our room without me. There are some very conniving men here."

"Like you?"

His eyes narrowed on her. "Some of these men will believe you are fair game just because you are my mistress."

"A position you forced me to play," she commented.

He smirked slightly. "A deal you agreed to."

"So I did. Go on," she said with a wave of her hand.

"Do not, under any circumstances, encourage Ancroft. His former mistress just ended their agreement."

"So he is looking for a new mistress?"

His eyes hardened. "Do not think it."

Smiling up at him, she said, "But our agreement is only for the week. Once that time is completed, I might be interested in such a position. He is, after all, a marquess and will be duke one day. Being the mistress of a duke is certainly an advantage."

She knew she should stop baiting him but couldn't seem to stop. "Besides, think of the money that would bring in for the poor children. I would be able to stop my criminal activities."

Suddenly, he hauled her out of her seat until she was up against his chest. Her heart thrummed.

"You will not take another man to your bed," he said deliberately.

"Indeed? You don't return to our bedchamber until late last night and after sleeping with—"

"Whom I sleep with is my business." He tilted her chin up.

"Just as whom I sleep with is mine. I can take any man I want to. You have no say in the matter."

"Oh, but I do," he replied in a menacing voice before lowering his hard lips to hers.

If she didn't know better, she might have thought his punishing kiss was a show of jealousy. But as she responded to his kiss, he softened his lips and punishment became seduction. Feeling his tongue lash against hers sent a strange tightening sensation to her belly. She wrapped her arms around his neck, attempting to get closer to him. She needed relief from this aching desire she felt for him.

His hand moved to cup her breast. She wanted so much more than a simple kiss. But she couldn't tell him that. Why couldn't he sense her desire for him? As he skimmed his thumb across her taut nipple, she moaned softly.

He trailed his lips to her ear as he pressed her hips to his. She could feel his erection pressing against her. Moisture pooled between her folds as she prayed he would touch her soon.

"Dammit!" he said, moving away from her. He walked to the window and stared out at the snowy expanse.

"Somerton?" she whispered.

"Don't say a word."

What could she say? The man kissed her as if he intended to take her to his bed then tore himself away as if she were the devil. So he didn't want her, but he didn't want her to take a protector, either. Something was completely wrong here.

"Somerton, we need to talk about what just happened."

He turned back to her with a frown. "There is nothing to discuss."

"Indeed? So why is it that I'm not good enough for you or your friend, Ancroft?"

"I never said that," he replied.

"You didn't have to. Your actions told me." Victoria walked toward the library door. Before she could reach for the door, she found herself spun around to face him again.

"We are not done with our conversation. Stay away from Ancroft and all the other men here."

"Then I demand the same respect. If I am to be the doting mistress, you had better be the adoring protector."

Before he could reply, she stormed from the room.

Chapter Eleven

Anthony stared at the open door unable to move.
Finally, he sank into a chair and stared at the embers
in the fireplace. Victoria could have sex with anyone
she wanted, once this job was finished and she was out
of his life forever. He combed his fingers through his
hair in frustration. She would never be completely out
of his life. Between the connection they had forged
ten years ago, and the fact that she socialized with
three of his friends' wives and his half sister, he would
always hear about her.

He would always see her. Even if it was just through
the window of her home as he went to see Lady Whitely.
He would know Victoria was there, possibly watching
and condemning him for walking into a brothel.

What the bloody hell did he care what she thought
of him? He was an unmarried man and could visit a
brothel if he wanted. What she thought of him did not
matter.

Victoria was pure temptation and passion. Moving
her into his bed had been a mistake last night. He'd
walked back into the room after playing cards with
Brentwood and noticed how uncomfortable she'd

looked on the sofa. He'd felt he had no choice but to move her. Of course, trying to sleep next to her had been impossible. He lay awake for hours as she dozed next to him.

"So what exactly is going on between you two?"

Anthony looked up to see Nicholas staring down at him. "Nothing is going on between us."

"Strange answer for a man who is supposed to be her protector."

"Stay out of this, Nicholas. You know nothing about her."

"I know you two are attempting to make people believe you are lovers and yet, I don't quite believe it. While you sit in here looking angrier than I have seen you in years, she went back to the breakfast room alone and looking miserable."

Anthony clenched his fists. "Stay out of this."

"I'm not a fool. I know you have done some work for people in high places." Nicholas must have seen the look of confusion on his face. "Selby told me."

Anthony nodded. Selby only knew because Anthony had used him once when he first started his dealings with Ainsworth. "I might have had some business in the past."

Nicholas laughed. "Or even now." He paused as if considering his words carefully. "I know you wouldn't be here unless there was a strong reason. Over the past two years, Farleigh has made his objections of you public. But he can't deny his wife anything. You wouldn't be here just to pay a call on her. If you need assistance, I shall help you. Let Mrs. Smith leave here."

Anthony glanced back to verify the door was firmly shut. "You cannot help me."

"Of course I can. If Mrs. Smith is here for—"

"Mrs. Smith is only here as my mistress. Nothing more."

"Somerton, you can lie to many people and they will believe you." Nicholas smirked. "But not me. I've known you far too long for that."

"I said, she is here strictly as my mistress."

"Somerton," Nicholas said roughly.

"All right, can you pick the pocket of a man without him feeling a thing?" Somerton demanded.

"No, but I highly doubt . . ." Nicholas's words trailed off. "You can't mean to say that Mrs. Smith can do such a thing."

"Better than anyone I have ever seen."

"Better than you?" Nicholas asked cautiously.

"Far, far better," Anthony admitted. "She is the best I have ever seen. Probably why she hasn't been hanged yet."

Nicholas took the seat across from him. "How did you find her?"

Anthony shook his head. This was a disaster. With Nicholas's connections to Elizabeth, Jennette, and Banning, he would soon discover Mrs. Smith was really Victoria. "You have to promise me what I am about to tell you will not leave this room."

"Of course."

"Have you ever heard Elizabeth or Jennette speak of their friend Miss Seaton?"

"Yes, she owns the home for . . . no, Mrs. Smith is not Miss Seaton."

"One and the same," Anthony replied. "She picked my pocket at the christening party for Banning's daughter. I never felt a thing until Jennette accidentally knocked into her."

"Then how can you be certain it was her?"

"Because she admitted it. We came to an agreement.

I needed a mistress with me to keep Farleigh from becoming an issue. With a mistress, he won't think I am after Hannah. So we agreed that she would help me, and I would not speak of her ability to her friends."

"Ah, a little case of blackmail."

"Perhaps," Anthony commented.

"Can I help you?" Nicholas asked.

Only Selby knew a little about what Anthony did for Ainsworth. And Selby most likely had no idea that so many of the rumors about Anthony were true. However, this was his last job and Nicholas already knew Hardy. Nicholas might be able to get closer to Hardy than he could.

"What do you know of Hardy?"

Nicholas shrugged. "Not much. We met a few times, mostly through Farleigh. He is the second son of Viscount Ellington. I have not heard much either way about his finances so I would assume he is secure."

Anthony lowered his voice to a whisper. "Any reason he might want to see prinny dead?"

"What?" Nicholas's mouth gaped in shock.

"You heard me."

Nicholas's brows furrowed. "I can think of no reason. His family is nowhere near the lineage of anyone of power. I'm far closer to the line of succession than anyone in his family. You are closer."

"I realize that. But is there anyone here who might be closer to the line of succession than you?"

"No one that I have seen so far. Has anyone warned the prince?"

Anthony blew out a breath. "I am not privy to that information."

"What can I do to help?" Nicholas asked. "I am not about to let the future king of England be killed. With Charlotte gone, the line is in question."

"Keep your eyes on Mrs. Smith. I cannot completely trust her. I fear she would turn for a large sum of money." He knew she would do anything for money.

"I don't see her doing that. Surely she has some loyalty to the king."

Anthony closed his eyes. Nicholas always had a soft heart when it came to women. Especially beautiful women. "I have not told her exactly why we are here."

"Then perhaps you should."

That would involve trusting her. And Anthony had yet to be able to do that.

"What an odious man," Victoria muttered as she left the breakfast room.

"Oh my, I do want to hear which odious man, of the many here, you are speaking of."

Victoria stopped at the threshold to the small salon and covered her mouth. Hannah sat in the room holding her daughter. "I am sorry, my lady. I did not know you were here."

"My lady? I told you to call me Hannah. Now come in and close the door so we are not disturbed."

"Yes, ma'am."

Victoria closed the door and took a seat across from Lady Farleigh. "Your daughter is beautiful. How old is she?"

"Suzette is three months old." She held the baby out. "Would you like to hold her?"

Victoria missed all her babies. The youngest was three and didn't require much holding. She reached for Suzette. Holding the little bundle made her homesick.

"Now to which odious man were you referring?" Hannah asked with a smile. "Tea?"

"Yes, please." Victoria had no idea what to tell this woman.

"The man?" Hannah pressed again as she placed the teacup on the small cherry table beside Victoria. "My first guess would be Lord Somerton. He is, after all, your protector and most likely to draw your ire."

Victoria nodded.

"Perfect, we shall start with him," she announced.

Start? What exactly did this woman want her to do? Gossip? Thinking back to the many conversations Victoria had had with Avis, Jennette, Elizabeth, and Sophie, discussing men had become more popular as each married.

"I take it you two had a row."

Victoria had no idea what to say. "I suppose we did."

"Get the man back into bed as quickly as possible. There he will forget the argument and after he is satisfied, he will give you anything you desire."

"It is not that easy," she blurted out before realizing her mistake. This would only encourage the woman.

Hannah frowned and picked up Suzette when the infant started to fuss. "Nonsense."

Victoria stared down at her wool skirt. She wondered again if Hannah and Somerton had been lovers. He would never answer that question, and asking Hannah seemed highly inappropriate. Somehow, she would have to get past this slight jealousy she felt on the matter. Hannah was in love with her husband.

Thinking back to her first time with Somerton, it had been anything but good. While ten years had passed, she still wondered if it would be different than before. If he attempted to seduce her, she doubted she would have the strength to resist him again. But would she feel the incredible magic she'd heard her friends speak of after being with their husbands?

"Anne, what are you woolgathering about?".

She shook her head. "Nothing important. I shall take your advice and do my best to get him into bed."

"Good girl. Once you get him back in your bed, I'll share my secrets for keeping him there and getting that ring on your finger."

Marriage? To Somerton? She could think of nothing worse than that. She highly doubted the man even had a heart. Besides, she didn't want marriage. Even though money was tight at times, she only had to answer to herself.

And Lady Whitely.

But in nine short years, Victoria would not have to do that either. Then the house would be turned over to her free and clear. She could keep the home open to orphans if she wished, or live in it on her own. She knew turning the orphans out wasn't an option but there were days she dreamed of having no responsibilities.

"Anne, you really should mind this penchant you have for woolgathering. A man wants to know the only thing you have on your mind is him."

"Yes, ma'am."

"Now, go speak with that man of yours. We have no activities planned until dinner. Tomorrow we shall decorate the mantels with the greens while the servants hang the mistletoe."

Victoria frowned. "I had always heard that bringing in the holly before Christmas Eve was bad luck."

"Oh, that is nonsense. I don't believe it at all. Now, we have several sleighs, and with the snow overnight, it would make for a romantic ride for you and Somerton."

Victoria did her best to keep from rolling her eyes at the romantic notion. "I shall think about that."

But instead of even attempting to get Somerton into her bed, she decided to do her best to ignore him the rest of the day. At lunch, Hannah changed the seating arrangements so everyone would have a chance to talk to each other. Victoria found herself sitting next to Mr. Hardy and Lord Bingham.

Victoria took her seat next to Mr. Hardy and smiled over at him warmly. "Good afternoon, Mr. Hardy. Lovely weather we are having."

"Good afternoon, Mrs. Smith." He slid a sly glance down the low bodice of her gown. "I will be far happier when spring comes. I am not one for snow."

She took the opportunity to examine the man. With sandy brown hair, small brown eyes, a bent nose, and slightly crooked teeth, he was not the type of man to inspire the sighs of a young girl. While not particularly handsome, he did have some good features. She supposed he might look handsome in a rough manner.

So what caused that sickening feeling in the pit of her stomach? Her skin crawled when he looked over at her.

"Tell me what you do with yourself, Mr. Hardy," she asked.

"I have an estate in Kent left to me from my uncle who had no sons. Unfortunately, no title came with the inheritance so I am merely a country squire."

"Hmm, there is nothing wrong with being a squire."

As the footman placed the plate of fish in front of her, she asked, "What type of amusements do you enjoy?"

He glanced over at her with an eyebrow raised and a smile on his face. Leaning in, he whispered, "I would be happy to show you the amusements I enjoy, Mrs. Smith."

She suppressed a tremble and smiled. "I am sure you could but I am with Lord Somerton right now."

"Of course." He slid another glance down the bodice

of her gown. "Should that situation ever change, I would be pleased to learn of it."

Victoria swallowed back the nausea. Somerton was right about the degenerate men at this party. She would need to be on her guard at all times.

The luncheon proceeded with dull conversation on the weather and politics. Not particularly interested in politics, she kept quiet and observed people at the table. Lord Farleigh appeared in a deep discussion with Lord Ancroft but she couldn't determine the topic from her position.

She looked over at Somerton who, while in conversation with Mr. Singleton, appeared to be listening in to the dialogue between Lord Brentwood and another man. What was Somerton about? He did not seem to be enjoying this party, so why did he insist on attending? She wondered if his reason stemmed from a desire to get Hannah in bed with him.

Although, Victoria had the impression that Hannah loved her husband. So why would Somerton attempt to take Hannah as a mistress? And if that was the case, there was no reason to bring Victoria along with him.

Something else was going on here.

Anthony glanced down the table to where Victoria sat next to Hardy. Perhaps he should have spoken with her as Nicholas suggested, but he could not do it yet. He knew her type. Money was everything. She would not hesitate to give information to another person who paid her more.

Nonetheless, she was sitting next to Hardy. She could have used her wiles to get information from him. Information Anthony desperately needed. No one at this party really seemed to know Hardy.

The only thing Anthony had heard is Hardy might have business with Farleigh. Yet, Anthony had not seen the two say more than a sentence or two to each other. He was starting to wonder if the information Ainsworth had given him was incorrect.

It wouldn't be the first time.

As the luncheon ended, Anthony decided to find out exactly what Victoria might have learned about Hardy. He rounded the table to catch her before she left the room. Clasping his hand onto her elbow, he led her toward their bedroom.

"What are you up to now?" she hissed.

"Am I interrupting some plans you made with Mr. Hardy?"

Reaching the top step, she stopped. "Perhaps you are. It is a beautiful day for a sleigh ride."

"Good, then we shall do just that." He led her down the hall and into their room. "Get your cloak and muff and we shall be off."

He'd had no intention of spending the afternoon with her when he should be watching Hardy. But knowing Nicholas hated the cold, Anthony could have him watch Hardy for an hour.

"I am not going . . ." Her voice trailed off as he glared at her.

"I am paying you to do as I say," he reminded her.

"Of course you are. I will get my things." She quickly returned with her black cloak.

He put on his greatcoat and headed for the door. Once he had the sleigh ride arranged, he escorted her outside. A biting wind took his breath away, and he wondered at this idea. It would have been far more comfortable to talk to her in their room.

With a big bed nearby. And a warm fireplace.

His mind quickly filled with all the wrong ideas.

He shook his head to rid it of all the erotic yearnings. He could not have her again. She was only here to pretend to be his mistress. If only there wasn't that shared past between them. He could have seduced her and started to become tired of her already. Just like every other woman he'd been with.

He tucked the fur blanket around them and then grabbed the reins from the stable boy. With a flick of the reins, they were gliding down across the fields. He looked over at her and smiled. Her eyes twinkled with excitement.

"Can I guess that you have never been on a sleigh before?"

She shook her head. "No," her voice sounded breathy.

Noticing her red cheeks, he asked, "Are you warm enough?"

"Yes." She looked around the open expanse. "It's so beautiful here."

He slowed the horses down and took the time to look around. A fresh coating of snow had turned all the trees to white. The only sounds were the birds chirping. It was as if they were the only two people in the world.

But he was here to do a job. That was all. And if she could assist him, even better.

"How did you find Mr. Hardy?" he asked.

"Do you know him?"

"No. Do you?"

She shivered but he didn't know if it was from the cold or the idea of knowing Hardy.

"I found him to be typical of the men at this party. A libertine only interested in his pleasure."

Anthony's hand fisted. "Indeed?"

"The man looked down the bodice of my dress even

though he knew I was with you. He told me it would please him to learn of our parting."

"Did he now?" The idea that Hardy propositioned her while Anthony sat only six seats away stirred his anger. He'd been unable to find a way to get close enough to Hardy without rousing his suspicion. "I am not certain why that bothered you so terribly. A woman in your position must get used to the leering looks of men."

Her jaw tightened but he waited for her retort disputing her occupation. When she said nothing but glanced away from him, he had no doubts about her.

"Oh, look!" Victoria pointed to a small deer at the edge of the forest. "He's beautiful."

"She is beautiful," he corrected.

"How do you know it's a she?"

"No antlers."

Her cheeks darkened from embarrassment. "Oh."

"How would you know if you have never seen one?" he asked softly for some reason wanting to ease her discomfiture.

"Shall we continue on? Or have you not received all the answers you needed regarding Mr. Hardy? Or perhaps you are not done disparaging my character?"

"Was anything else mentioned?" Ignoring her last comment, he gave a quick slap of the reins and the horses started down the road.

"No. He started to speak of the weather and politics to Mr. Singleton."

"Politics?"

She shrugged under the fur rug. "I didn't really listen at that point."

"Why ever not?" he asked harshly.

She turned her head and stared at him oddly.

"Because I have no interest in politics or Mr. Hardy. Why ever would I listen?"

Since he had told her nothing about his mission, she would have no idea why he would be interested in anything Mr. Hardy said. He released a long breath. The air swirled around him like a mist.

"Of course, you would not be interested in politics," he finally replied.

She tilted her head. "Should I have listened in?"

The woman was far too intelligent. "It might have been useful."

"Will you tell me why?"

"I cannot do that, Victoria. I'm sorry." He actually did feel bad that he couldn't tell her the truth. An intelligent woman might get farther with Hardy than him. But that was out of the question. He could not risk her safety.

"Very well," she said stiffly. "Will we need to stay the entire week?"

"I am not certain yet."

"When will you be certain?"

"I will let you know when I know." He slapped the reins a little harder, eager to be back to the house. "Why are you so impatient to return to London? I thought you would like your adventure out of town."

"I miss my children."

Of course she did, he thought sarcastically. More than likely her reason to return was to get away from him. "I understand."

"If there is something I can do to help us get home faster, will you let me know?" she asked in a soft voice.

He wanted to say no. He wanted to say yes. But in the end, he said in a vague tone, "Perhaps."

Chapter Twelve

After returning from the strange sleigh ride, Victoria walked to her room. Thankfully, Somerton decided to stay downstairs with Lord Ancroft. She wondered what Somerton was truly about today. More and more, she believed he had an ulterior motive for being at this party. And somehow, both Ancroft and Hardy were involved.

She walked slowly from one end of the room to the other. Why would Somerton be interested in Hardy? She knew Somerton would never tell her the truth. Perhaps she could glean some information from Lady Farleigh.

That might work. Talking with Hannah might give her some more insight into Somerton, too. Victoria sat down at the desk in the salon and wrote a quick note to Somerton, telling him she intended to meet with Hannah.

She just hoped she could get to Hannah before it was time to dress for dinner. As she made her way to the door, she realized she needed to relieve herself first. After finishing behind the screen in the bedroom, her breath caught when she heard the door open.

"If she is not in our room, we can talk privately in here," Somerton said quietly.

She heard footsteps walking around the salon and then they stopped. She sat down on the stool behind the screen and waited for them to leave.

"She is with Hannah," he said.

He must have read the note she left on the desk for him. This might give her the opportunity to find out exactly what they were looking for.

"Why haven't you told her yet?"

That was Lord Ancroft's voice. Her cheeks burned with mortification. *Please don't let them walk into the bedroom,* she prayed silently.

"I cannot trust her," Somerton replied. "She's a thief, Nicholas."

"You can't trust any woman," Ancroft commented. "But I think she might be able to help you."

"How?"

"Use her to get to Hardy."

Victoria's eyes widened. So she was right!

"She finds the man to be a lecher," Somerton said. "He was looking down her bodice at the luncheon table even though he knew she was under my protection."

Nicholas laughed. "Sounds like something you would do and yet, she doesn't find you lecherous."

"No, I'm far worse than that in her opinion," Somerton muttered.

"What are you talking about?"

"Nothing important."

Why would Somerton believe she thought so poorly of him? While he hadn't always been a gentleman, he certainly didn't turn her stomach like Hardy. With Somerton nearby the air was always charged with excitement and tension.

"I can't get close to Hardy to find out if he's received

the missive. I checked his room this morning and
found nothing in there."

"If you're not willing to use Miss Seaton, then I
would suggest you engage him in cards tonight. Perhaps attempt to befriend him."

Ancroft knew her name! How did he find out . . .
unless Somerton told him? Somerton knew how
important keeping her name secret was to her.
She pressed her lips together as disappointment cut
through her.

She pushed away her feelings of betrayal and listened to them again.

"All I need is that missive, and then I can get out of
this place."

Nicholas chuckled. "And away from temptation."

Somerton muttered something that Victoria couldn't
decipher.

What was this note he was looking for? If she could
help him find it then they could leave this dratted
party and return to London. She would be away from
him before she let her defenses crumble. There had
to be a way she could assist him.

Ancroft had said they could use her to get close to
Hardy. True, if the note was on his person, she could
probably pinch it from him. But how would she know
if Hardy had the note?

"Get Miss Seaton to pick his pocket, Somerton."

Ancroft knew about that, too!

"I will not use her for this. She is only here to keep
Farleigh off my back about Hannah."

"When will he understand that Hannah loves him?"
Nicholas asked.

"It doesn't help that she will still look at me as if she
wanted to take me to bed right in front of him."

Victoria listened as they both moved in the room.

She prayed they were not walking toward her. The door creaked open and then closed behind them. At least she hoped they had both left. Somerton would be furious if he discovered her eavesdropping on his conversations.

Sitting quietly, she waited for some noise, which would indicate his presence. After a minute, she stood and peeked around the room. He wasn't in here. She tiptoed to the doorway of the salon and peered around the corner. The room was thankfully empty.

She tossed the note for Somerton into the fireplace since she no longer needed to speak with Hannah. Taking a seat by the warm fire, she wondered at that. Hannah might be able to give her information on Hardy. But somehow, Victoria would need to get those details without making Hannah suspicious of her actions.

And as the door opened and Somerton walked inside the room, she knew she had to do something because every time she saw him, her defenses crumbled a little more.

"What are you doing in here?" Anthony asked after closing the door behind him. "I thought you were with Lady Farleigh."

She shrugged. "I needed to think so I decided to return for some privacy. Besides, it will soon be time to dress for dinner."

"Wear the blue velvet tonight," he said then tossed his jacket on a chair.

"Why?"

Could she not know how beautiful she looked in that gown? Perhaps she was acting coy with him. "It matches your eyes."

"Somerton," she started then paused.

"Yes?"

"Do you think we could talk for a few minutes?"

He took the chair across from her and stared at her. "That might depend on the topic."

"I am sleeping in the same bed with a man I know practically nothing about. I thought it might be pleasant if we became better acquainted."

"Why would it matter? You are only here to pretend to be my mistress." Yet even as he gave his usual retort, he wondered at her intent.

She glanced at the fireplace and nodded. "Of course," she mumbled.

"What do you want to know?" he asked in a resigned tone.

"Anything. I know nothing about you. Are your parents alive? Do you have any siblings?"

He supposed it wouldn't hurt to give her a small amount of information. "My father is alive and I have a sister who is twenty."

"Oh," she replied flatly.

How much detail did she need? "Genna, my sister, is engaged to Lord Lindal. They are supposed to marry after Christmas."

She tilted her head and looked at him with a little smile. "Something in your voice tells me you are not completely happy about that."

The woman was far too smart. "Lindal is a good man."

"But . . . ?"

"I am not certain of her feelings for him."

She leaned forward in her chair. "Then you must stop them. You cannot let your sister marry someone if she is unsure of her feelings for him. Marriage is a lifetime commitment. It is vitally important that she love her husband."

Thinking back to the comments from his mother,

he wondered if love was the answer. Loving her
husband had caused her nothing but pain. Perhaps it
would be better if Genna married Lindal, then. If she
didn't love him then he could not hurt her.

"Love is not the answer," he muttered, staring into
the fireplace.

"Who hurt you so badly?" she whispered.

He turned his head and glared at her. "No one."

She looked as if she were about to question him further on that topic but quickly closed her mouth.

"And what about you, Miss Seaton?"

"What about me, Lord Somerton?"

"I am still curious how a woman of no means goes
from selling oranges to living in a home and taking
in orphans."

She stared at him. Her blue eyes hardening. "I
thought you had that all figured out." She rose from
the seat and headed into the bedroom.

Dammit! Why couldn't he let her former profession go? Unless it wasn't her former occupation.
He watched the flames lick the firebox. He didn't want
to know the answer to his question. Because he blamed
himself for what she'd become. If he had never
touched her that night, her life might have turned out
completely different.

He shook his head and walked into the bedroom
to find out what she was doing now. He found her
behind the screen, attempting to unbutton her dress.

"Why didn't you call for a maid?"

"I can do it," she mumbled, straining her arms to
reach the buttons.

"No, you cannot."

He walked behind the screen and swept her hands
out of the way. Just being this close to her sent far too
many erotic thoughts into his head. He unbuttoned

the small buttons one at a time savoring the hint of lavender on her skin. Desire surged in him as he exposed more of her pearly skin.

Hearing her swift intake of breath, he wondered if she felt this same tension. She could not want him after what he'd done to her. But it never stopped him from desiring her. He hadn't stopped thinking about it for days.

"Are you finished yet," she asked in a breathy voice.

He didn't want to be finished. "Yes."

"Would you mind leaving so I may remove my dress?"

"Of course." He walked to the linen press and pulled out his own clothing. He should have hired a lady's maid for her. Hannah said Victoria could use hers but he knew Victoria would not want to bother Hannah just for dressing. Instead, he had no choice but to play lady's maid.

"Somerton?"

"Yes?"

"Could you get these blasted buttons?"

At least this time he would be buttoning her and not undressing her. "Very well."

Restraining his desire for her, he walked back behind the screen and made quick work of the buttons. He waited for her to turn around. What the bloody hell had he been thinking when he ordered that gown for her? The sapphire blue matched her eyes perfectly. The bodice of the dress curved low displaying just a hint of a valley between her small breasts.

"Somerton, are you all right?"

He would never be all right after seeing her in that gown. He had the strangest urge to lock her in the room so no one else would see her.

"I am perfectly well," he said a little too harshly.

She moved past him with a slight shrug. "Very well, then."

He stood behind the screen for a moment to collect his breath. She had absolutely no idea what she did to him. And she could never find out. She would hate him for his lusting after her again. Although, he believed she already suspected it.

After changing into his dinner attire, he held out his arm to escort her to the large salon. They entered the room and a footman handed them both a glass of sherry. Anthony watched as she sipped the liquid vaguely remembering the night she sipped brandy from the bottle at St. George's Church.

Hannah approached them both, a secret smile on her face. "Good evening, Mrs. Smith, Lord Somerton."

"Lady Farleigh, you look lovely tonight," Somerton replied.

Victoria mumbled some response but leveled him with a glare.

"How was the sleigh ride this afternoon?" Hannah pried.

"Very nice," Victoria answered.

"A touch frigid," he replied with a brow arched at Victoria.

"Oh, Somerton," Hannah said with a soft laugh. "Perhaps you should return her to your room and melt her heart."

Victoria tensed.

Somerton looked over at Victoria with a little grin. "Perhaps I should."

Hannah walked away with another light laugh.

"How dare you embarrass me like that," Victoria hissed.

"Haven't you learned by now that I dare to do just about anything?"

She pulled her arm out of his grip and walked away. He watched as she realized her mistake. She glanced around and then sulked back toward him.

"Do not say a word to me," she whispered. "I am only back with you because I know no one else here."

"Do not forget that you are supposed to be my mistress. I believe you should remember that and stop glaring at me."

"Of course," she snapped. "How could I forget about the man who is paying me?"

He almost chuckled at her waspish tone. "Exactly, Mrs. Smith. You will do what I say and when."

"Only if it is part of the act."

He escorted her into the dining room and noticed she was sitting near Hardy again. His brows furrowed in confusion. Had Victoria asked that of Hannah when she went to speak with her this afternoon? Hannah would never agree knowing Victoria was his mistress.

Unless Victoria had confided in Hannah!

They were going to have a long talk tonight. He would get answers from her.

Victoria took a forkful of her pheasant and chewed slowly. Anything to avoid too much conversation with Mr. Hardy. Although, she really should engage him to see what she could learn.

She slid a glance up the table where the exasperating Somerton sat next to Lord Bingham. The old earl could barely keep his eyes open, leaving Somerton with one less person to talk with. He arched a brow at her when he noticed her gaze.

She wondered who had hurt the man so dreadfully that he couldn't respect women. A part of her wanted to tell him the truth about her background. But she could not spill her secrets to him when he wasn't about to spill his.

"Mrs. Smith, I have heard there will be dancing tonight," Mr. Hardy said after a sip of wine. "Will you save me a dance?"

Dancing! Oh, God, she just didn't belong here. "I am sorry, Mr. Hardy but I cannot."

He frowned at her and most likely thought her rude. But it wasn't incivility that made her say no. She might be able to pretend to be a mistress but she would never be able to pretend to be a proper lady.

"Perhaps another time," she added to make him feel better.

"I suppose you will save all your dances for Somerton."

She could have sworn she heard a slight note of jealousy coming from him. If she could find whatever missive Somerton needed then she could return home sooner. Unfortunately, that meant flirting with Hardy.

"I hurt my foot this afternoon, Mr. Hardy. I will not be dancing with anyone tonight."

"Are you all right?"

She smiled at him but felt Somerton's burning gaze from several seats away. "I will be very well. It was just a little twist. I must have lost my footing on a small rock hidden under the snow."

"You should stay inside where it is safe."

She felt far safer alone in a sleigh with Somerton than sitting next to Hardy in a crowded room. "I shall have to remember that."

"Tell me, Mrs. Smith," he paused and looked up the table as if to determine Somerton was not watching. "How long have you been with Somerton?"

"Only a few weeks."

He leaned in closer to ask her. "Are you happy with him?"

"Somewhat," she said trying to be vague. "He does not always please me."

"I could please you," he whispered. "Let me please you, Mrs. Smith."

"I shall think upon it."

"Do that," he said with a leer.

Thankfully, dinner ended before he could proposition her any further. The women walked into the large salon for tea and mulled cider while the men had the brandy and cigars. Lady Farleigh took her spot on the sofa and then patted the seat next to her.

"Mrs. Smith, please join me."

Oh dear, what could Hannah wish to speak with her about? "Yes, ma'am."

"Now, Anne, we do need to talk." She waved her hand at the other women in the room so they would go about their business. "I could not help but notice the tension between you and Lord Somerton."

Victoria only nodded slightly at her.

"I also could not help but notice Mr. Hardy's glances." She leaned in closer to Victoria. "Do you have an interest in Mr. Hardy?"

"I cannot determine much information about the man." Victoria reached for her cider and wished this conversation and party was over. Inhaling, the spicy scent of the cider lifted her lips upward. This was the one indulgence she made every year at Christmas, no matter how tight the money.

"Mr. Hardy is a second son. You are far better off with Somerton. He is a much wealthier man."

Why was Hannah pushing her toward Somerton? It was obvious that she had been intimate with Somerton so why would she want Victoria to be with him? It made no sense. Unless it was strictly to make her husband feel better about Somerton being here. Perhaps that was the answer.

"True, but wealth does not always make the man," Victoria replied. "I might enjoy Mr. Hardy's company more than Somerton's. Though, Mr. Hardy doesn't seem to socialize with anyone here except at the dining table."

Hannah laughed softly "And Somerton does? Hardy is only here with some business proposition for my husband."

"What type of business proposition?"

Hannah tilted her head with a frown. "I would not dream of interfering with my husband's business."

"Of course," Victoria murmured. Believing she had incurred Hannah's curiosity, Victoria changed the topic to the Christmas decorating Hannah had planned for tomorrow.

Finally, the men joined them and Lady Farleigh announced the ballroom was open with musicians for dancing and tables for gaming. Somerton strolled to her and offered her his arm in escort. They walked arm in arm and in silence toward the ballroom.

"Did you enjoy your dinner?" Somerton finally asked, breaking the uncomfortable silence.

"Did you not see who I was sitting next to? How could I enjoy my dinner with Hardy leering at me?" Every time she thought of Hardy, she felt nothing but revulsion.

His brows furrowed. "Did you ask Hannah to seat you next to him?"

She stopped once they entered the room. "For what purpose?"

"There are just so many I can think of. Perhaps you are looking for another protector. Someone who would give you more than just a quick tumble and a few pounds."

She stiffened. She told herself again that it did not matter what he thought she was because she knew the truth. As much as she wanted to throw the truth back at him, she couldn't without the risk of him discovering the secrets she'd promised to keep.

Instead, she decided ignoring him was the best option. She turned her attention to the dancers who had taken the floor. They glided across the dance floor in perfect unison as the musicians played. Oh, how she wished she could dance. To have Somerton hold her close as they crossed the floor would be a dream. The musicians stopped and some couples left the dance floor while others moved onto it.

Lady Farleigh and Mr. Hardy lined up for a dance. Somerton glanced over at them and then down to her.

"Dance with me," he said in a tone far more like an order than a request.

She swallowed the lump of fear in her throat. Why would he imagine she could dance? Was he trying to humiliate her?

"I cannot."

"Excuse me?"

"I cannot dance with you."

"I am paying you to be my mistress. As such, you will dance with me." He started to move them toward the dance floor.

She stopped and glared up at him. He had to be trying to embarrass her. There could be no other reason for his attitude. "I will not dance with you."

He looked down at her and then smirked. "Of course, I should have realized what a good whore you are. Don't worry, I will pay extra for the dance."

Chapter Thirteen

Victoria ran from the room with tears blinding her eyes. His words had cut straight to her heart. Instead of returning to their room where he could easily find her, she sought refuge in the library. She closed the door behind her and walked toward the small fire still glowing in the fireplace.

"Good evening, Mrs. Smith."

She started and then turned to the seat where Lord Ancroft sat with a glass of brandy in his hand. "Good evening, my lord. I had no idea anyone was in here."

"Have you been crying?"

"No," she said, quickly wiping an errant tear away.

"Of course not." He inclined his head toward the seat next to him. "Why aren't you with Somerton?"

She sat and looked over at the handsome man. For a quick moment, she wondered what was wrong with her that she found Somerton so irresistible and not this handsome man. Ancroft was kind, personable, and warm. He actually seemed to enjoy talking with her.

"He said a few unkind words so I decided to steal away for some privacy."

Ancroft nodded in understanding. "Somerton is

not an easy man." He stared into the fire. "I wish I knew why he is so indifferent now."

"Now?"

"I should not have said anything." He lifted up his glass and sipped the brandy slowly. "I apologize. Would you like some brandy or a sherry?"

"No, thank you." She straightened out her skirts. "But I would be interested in learning more about Lord Somerton. You implied that he has changed. Did he?"

Ancroft stared at her for a long moment as if trying to decide what to tell her. "Yes, he was very different. Maybe it was growing up that changed him."

"Most people don't change that drastically."

"Something happened to him." He looked to the fire again. "It was ten years ago. I can't place the exact date but not far from his birthday. Whatever happened changed him from a man who used to care about people and what they thought of him, to a hard, indifferent man."

Ten years ago. She wondered if it was before or after their night together. The times she had seen him before that fateful night, he'd always smiled at her with kindness in his eyes. She hadn't seen that gentleness once since they had reunited.

"He won't tell you what happened?" she asked quietly.

"No, I tried a few times and then gave up. Whatever scarred him so terribly is not something he will speak of."

"Thank you for telling me what you know, Lord Ancroft."

"Don't fall in love with him. He will only hurt you."

She knew she could not fall in love with a man who only wished to hurt her. Lust and desire were not the same as love. But she wished she could help him overcome his demons.

"I will not do that, my lord. May I ask a favor of you?"

He drank down the rest of his brandy and looked over at her again. "Of course."

"I know you were told who I really am." She shook her head when he started to protest. "Please, the only thing I ask is that you keep my secret. I could not bear to have my friends know who I am and what I am doing here with Somerton."

He closed his eyes and nodded. "I can do that, Miss Seaton." He opened his eyes with a smile for her. "How is it that we have never met until now?"

"I honestly don't know. We have always tended to go to Avis's home more than anyone else's home. Now that she, Jennette, and Elizabeth are married, our social time is rather limited."

"That must be it, then."

"Thank you, Lord Ancroft."

He smiled over at her and again she wondered at her fastidious heart. Here was a man who was kind, gentle, and handsome and she felt nothing but friendship for him. There was no tension when he walked in the room as there was with Somerton.

"Nicholas, are you in here?"

Speak of the devil and he appears. Victoria kept her eyes on the fireplace as Somerton entered the room.

"I'm by the fireplace."

"Damn shadows, I can't see a blasted thing." Somerton took a few more steps toward the light. "Have you seen Victoria? I cannot find her anywhere."

Ancroft stood and turned toward Somerton. "Perhaps if you treated her with the kindness she deserved you would not lose her so easily."

"What the bloody hell is that supposed to mean?"

Ancroft walked past Somerton. "I shall leave you two to figure that out."

Damn him, she thought.

"Victoria?" Somerton called out as Ancroft closed the door leaving them completely alone.

"What do you want?"

He walked to the fireplace and took the seat Ancroft had deserted. "Why did you run from me?"

"You really need to ask that question?"

"I would like the truth, Victoria."

"You called me a whore." She stood and walked closer to the fireplace to escape his prying gaze. The last thing she wanted was for him to see how much that remark had hurt her.

"I apologize for that." He rose and closed the distance between them until he was directly behind her. "Why would you not dance with me?"

"I did not wish to dance."

"Did not wish to? Or did not know how?" His hands closed over her shoulders.

"When would I have learned to dance? In between pinching coins from people? Or maybe I hired a dance instructor from all the money I made selling oranges."

"I'm sorry," he whispered, then kissed the spot where her neck met her shoulder. "I was an insensitive lout for not realizing you had never danced before."

She tried to ignore the sensual feel of his lips on her bare shoulder. "No, you were an insensitive lout for calling me a whore."

He smiled against her skin warming her entire body. "You are right, of course."

Anthony had never felt like such a fool. When she ran away from him, he was certain it was for calling her a whore. It had taken him several minutes to realize that she had probably never learned to dance. But he honestly knew so little about her that he didn't know what to believe about her.

"I find I am fascinated by you, Victoria. I want to know so much more about you but every time I question you I don't get the truth."

"I could say the same about you." She pulled away from him and sat back down. "Perhaps I am ashamed."

"Of what?" he asked softly.

"My upbringing."

"I have done plenty of things in my lifetime that I am not proud of. If you ask any of your friends, they would probably tell you to stay away from me because of my reputation. You were a child forced to pick pockets in order to survive."

"Just because I was a child doesn't make it any easier to accept what I've done. And I certainly wasn't a child last week."

He looked back at her and smiled. "But you have made up for your upbringing by taking in orphans and keeping them from making the same mistakes you made."

She fell silent for a moment as if pondering his words. "Tell me about some of the mistakes you made," she whispered.

Why would she want to know about his errors in life? She was the biggest blunder he ever made. "If I do, will you tell me more about yourself?"

She nodded. "I will tell you what I can."

"Very well. I believe one of the biggest mistakes I ever made was how I treated you that night ten years ago."

"Tell me something I don't already know."

He leaned back against the chair and looked at the ceiling in thought. "I sometimes do some jobs for a man in the government. Several years ago, I was in France and Lord Selby and Trey, Lord Kesgrave were assisting me. I was supposed to get some information to them in a timely manner. They decided to finish the job earlier than I had expected. Because I didn't get there in time, a child was killed and Lord Selby shot."

"But you said Selby and Kesgrave went in early. There was nothing you could have done to prevent that."

Anthony stared over at her and shook his head. He closed his eyes so he would not have to see her repugnance. "I didn't get there in time because I stopped at an inn and . . ."

God, he hated admitting what he had done.

"And what?" she asked quietly.

"I was with a woman. If I hadn't stopped for that, I would have been at the location early—before they went inside. Then they would have known about the child."

She reached over and caressed his leg before slowly returning to his knee. Opening his eyes, he stared at her slender fingers on his leg. She had no idea what she did to him physically and mentally. He had told no one his side of the story. Only saying that he'd been delayed getting to Selby and Kesgrave.

"I'm sorry," she whispered. "You could not have known what would happen."

"It does not change things, does it?"

She sat back and shook her head slowly. "No, it does not. Is that why you are here this week? Doing a job for that man in the government?"

He supposed it would not hurt to tell her some of the truth. "Yes."

She smiled at him until his heart started to pound.

What was it about her smile that stirred all sorts of improper thoughts?

"Yes? That is all you can tell me?"

"Unfortunately, that is it. I cannot let anyone know too much information, Victoria." He rose and then poured two glasses of brandy. He handed one to her. Now that he had answered her question, it was his turn. "Can I ask you something?"

She bit her lip and stared at her snifter of brandy. "Very well."

Knowing he could not ask too personal a question to start, he began with what he thought was an easy question. "Who taught you to read?"

She glanced back at him quickly then looked away. "No one of importance."

"Then why is it a secret?" He wanted to know more about her life. How had what they'd done together influenced it? For some reason, he knew it had.

"It was just a woman who lived in the house."

"Mrs. Perkins, then?"

"No, she died when I was sixteen," she replied then covered her mouth with her hand. She looked away as her cheeks turned red.

"So what did you do after Mrs. Perkins died?"

Victoria closed her eyes. She shouldn't be telling him even this much about her life. But he did tell her about a part of his life. Perhaps if he learned the dirty truth, he would be repulsed and leave her alone. Then she wouldn't have to fight this damned attraction to him.

"Mrs. Perkins had no family. So when I found her dead one morning, I called on a man I knew to take her body."

Somerton grimaced. "What type of man?"

"A body snatcher." She stared at him. "A man who would pay me for her corpse. The money he gave me helped me live in her rooms for another three months."

"Why?"

She turned and faced him with all her fury. "Are you jesting with me? My choice was stay in her rooms for as long as I could or go sell my body on the streets. I was trying to find some type of employment but no one wanted a girl with no references, except for their sexual pleasure, of course. Then having no experience was a boon."

"I'm sorry," he muttered and looked away. "What happened after three months?"

How much could she tell him? Knowing he frequented the place, she had to be careful. "I went to work in a brothel," she admitted slowly.

Somerton looked over at her. "Now I know you are lying to me. You were a virgin when I . . . we . . ."

"When we had sex, Somerton."

"I would hardly call it that." He stood and started to pace the width of the library.

Watching him, she realized that her story might be repelling him. But nothing seemed to change her desire for him. Even when he told her about that poor child, she had only wanted to comfort him. Wrap her arms around him and ease his anguish. She had to tell him some of the truth of her time with Lady Whitely.

"I didn't say I worked as a prostitute, only that I worked in a brothel. I kept the rooms."

He stopped by the sofa and grabbed the back of the upholstery. "Why did the owner of the house let you do that? You were young and beautiful and could have brought in plenty of money. Especially for your virginity."

"Believe it or not, she was a kind woman. She never forced a girl to do something she wasn't ready for yet. She told me if I changed my mind she would let me work upstairs."

"So after you and I had sex, as you so eloquently put it," he bit out, "you went to work for her upstairs."

She struggled with how to answer his question. The truth finally came out. "No. I never went upstairs to work for her."

He walked past her, anger seemed to accentuate each word, "Then, how did you end up affording a home on your own?"

"Someone else pays for it."

"Of course," he muttered with disgust.

"Why does my background concern you so? I mean nothing to you."

"You're right," he replied and walked out the door.

Victoria wanted to scream in frustration. Every time she thought they were starting to be honest with each other, something came between them. Part of that was her fault. But she had a promise to keep. She had never met such an exasperating man. He had no right to question her about her life. Everything she had ever done had been out of pure survival, something he would know nothing about as a pampered young buck.

She would never understand the man. Leaving her untouched brandy on the table, she walked to their room. She wondered if Somerton could speak honestly with anyone. And why was he so concerned about her background? She was no one. As soon as this week finished, they would only see each other occasionally.

The idea of seeing him once or twice a year made her heart sink. She wanted to help him, make him see there was still good somewhere deep inside him. But

if he could never be honest with her, she wondered if
there was any hope for him. She stopped at the door
to her room.

If she could not be honest with him, was there any
hope for her?

Anthony crept into the bedroom and breathed a
sigh of relief when he saw her sleeping in their bed.
After stripping out of his eveningwear, he slid into bed
quietly so as not to wake her. She rolled over and now
faced him.

He couldn't look away from her. Her square face
softened and her lips opened slightly. She was driving
him mad. No matter how much he tried to control
himself, he wanted her more than any other woman.
A part of him knew the reason he baited her into ar-
guments was to force a wedge between them. Because
one sign of encouragement from her and he'd have
her on her back.

The glow of the fire reflected gold tones on her
face and neck. She looked like a sleeping angel not a
woman who gave herself to anyone for a few pounds.
Just being in the same bed with her sent blood to his
thickening cock. Knowing he could never have her
was driving him mad.

He only needed a few more days then this hellish
desire would be finished. He could return to London
and sate himself with as many women as it took to
forget her face. Staring at her lush lips, he wondered
if he could survive even one more day without having
her. He could have any woman he wanted. Why did he
have to want her?

He reached out and let his finger softly draw across
her jaw. She sighed. He wondered what she would do

if he attempted to kiss her while she slept. Withdrawing his hand, he knew she would not be pleased.

As the night progressed, he continued to watch her sleep and agonize over his reaction to her. No matter how many times he told himself this obsession over her had to stop, it only seemed to increase. When he discovered she had gone to Nicholas tonight, he could barely contain his jealousy. And he had never been a jealous man with any other woman.

There was just something about her.

Chapter Fourteen

Victoria spent the next morning outside with Hannah cutting holly and evergreens for decorating the house. As she cut another sprig of holly, Victoria wondered why Hannah didn't have the servants do this chore.

Hannah walked to her with a smile. "Smell this," she said, holding out a fresh cut branch of pine.

Victoria inhaled the fresh pine scent and sighed. "It smells wonderful. But don't you think it's bad luck to bring them into the house before Christmas Eve?"

"Utter nonsense, Anne. There is no such thing as bad luck"

Victoria didn't agree. She had seen enough bad luck while living in Whitechapel that she didn't believe in taking chances.

"Come along," Hannah said happily. "I believe we have enough. If we need more I'll send the servants out to cut it. Right now, I need a cup of warm tea."

Victoria nodded and walked with Hannah toward the house. She'd hoped to spend the morning watching Hardy, but Hannah had insisted that Victoria should help her with the evergreens. Finally inside the house, she left her cloak with a footman and walked toward the library in search of Somerton.

But as she turned the corner of the hall to walk to the dining room, she spied Mr. Hardy walking out of the library, slipping a paper into his waistcoat pocket.

That had to be what Somerton was looking for. He'd told Ancroft it was a missive. If she told Somerton, he would most likely be angry with her for eavesdropping. However, if she handed him the note herself, they could be done with this insane mission he was on. She could return home to her children and life might become normal again.

As Mr. Hardy walked toward her, she smiled at him. "Good afternoon, Mr. Hardy."

"Good afternoon, Mrs. Smith."

And if her luck held, she would be seated on his left again, exactly the side on which he placed that note.

"Are you on the way to the luncheon?" Mr. Hardy asked her as he stepped closer.

She had to encourage him on the off chance she wasn't near him during the meal. She smiled at him. "Yes, I am."

He held out his right arm for her. "May I escort you?"

"Yes, I would like that." She prayed Somerton was not in the dining room yet. He would be furious to see her walking in the room with Hardy.

She focused on the lovely landscape paintings that lined the walls as they walked to the dining room. If she thought about how her skin felt like it was crawling with bugs, she might just run. As they strolled into the room, she cringed at the sight of Somerton speaking with Ancroft.

Somerton looked over at her with the coldest gaze she had ever seen. He started to step forward until Ancroft placed a hand on his arm.

Hardy seemed to ignore the sudden tension and said, "Here you are, Mrs. Smith. Unfortunately, we will not be near each other."

"Perhaps after the luncheon we could talk?"

Hardy's eyes lit up. "Where would you like to meet?"

"Farleigh's study."

"I will meet you in there," he replied and then walked to his seat across the table.

Now she just had to get through this meal sitting between Somerton and Lord Bingham. Since the old earl appeared to sleep through half his meals, she doubted he would rescue her with conversation.

Somerton strolled over looking casual to all observers, except Victoria. She noticed how tight he clenched his jaw and the slight tic in his cheek. He pulled out the chair for her. His hot breath burned her shoulder.

"We will talk about this after the luncheon," he whispered in her ear.

"I have plans." She sat in the chair and smiled at the couple sitting across from her.

"You will meet me in our room."

"Of course." But not until after she had met with Hardy. If all went well, she could hand Somerton the note and pack her bags.

Somerton sat beside her. After being near Hardy, Somerton's presence felt oddly comforting. It made no sense. Somerton was a far more dangerous man than Hardy.

Sitting between Somerton and Lord Bingham, the meal seemed excruciating. Somerton barely spoke to her. Bingham's head nodded a few times as if he were sleeping. The couple across from them appeared so devoted to each other that they scarcely conversed with anyone, save themselves.

As the luncheon finished, she rose and started for the door only to have Somerton clasp his hand around her elbow. "I believe we have a meeting."

She yanked her elbow out of his grip. "I must speak with Lady Farleigh first. She asked for my assistance with the decorations for the ball."

"You have one hour," he replied in a harsh tone. "If you do not return to our bedchamber by then, I will find you."

"I understand." Although, she didn't feel terribly relieved. Too much could happen in an hour alone with Hardy. She had to find a way to get that missive quickly.

She walked away from Somerton toward Lord Farleigh's study. She entered the room to find Mr. Hardy sitting in a wingback chair with a glass of brandy in his hand.

"Good afternoon again, Mrs. Smith." He held up his glass of brandy. "Would you care to join me?"

"No spirits for me." She strolled to the chair across from him with a smile.

"So," he drawled. "What exactly did you wish to speak with me about?"

She adjusted the line of her silk skirts. "Lord Somerton and I have not been getting along as of late. I was curious about your reason to know about the ending of our relationship."

"I believe you know." He sipped his brandy. "Are you certain you would not like some?"

"I prefer a clear head when making decisions such as these."

He smiled at her in a leering manner. "I am glad to see how seriously you take such negotiations."

"I must. After all, this is my life and income we are discussing. A head muddled with spirits would let you take advantage of me." She smiled back at him. "And I will never allow that to happen."

He nodded. "I do like an intelligent woman."

"So tell me, Mr. Hardy, what can I expect from you?"

"I shall be anything you would like. A gentle lover, a demanding lover—"

"I meant," she interrupted, "Exactly what type of benefits would I enjoy. After all, I am giving up a very generous man."

Hardy tilted his head slightly and stared at her with probing brown eyes. "Yes, you are. Tell me, Mrs. Smith, exactly why are you looking to leave a man like Somerton for someone like me? After all, he will be an earl someday, while I am a lowly second son."

Victoria laughed in a light tone. "Lord Somerton is . . . shall we say, not an easy man. He demands perfection in everything and expects me to comply with his every whim. I prefer a little more give and take in such a relationship."

He smiled slowly "I agree. If I wanted a woman who only did what I told her, then I would marry."

Victoria tried not to show her disgust. She glanced at him once more attempting to find something redeeming about the man. She found nothing. As her gaze fell to his striped waistcoat, she noticed the slip of paper sticking out of one pocket. Now it was just a matter of getting the note. Then her job would be done and she could return home.

Hardy cleared his throat as if he noticed her woolgathering. "I will furnish you with a house in Mayfair and as many servants as you need. Your clothing will be paid for along with any other thing you require. In addition, I will send a monthly allowance to you. Does that satisfy your needs?"

"Mr. Hardy, you are more than generous," Victoria

said softly. "However, I must not enter into a new relationship until I break things off with Lord Somerton. I should hate to do that in a public place like this party. Upon my return to London, I shall inform Lord Somerton of my desire to end our relationship. Therefore, until we return to London, I believe we should be circumspect in our behavior. I would feel dreadful if something happened to you because Somerton discovered our newfound friendship."

She stood to leave, but knew she had to get closer to him first.

"I agree, Mrs. Smith." Hardy stood to take her elbow to escort her out the door.

Victoria stopped and turned toward him. His eyes darkened with unmasked desire. "Perhaps we should seal our upcoming arrangement with a kiss?"

His smile turned to a leer. "I could not agree more."

Before she could take a step closer to him, he yanked her to him and pressed his wet lips to hers. Tampering down the nausea in her stomach, she wrapped her arms around his neck and returned his kiss. The disgusting sensation of his vile kiss was nothing like the sensual feel of Somerton's lips on hers. Not wanting this kiss to last any longer than necessary, she slowly brought her arms down, slid the paper out of his waistcoat and into her pocket before pushing him away with her hand.

"You are a very eager man, Mr. Hardy." She plastered a smile on her face and turned to the door.

"When will I see you again in private?"

"Hopefully soon." *Hopefully never!*

As she reached for the door, she realized he was directly behind her. He pulled her up against his chest and kissed the nape of her neck. "Very soon," he murmured.

"I must leave now, darling."

"Of course." He backed away and let her open the door.

Once out in the hallway, she stopped and breathed in deeply. Eager to find Somerton and show him the paper, she raced to their bedroom. She opened the door to find him pacing the room with a look of dark fury on his face. She stepped inside, and he halted his stride.

He turned to her, his eyes a dark shade of green. "You let the man kiss you?"

That was why he was furious? And how did he discover that fact? "You were listening in on my private conversation?"

"Yes. When I saw you going into Farleigh's study and Hannah walking up the stairs, I knew you were not meeting with her to discuss ballroom decorations."

"So you followed me and eavesdropped?"

He stepped menacingly closer to her. "It is what I do. Now why did you kiss him?"

His anger had caused her irritation to grow. "Why does that concern you? Are you the only man allowed to kiss me now?"

"Yes," he said as he dragged her to him and lowered his lips to hers.

His lips felt hard and punishing against hers. And somewhat wonderful. As his tongue slashed across hers, she responded to his demands. A jealous man had never kissed Victoria, but if she had to guess what it felt like, this would be it. Although she was certain, Somerton would never let such an emotion control him.

Anthony poured every bit of frustration and jealousy into his kiss. Never in twenty-eight years had he felt anything like the reaction he had when he realized she had allowed Hardy to kiss her. He'd listened to their conversation from the secretary's office, clearly overhearing every word. But the moment he comprehended the silence in the room, his world had spun around him.

He pulled away from her and then turned toward the windows. His heart pounded in his chest. How could she have kissed Hardy?

"Would you mind telling me exactly what that was about?" she ordered.

"No."

"Would you like to know why I kissed him?"

Anthony clenched his fists as his frustration with her grew. "I believe it was obvious that you were making the proper arrangements for when we are finished."

She had the audacity to laugh. "You can't possibly believe I would have anything to do with that disgusting man, do you?"

"You sounded damned convincing to me."

"Thank you," she replied.

He turned to face her again. "What?"

"If I hadn't been able to convince Hardy, I never would have picked this out of his waistcoat," she said as she pulled the paper from her pocket.

"You pinched a note from him?" he almost shouted at her. He couldn't remember the last time he felt so much anger coursing through him.

"You were having trouble getting close to him. I saw him place a note in his pocket, and knew I could get it from him. Now we can get back to London."

"Give me that," he said, snatching it out of her hand. He didn't want to think about just how foolish he must look to her. He'd never let jealousy get the upper hand with him. Until now.

As he read the letter, his jealousy turned to rage.

"How could you have done this without letting me know beforehand?"

"I overheard you talking with Lord Ancroft and learned you were looking for a note on Hardy." She sat in the chair looking far too pleased with herself. "So I picked it from him."

"You stupid little fool," he said in a low tone. "You might have just cost me this entire mission."

Her eyes opened wide with fear. "What do you mean?"

He tossed the note on her lap. "It is a letter to his mother. Nothing more. Now he will suspect you took it from him. Now he will believe we are working together on this."

She bit her lower lip and scanned the letter. "I'm so sorry," she whispered.

"You ruined everything, Victoria. You with your impatience to get away from me. Are you desperate for my money so you can leave your current lover? Will Hardy be the next one in your bed?"

"What?" She strode to the door, but he was not done with her yet. He turned her around and forced her against the door.

"How could you let him kiss you?" he demanded again before bringing his lips down on hers. He wanted to punish her. He wanted her to know that he was the only man who should kiss her.

As her velvety tongue touched his, desire and need clawed at him. He wanted to be the one she offered herself to, not Hardy or any other man. Bringing his hands around to her back, he ripped the back of her dress. He kissed her harder until she whimpered.

He wanted to feel her breasts against his chest. Feel her soft body riding him. As he attempted to pull her dress down, she pushed him so hard he stepped back.

"Is this the only way you can make love with a woman?" she cried. "Forcing her up against a door or the wall of a church?"

Her words were like a bucket of cold water dousing him and his desire. What the bloody hell was wrong with him? She ran to the bedroom and fell to the bed. He strode from the room unable to face what he had almost done.

Again.

Why?

Victoria sat up on the bed and wiped her tears. Why would he treat her like that? All she'd done was try to assist him. And he thought to force her. She thought back on the interaction and suddenly realized something absurd.

He had been angry with her about the note, but he seemed far more furious over the fact that Hardy kissed her. Somerton was jealous. Angry and jealous and possessive. Those punishing kisses had come from jealousy.

A little smile lifted her lips. He wanted her. Her heartbeat increased with the idea. If she had let him, he would have made love to her. Perhaps not in the manner she would have preferred, but he would have nonetheless.

Still, anger simmered within her at his method. If he'd told her of his jealousy, she could have eased his mind. He should have talked to her. Not that he seemed to have the ability to speak with her honestly about anything.

Well, she was not about to soothe him now. He would have to come to her. She almost laughed aloud at the thought of Somerton apologizing to her. The man was more stubborn than a mule.

She rose and rang for a maid. She wanted a bath and change of clothing before he came back into the room. In truth, she wished to be done and departed from the room before he returned. She had no desire to speak with him for a while.

As soon as she finished with her bath and dressing, she picked up the letter to Hardy's mother and placed it in her pocket. She needed to return this to the study where he could find it, and not suspect that she'd taken it. Leaving the room, she paused and listened for any sound that might indicate Somerton coming nearer.

Victoria checked the stairs and then strolled down them. The door to the study was open so she cautiously entered the room. Finding no one there, she placed the note on the floor by the chair Hardy had sat in. She crossed the room eager to leave and find a quiet place to read for now.

"Mrs. Smith, what are you doing in here?"

She stopped and stared at Hardy. What was she doing here? "I came in to see if I had left my book of poetry here earlier. Have you seen it?"

"No. I don't remember you coming in here with a book," he commented.

She frowned as if truly pondering this situation. "Indeed? Then where could I have left it?"

"I do not know. I came here looking for a letter I had on my person before we spoke. It seems to have gone missing from my pocket."

"Oh, perhaps it dropped out when we . . ." She looked away as if embarrassed by talking about kissing.

"Perhaps." He walked to the chair and glanced around. "There it is." He picked it up and placed it back into his pocket.

"Well, I must continue searching for my book. Good day, Mr. Hardy."

"Mrs. Smith, wait." He walked closer until he was next to her. "Do you think we might meet later?"

She smiled at him. "No, Mr. Hardy. As I said earlier, I must break things off with Lord Somerton first."

"Is that right?" Somerton's voice sounded from the threshold.

A part of her was relieved that Somerton entered the room before Hardy attempted to kiss her again. But another part of her felt a sudden stab of anger.

Somerton leaned against the door in a casual manner with his arms folded across his chest. "Perhaps one of you would like to explain what is going on?"

"Mr. Hardy, you should leave while I speak with Lord Somerton."

"I think I would prefer to stay."

"Oh, do stay, Hardy." Somerton stalked into the room like a panther. "But let us get one thing out of the way. Mrs. Smith is my mistress. She is not yours, nor will she ever be yours."

As Somerton approached Hardy, she noticed Hardy's eyes widen with fear.

"I understand." Hardy strode from the room before Somerton stepped closer.

She waited until Hardy was out of earshot. "Well done, Somerton. I am certain he will not bother me again." She walked toward the door only to have him spin her around to face him.

"We are not done talking."

She arched a brow at him and twisted out of his grip. "After this afternoon, we are absolutely finished."

Chapter Fifteen

Victoria took her seat for dinner just as Lord Ancroft walked in with Somerton at his side. She looked away as Somerton glanced toward her. She could never remember feeling so disappointed in a person. And yet, the idea that there was something redeeming about Somerton would not leave her. She still wanted to discover that part of him.

Hardy took his seat next to her and rubbed his leg against her thigh. She had the greatest urge to inch her seat next to Lord Bingham and away from Hardy. She doubted the old earl would even notice.

Somerton's icy glare blasted her from across the table.

"Are you all right, Mrs. Smith?" he asked with concern lacing his low voice. "You look a little pale."

Victoria blinked and looked away from Somerton. "I am quite well. I just remembered it was my sister's birthday and I have forgotten to send her my wishes for a happy year."

"Ah, of course."

She ate far too quickly in an attempt to get away from Hardy. Not that it mattered since dinner was a five-course event that took hours. Then she would have to wait for Lady Farleigh to rise and call the ladies to the salon. She poked at her roast duck but could not stomach it tonight.

"Mrs. Smith, will you attend the mummers' play this evening? Lady Farleigh has been planning this for months. Or would you prefer to play a card game tonight?" Hardy asked and then stuffed a large piece of duck into his mouth.

She couldn't believe after the confrontation in the library that he would ask such a thing. Hannah had brought in a mummers' troupe to perform a midwinter play but also promised a full selection of cards and games to keep everyone occupied. All Victoria wanted to do was escape from the noise and people, mostly Hardy and Somerton.

"I do not believe it would be wise to do either. Besides, I may retire early tonight, Mr. Hardy. I feel a most dreadful headache coming upon me."

"Would you like me to escort you to your room?"

The man just did not know when to stop. Was he trying to provoke Somerton? "I do not believe that would be proper."

"Of course. It is only proper if Somerton escorts you."

"Tsk, tsk, do not show your jealousy to me."

Would this meal ever end? She slid another glance toward Somerton. If only he would tell her of the demons he fought. Even after this afternoon's debacle, she was certain there was something else behind it. Some need of his to control the situation, but why? A need to control her, perhaps? All women?

Finally, dinner ended. As the ladies strolled into the salon, she caught up with Hannah.

"Hannah, I must get some air."

Hannah frowned. "It is frigid outside."

"I shan't be gone for long. I need some time alone to think."

"Is Somerton still giving you trouble?" Hannah asked.

She nodded. "And Hardy too."

"Very well, then. I will think of some excuse for you. But not too long, or I shall be forced to send a footman out to find you."

"Thank you." She raced upstairs to get her wool cloak and then outside.

The peace and darkness enveloped her like a cave. She walked a little ways down the path until she found a seat in what must be a garden in the summer. She brushed powdery snow off the bench and sat. With the stars twinkling down at her, for the first time in a very long time she was alone.

If only her biggest problem could be solved by sitting out here by herself. At some point tonight, she would have to face Somerton again. While she should be furious with him for his actions, and a part of her was, she felt his pain too. Something was eating at him and it had to do with her.

"What the bloody hell are you doing out here in the cold?"

She turned slightly to see him staring at her as if she must have lost her mind. "I needed some time alone. Now, if you do not mind, I would like to continue to be alone."

Instead of listening to her, Somerton stepped forward and then took a seat on the far end of the bench. If he moved only a few inches, they would touch.

"Did you know I was out here?" she asked.

"Lady Farleigh mentioned that I might need to go for a walk tonight. She said the cold air might do me good."

"I see." She wondered why Hannah would do such a thing.

They sat silently for a few moments before he finally shifted in his seat.

"I can't apologize enough for my actions, Victoria," he whispered, staring at the frozen ground in front of him. "I was a bloody idiot."

"Yes, you were. But why?"

"I was angry."

"Why?" she pressed.

He blew out a breath and she watched air swirl around him. "My entire life has been nothing but secrets and lies. You have done nothing but lie to me or keep things from me. Hearing you make plans with Hardy sent me over the edge. I know it is no excuse."

"No, it is not. Especially when you are keeping secrets of your own." She inched a little closer to him. "Were you jealous of Hardy?"

"Yes," he admitted softly. "When I close my eyes and think about him kissing you, I want to strangle the man."

"I was only trying to help you," she whispered.

"I know that now."

She desperately wanted to keep him talking to her. Maybe then, he would disclose something of himself to her. "Do you think there is any way we could reveal some of our secrets without divulging everything?"

He turned his head slightly and looked at her with a small smile. "I would like to try."

"Very well, I shall start," she said. "A woman paid me to take her baby in after she discovered she was with child. She was a wealthy woman who could not afford to let her secret get out. She bought the house for me to stay in while raising her child. Once her daughter is eighteen, she promised to turn the house over to me."

"A woman," Somerton said, shaking his head with a long sigh. "I should have assumed that was the case. What if her husband discovers the truth?"

"She is not married. At least, not to my knowledge. She might have been at one time. Honestly, the topic never came up."

"Is she the one who taught you to read?" he asked, then moved a little closer to her.

"Yes, and she taught me to speak correctly and my manners. She wanted me to be able to teach her daughter all these things, too. Once I learned to read, I went to the lending library and brought home books on history and mathematics. It was as if a whole new world had opened for me." She looked over at him and smiled. "I did discover that I don't like mathematics much."

He laughed softly. "I loved mathematics in school. Poetry bored me, but with numbers I was happy."

"I cannot tell you any more than that. I promised the woman I would never reveal her name."

"Thank you."

Anthony knew she was waiting for him to admit his secret but he had no idea how to do so without telling her everything. But as she said, they could reveal some of the secrets without telling the entire truth. He could at least try.

"When I was ten, two days before Christmas, I was told my mother died in a carriage accident."

Her eyes widened and she reached for his hand. "I'm sorry."

"You had lost both parents by then." He squeezed her hand. "For eight years, I lived with my father believing what he'd told me. Then that night ten years ago, I found out differently."

"What do you mean? Your mother didn't die in a carriage accident?"

He closed his eyes to block out the pain he felt whenever he thought about that night. "I found out my mother was still alive."

"Are you certain?"

"Very. After I found out the truth, I picked up a bottle of brandy and ended up at St. George's."

"Well that explains quite a bit. But did your parents reconcile?"

He almost laughed aloud. "No. She wants nothing to do with my father. She left because he had kept not just one but several mistresses and one even had his child."

"Does he know that she is still alive?" she whispered. "It must have been dreadfully hard when he found out the truth."

This time he did laugh, albeit scornfully. "Yes, it must have been hard on him especially since he'd known for eight years. He is the one who made up the story about the carriage accident."

She covered her mouth with her hand. "Oh, my God," she mumbled. "Did she run off with another man?"

"Not quite." Men, maybe but not just one. "I'm afraid I can't tell you more about her without disclosing things I have promised to keep secret."

She put her finger against his cold lips. "Then do not say another word."

He kissed her finger and then held it in his hand. "I must. There is no justification for how I treated you this afternoon. But I am more sorry than I can ever express to you."

He cupped her frigid cheeks and kissed her softly. "I promise I will never treat you like that again."

"Thank you, Somerton."

"I would not mind if you called me Anthony."

She smiled against his lips and kissed him again. "Thank you, Anthony."

"Ancroft told me I should have told you days ago why I am here."

She looked up into his eyes. "You have decided to trust me?"

He smiled down at her. "Perhaps just a little. A man I do some work for asked me to watch Hardy. There is a rumor that there may be an attempt on the regent's life. Hardy is suspected of being the messenger."

"That is why you are looking for a note on him."

"Exactly."

Her brows furrowed deeply. "But why didn't you come to me? You know I can pick his pocket. And being a woman, I can get much closer to him without drawing suspicion."

"I didn't want to drag you into this, Victoria. I have no idea what Hardy is capable of doing."

"Thank you for telling me this. If I see Hardy with anymore notes, I will tell you."

"We need to go back inside before you freeze completely." He rose and held out his hand for her. Once she stood next to him, he said, "I need you to do me an important favor. I know I don't deserve your assistance after this—"

"What do you need?" she interrupted.

"Can you keep Hardy busy downstairs while I check his room again?"

"He asked me to either attend the mummers' play or join him in cards tonight. I will determine which he has decided to do and try to engage him while you investigate his room. How long will it take you?"

He pulled out his pocket watch and held it out to see in the moonlight. "I will need at least thirty minutes. I will return to the salon once I am finished."

"Very well." She brought her hand up to his cheek. "Be careful tonight."

"I plan to. Do not let Hardy take you to a room alone." As much as he tried, there was still a slight tone of jealousy to his voice.

"I have no intention of doing that."

They walked together in a comfortable silence toward the house. He wondered if she could ever truly forgive him for his actions of both today and ten years ago. He wanted to make it up to her in some way but knew of nothing that would help. Perhaps some day, she could tell him more about her past. There were still things she kept from him whether from a promise to another or not.

Asking her for more was hardly fair when he could never reveal the identity of his mother . . . or half sister.

Victoria first entered the ballroom where the mummers were set to entertain. Old Father Christmas stepped across the stage to introduce the play and the characters. She glanced at the people seated and could not find Hardy.

Praying that he hadn't retired to his room, she entered the salon where card games along with chess and backgammon were set out for the guests. She found Hardy standing near a window, watching the games in play. Slowly, she made her way over to his location.

"Mr. Hardy," she said as she neared him. "I am feeling much better now and would love to play cards."

"How about backgammon instead? There is a table set for two over there," he replied, pointing to a small table set away from most of the others.

"All right, but I have to admit I am not very skilled at that game."

"I shall teach you some strategies." He held out his arm for her to link.

After a moment of hesitation, she took his arm and they walked to the table. She took her seat and stared at the board. Lady Whitely had taught her to play several years ago, but Victoria hadn't touched the game since.

"Why don't you go first since I haven't played in awhile?"

"Of course," he answered, then quickly reviewed the rules of the game and some simple strategies.

Victoria sneaked a quick glance at the clock on the mantel. It was already half past ten, so she needed to keep him occupied until at least eleven.

"Bored with the game already? Or are you bored with me?" he asked when she returned her gaze to the board.

"Neither. I was just checking the time. I did not realize how long I had been gone from the house."

He sat back as she took her turn and smiled. "Yes, did the fresh air help your headache or did Somerton's company help?"

She tried to hide her shock by staring at him directly and arching an eyebrow. "Somerton joined me outside without my permission. However, I did take the time to speak to him about my desire to end the relationship."

"Was that before or after he kissed you?"

The man had outright admitted to spying on her! "That peck on my lips was nothing more than a kiss good-bye."

"Is he leaving, then?" Hardy glanced around the room as if to verify that Somerton wasn't in the room.

She took her turn and moved her checkers. "He said he preferred to stay. Unfortunately, Lady Farleigh is out of bedrooms so we will continue to stay in the same room. He did offer to sleep on the sofa."

"You could stay with me," he offered as he rolled the dice.

"I could, but I would not wish to embarrass Lord Somerton in front of everyone. Besides, he is a very jealous man."

"So I have heard. Did things end well?"

She watched as he moved his checkers and then moved one of hers off the board. "As well as could be expected. He was not surprised since we have been arguing more than ever lately."

"I see. How soon after we return to London can I call upon you?"

She needed an excuse to keep him away! "After the new year. I must spend Christmas with my sister."

"Ahh, the same sister who is having a birthday today?"

"Yes."

"And what is her name?"

Name? He wanted a name! Why was the man interrogating her? "Mrs. Lillian Johnson. She and her husband David live in a small home on Hereford Street." She leaned in closer to the table and him. "She married beneath herself. My father wanted her to marry a squire near Carlisle."

"Why didn't she do as her father expected?"

She really was far too good at telling stories. Perhaps

she should speak with her friend Avis upon her return and talk with her about writing. "She and David skipped off to Gretna Green. By the time they had returned, she was already with child. My father was scandalized."

"And I would guess your mother, too," he added.

"Alas, my mother passed before that happened."

"I'm sorry," he said, then took his turn.

Victoria glanced up again at the clock. Somerton said thirty minutes and already thirty-five had passed with no sign of him. She looked down at the board and realized Hardy had several of his checkers already in. He could win the game in a turn or two. She had to come up with something to occupy his time until Somerton returned.

"So do you plan to visit your mother over the Christmas season?" she asked to keep their conversation going.

"It will depend on some things I have in progress."

What an odd answer. "What type of things do you have in progress?"

He waved a hand at her and shook his head. "Just business things. Nothing that would interest you."

She smiled in what she hoped was a seductive manner. "Oh, you might be wrong. I find everything about you fascinating."

"Do you now? Perhaps when I get to know you better I will confide in you. But not until I know I can trust you."

She blinked in surprise. "Trust me? Why wouldn't you trust me?"

"You are still far too close to Somerton. And I do not trust him. He has barely given Farleigh the time of day for years because of his marriage to Hannah."

"Why would Somerton care about that?"

"She and Somerton were close before she met Farleigh. Then he shows up here with you. There is more to his being here than just wanting to be at a party."

"Such as?" she prodded.

"I believe he wants Lady Farleigh back in his bed."

She tried to ignore the way her stomach clenched. "But Lady Farleigh seems very much in love with her husband."

"All just an act to make Farleigh believe that the little slut is faithful to her husband."

"Then why would Somerton bring me along?"

Hardy sneered at her. "To make Farleigh believe that he is not a threat to the Farleighs' marriage. But as you say, you and Somerton have been arguing more. Perhaps that is because he planned to break it off with you to get Lady Farleigh again."

Victoria chewed on her lower lip in thought. She wanted to believe Hardy was lying about this matter. But as she watched Somerton cross the threshold and glance over at Lady Farleigh, Victoria wondered if Hardy was speaking the truth.

Chapter Sixteen

Anthony watched as Victoria and Hardy continued to play their game of backgammon. After searching Hardy's room for close to forty-five minutes, he had come up with nothing. Either Hardy was keeping some information on him or the missive had yet to be delivered to him.

Anthony's frustration with the situation grew with every moment he spent at this damned party. He had to find the note and return Victoria to London before he did something they might both regret.

Nicholas walked up to him casually. "They have been playing backgammon for nearly an hour. Before that, he played a game of cards with Lord Bingham."

"Thank you, Nicholas." Anthony lowered his voice to a mere whisper. "I just checked his room and found nothing to incriminate him."

"Do you think you might have been given the wrong information?"

"It wouldn't be the first time."

Anthony noticed the strange side glances that Victoria kept giving them. He would have to remind her to be more careful. Hardy might get suspicious. Slowly, she rose from her seat and gave Hardy a secretive smile. The urge to storm over there and kiss her in front of everyone grew.

What was wrong with him?

He had never felt such a strong reaction to a woman before now. Jealousy had never played a part in any relationship he'd had with other women. So why now? Especially when she was merely playing a part.

She walked past him without a look toward either him or Nicholas. He listened as her heels clicked down the marble hall. Noticing Hardy's gaze on him, Anthony knew he had to wait before following Victoria to their room.

Hardy walked over toward them with a smug smile. All of Anthony's senses heightened. The man seemed far too comfortable right now. As if he knew something Anthony did not. A slice of fear tracked down his back. Something was wrong.

He didn't wait any longer and hurried back to his bedroom. Opening the door, he found Victoria sitting in the wingback chair with shoes off and her legs curled under her. He backed up against the door. The sheer beauty of her captivated him. He was a fool to think he could resist her.

"What are you about, Somerton?" she asked though her voice held the tiniest quaver.

"Nothing at all," he replied.

"Did you find anything in Hardy's room?"

"No."

"Somerton, why are you still standing against the door?" she asked. "Are you feeling well?"

Bloody hell, he was not all right. Just seeing her sitting there in that chair had him hard with desire.

How was he supposed to sleep in the same bed with her tonight?

"I need to leave," he mumbled.

"Why?"

He turned toward the door and pounded his fist on it. Why couldn't she understand how difficult this was for him? Because she did not know.

"If I don't leave here right now, I am going to pick you up and take you to that bed." He glanced back at her shocked face. "And we will not be sleeping."

She licked her full lips sending another rush of blood to his cock. "What if I said that was all right?"

"It isn't all right, Victoria." He pounded on the door again. "After what I did to you ten years ago and then almost did today!"

"I thought I meant nothing to you," she whispered.

He turned and stalked her. Stopping in front of her, he pulled her out of the chair and grabbed her shoulders. "What happened that night forged a bond between us that quite possibly neither of us wants to admit. I never stopped thinking about you or what I did to you. So do not ever think you mean nothing to me. I searched for weeks all over the streets of London, trying to find you again. No one knew of you."

Victoria's heart skipped a beat. *He'd searched for her.* She'd spent weeks believing she had been nothing to him but a release of sexual frustration.

Blinking back the tears that suddenly sprung up, she whispered, "Why?"

"Because what I did that night was criminal."

"It was hardly criminal, Somerton. Ungentlemanly without a doubt but not an unlawful act." She tried to wiggle, unsuccessfully, out of his grip.

"Since when isn't rape a criminal offense?" he demanded.

"Oh, my God," she whispered and then covered her mouth. How could he have thought such a dreadful thing?

"What?"

"Somerton, you never raped me."

He released her so quickly she fell back against the chair. "I was there. And while I'd had far too much to drink that night, I succinctly remember you saying no."

He turned and headed back to the door. Victoria struggled out of the chair to catch him before he left. She could not let him think that he raped her. Just as he reached for the doorknob, she threw herself against his back and held on to him.

"Dammit, Victoria," he growled. "Let me go. I cannot stand being in here another moment. I know what I did, and if you think back, you will remember exactly what happened. I just can't be around when you do."

"Somerton," she cried, tears dampening his jacket. "You did not rape me. I only had a few sips of your brandy. I wasn't drunk. I remember everything that happened that night."

"Then you must remember telling me no. I heard it and remember it like you said those words only yesterday. Only that night I was too foxed to think coherently and acted like a bloody fool."

She rested her head against his strong back and felt his heart pound under her left hand. The urge to ease his pain had never been stronger. "I only said no because I didn't want my first time with you to be on the steps of St. George's Church."

He dropped his head to the door. "Victoria, you were an innocent. You said no and I should have stopped."

"I wanted you that night," she whispered. "I wanted you so badly that instead of trying to get you to understand that I wanted to go some place private, I let you do as you pleased."

"It was rape."

"No, I wanted you that night almost as much as I want you now."

Slowly Anthony turned around and faced her. Hearing her tell him that she wanted him changed everything.

"What did you say?" He slid his thumbs across her cheeks, wiping away the tears she'd shed for him.

"I wanted you desperately that night. There was no one else that I wanted to be with for my first time."

And he had treated her like a common whore. While inexperience might have been an excuse, he should have known better. "I'm sorry."

"You were obviously upset about something that night."

"Yes. And it might have been better if I'd had more experience," he muttered.

"Like it would be now?" she whispered so quietly he almost didn't hear her.

He brought his lips to her cheeks and trailed a path to her ear. "Would you like to find out?"

"Oh, God, yes."

Bending down, he wrapped his arm around the back of her legs and picked her up. As he walked her to the bed, he stared at her, waiting for any sign of second thoughts. But her blue eyes sparkled with desire.

He placed her beside the bed and kissed her softly until she moaned. Breaking away from her tempting lips, he turned her around.

"The past few days of having to act as your lady's

maid has been torture," he admitted as he worked at the buttons on her dress.

"Good. I didn't want to be the only one in the agony of unrequited desire."

As her dress slid down her body, he kissed the nape of her neck. She shivered as he moved his lips down her shoulders to her shift. He quickly unlaced her stays and removed the garment. Eliminating her shift and petticoats, left her standing in front of him with just her stockings on.

"Take your hair down for me," he whispered. "I want to see all your glorious hair."

"Now?" she squeaked.

"Yes." He stared down at her small rounded breasts, itching to cup them in his hands.

He watched as her breasts moved when her hands went to the pins in her hair. As each pin dropped to the floor, his desire increased. He wanted to lay her down and sink himself into her warm depths. But this time was for her. He'd botched the first time so badly that he would do everything in his power to make this the best she had ever had.

Once all the pins were gone, her blond hair flowed down her back. Anthony spread his hands through her silky tresses. The sight of her with her hair down, standing in just her stockings almost did him in.

"Can I undress you?" she asked.

He smiled at the timid tone of her voice. Was it an act she played to convince him that she was still an innocent young girl? He honestly didn't care how many men she'd been with. He could not judge her.

"Yes," he replied.

Even though he knew it was going to kill him to have her hands all over him, he let her have her way. She removed his jacket and waistcoat, throwing them over to the chair in the corner, then set to work on his cravat. Once that binding was gone from his neck, she unbuttoned the small buttons on his linen shirt. His pulse thrummed in his veins when she reached to pull the shirt out of his trousers.

She had him down to just his trousers and boots. Her fingers glided down his chest, making him tighten his muscles against the desire scorching him.

"Let me take my boots off first," he said in a husky voice.

"Very well, but I do get to remove your trousers."

He smirked at her. "Oh?"

"I would very much like to see exactly what was inside me ten years ago."

He gripped the bedpost for support. It was as if she knew exactly what to say to make him lose control. He yanked off his boots faster than he ever had and stood before her.

"I'm all yours," he said.

She swallowed and stared at his chest. Once more, her fingers reached out tentatively, this time sliding over his nipples. He moaned and grabbed her hands.

"Sweetheart, you need to stop."

"I'm sorry," she replied with a frown.

"Take off my trousers because if I don't get my hands on you soon, I will embarrass myself."

He wondered at the confusion on her face but closed his eyes as she unbuttoned his trousers. If he opened his eyes, he would be done for, so instead, he pictured her in his mind. Her soft hands brought his trousers down to his knees.

Hearing her soft intake of breath, he forced his eyes open. She was staring at his erection with a stunned look on her face. He almost laughed.

"Am I that much bigger than most other men?"

"I don't know," she whispered. Slowly, she reached a hand out to touch him.

As she did, he tilted his head back and enjoyed the sensation of her soft hand on him. He clasped his hand over hers to stop.

"I am too far gone for that tonight, sweetheart."

Victoria wished she had a little more experience with men and understood what he was talking about. She had heard the women in the brothel talking, but her first time had been so quick that none of it made any sense. As she stroked his long cock, she shivered at the idea of it being inside her.

"Let me make love to you tonight," he whispered in her ear. "I want to hear you moan my name as you reach your climax."

He kissed her neck and then her mouth. The feel of his tongue on hers caused wetness to form between her legs. She moved her hips against his, savoring the hard length between them.

He picked her up and placed her gently on the bed. Smiling down at her naked body, he undid the garters holding up her stockings. He slowly slid her silk stockings down her legs then slipped his tongue across the arch of her foot.

"Oh, my God," she whispered.

He smiled against her foot. Kissing his way back up her body, he stopped only once to stare at her breasts. With him on top of her, she felt petite and for once in her life, safe. When she moved her hands to skim through his short hair, he kissed her again.

Victoria deepened the kiss, demanding as much of him as he demanded of her. He finally broke away only to move his mouth to her erect nipple. She arched against his mouth. Never had she felt a sensation as sinful. Her body ached for more, and suddenly she had it as his hand slid down her belly until he reached the apex of her thighs.

His fingers split her folds open for him. As he rubbed his thumb against her, her desire climbed higher. He continued to stroke her, all the while his mouth kissing a path downward. When his mouth replaced his fingers, Victoria moaned.

Passion spiraled upward until she arched her back, closed her eyes and shattered. Slowly, he stopped and she fell back to reality. Opening her eyes, she saw him with a smile on his face, staring intently at her.

"I want you so badly right now," he whispered.

"Then what are you waiting for?"

"You to tell me you want me."

Victoria blinked back the tears that welled in her eyes. She understood his request. After ten years, he still felt remorse over what happened and wanted to make certain she wanted him. She cupped his cheeks and kissed him tenderly.

"I do want you, Anthony. More now than I did ten years ago."

With a groan, he was over her. His erection pressed to her opening. She shifted her hips to allow him better access and felt him slowly slide into her wetness. He eased into her slowly, allowing her body to stretch to his size.

"Dear God, you are so tight."

She watched his hazel eyes, which were more green than any other color, as he filled her.

"Put your legs around my hips, sweetheart," he whispered as a bead of sweat broke out on his forehead.

As she did what he'd told her, Anthony realized something that made him stop. This was not an experienced woman. In fact, he doubted that anyone had made love with her since him. The idea that she hadn't been with another man sent a strange sensation to his heart.

He filled her completely and then stretched out over her. Gripping her hands, he brought them over her head and clasped her hands.

"Liar," he whispered in her ear before sliding out of her and then back inside of her warmth.

"What?" she gasped.

He repeated the movement faster this time, watching her eyes sparkle. He'd never felt anything as exquisite as her body under his. This slip of a woman had a hold over him unlike any other woman. As her eyes shuttered, he knew she was nearing her climax. Thrusting into her again, he felt her tighten around him until he couldn't help but follow her over the precipice.

He lowered himself down on her and then rolled them both over. Her head rested on his shoulder as he stared at the ceiling. For ten years, he'd taken his satisfaction from all types of women, and yet, none had left him this fulfilled. And it scared the hell out of him.

His mother's words about marrying a reputable woman came back to him. Victoria was anything but reputable. She was a pickpocket, had worked as an orange seller and cleaned rooms in a brothel. She was not the marrying type.

Victoria was the mistress type.

Listening to her rhythmic breathing, he knew she had fallen asleep on him. He'd never had a real mistress before, only women here and there. With his job, he hadn't wanted the complication of a woman who expected him to visit several times a week. But now that he was soon to be finished, he could take Victoria as his mistress.

He could buy her a house of her own. Set her up with a large allowance for expensive dresses and servants, and anything else her heart desired. She would make the perfect mistress. She was intelligent and a little smart in the mouth, but he liked that about her. He liked the fact that she didn't agree with everything he said.

She blinked her blues eyes open as he stared down at her. A shy smile formed on her lips. Unable to stop himself, he pulled her a little closer and kissed her forehead. She pulled back and frowned at him.

"Why are you frowning at me like that?"

"I'm just wondering why you called me a liar during the middle of . . ."

He smiled as her cheeks grew red with embarrassment. "Of making love?"

"Yes."

"Because I quickly realized that you have not been with many men if any other than me."

She pushed herself up to the pillow and put her head on her hand. "I don't remember telling you that I had been with many men. That was your assumption."

He lay back against the bed and stared at the ceiling. "Will you ever be completely honest with me?"

"Will you with me?" she asked softly.

"What are you talking about? I have been honest with you." He turned back on his side to face her again. "I even told you about what happened in France. I've never told a soul about that!"

"You haven't told me who hurt you so badly that you don't trust people, especially women." She reached out and rubbed the back of her hand down his cheek.

"My job demands that I trust no one."

She closed her eyes. "I understand you have things you can't tell me just as I have things I can't tell you." She opened her eyes and looked at him. "Hardy told me that you and Lady Farleigh were intimate. Is that true?"

How much of this story could he divulge to her? He doubted Hannah would mind. "It was only a few times. I haven't been celibate for the past ten years."

"Are you trying to get her back into your bed?"

Anthony laughed. "The only woman I have wanted in my bed for the past week and a half is you. I actually introduced Hannah to Farleigh."

"Then why would Hardy say such a thing?"

"He must know some of the truth," Anthony said. "Before Hannah became Farleigh's mistress, she worked in a brothel."

She pulled back and stared at him. Her blue eyes questioning him. "A brothel?"

"Yes. I paid for her services two or three times." He placed a finger over her mouth. "The last night we were together we ended up talking all night. I convinced her that she could do far better for herself than working as a prostitute."

"How is a mistress better than a prostitute?" she exclaimed.

"You worked in a brothel. Surely, you have an idea of what those women go through every night. They are forced to have sex with whoever picks them. The man might be pleasant or might be abusive. They don't have a choice. At least as a mistress, they can get to know the man before making the decision to be with him. Then they only have to be with him."

Victoria knew he was right. When she worked at Lady Whitely's she had seen a few women with bruises. She did give Lady Whitely credit, once a man had bruised one of her ladies, the man was denied entrance into her home. Unless the lady didn't mind the rougher sex.

"I suppose you are right," she finally said. "I'm sorry I even mentioned it."

He turned toward her with a little smile. "I'm not. If you have a question about me, ask it. I will do my best to answer your question truthfully. But you have to understand that because of the work I do there will be some questions I cannot answer."

"I do understand that." Still, she wondered how many secrets he kept inside. And would he ever tell her about who had hurt him so badly?

For a long moment, he just stared at her. "What are you thinking about?"

Not wanting to bring up the topic of his past, she said, "How wonderful the Christmas season is."

Anthony looked away and muttered, "I hate this time of year."

Sitting up, she looked down at him as she held the coverlet over her breasts. "How could you hate this season? It's always been my favorite time of year."

"Nothing good ever happens in December."

"You were born in December."

"My mother left us in December. I found out she was still alive in December. And until tonight, I'd thought I raped a woman in December." He looked up at her and scowled. "What is so good about this damned time of year?"

A slow smile lit her face. "People are more generous and they carry more money with them. They are willing to buy more oranges and don't mind so much if a pickpocket takes a little for some coal. I have always loved Christmas. There is just something magical about it."

"Perhaps you can change my mind," he whispered

and then kissed her softly as if making certain she wouldn't reject him. Not that she could. His lips and tongue triggered a warm liquid throughout her body that always made her knees weak. Slowly, he pulled away and stared at her blue eyes dark with passion.

"Perhaps we should continue our conversation later."

Chapter Seventeen

Victoria slowly opened her eyes and adjusted to the dim light coming in from the windows. A strong arm held her tight against an equally strong chest. She closed her eyes again and relished the sensation of safety and comfort. How could she feel so comfortable with him?

She had only known him for just over a week. Yet, here she lay, naked in bed with him. She wondered what would have happened if he'd found her ten years ago after that night. She wasn't foolish enough to think he would have bent down on one knee and professed his undying love to her. Most likely, he would have apologized, given her some money and sent her on her way.

Just as he would in four more days.

She sighed. The only difference now was he associated with her group of friends. She would see him every few months at occasions. As a viscount and future earl, he would have to marry before long. Then she would see him doting on his wife and possibly even his children.

Her heart suddenly ached.

She might have to give up her friends to save her heart from destruction. Turning slowly in his arms, she stared at his face. In sleep, he appeared content, not tense. His strong cheekbones and jaw line was covered in a light beard. She brought her hand to his cheek and gently caressed his face, enjoying the scratchy feeling of his morning growth.

Hazel eyes stared down at her and a smile formed on his perfect lips. "Good morning," he said with a hoarse voice.

"Good morning," she whispered in return. She would miss waking up in his arms.

"We could have our breakfast up here." He kissed her softly. "Have breakfast in bed and maybe then a long hot bath . . . together."

"That sounds heavenly."

"I hear an objection in there," he commented and then kissed her again.

His suggestive kiss had sent a tingle down her back. "I have given Hardy the impression that you and I are not on the best of terms."

"So I noticed. Now why would you do that?" He nipped her shoulder with his teeth.

"Should you decide you need my help, this would let me get close to Hardy."

He lay back against his pillows and stared at the ceiling. "Victoria, I cannot risk it. Hardy might be extremely dangerous."

She turned on her side to look at him. "But it doesn't hurt to keep the farce going. You might not need my help. But you might. If you do, then I can step in and pinch the note from him."

"You know I won't let you get involved."

"Why?"

"What I do is dangerous work. I cannot put your life

in jeopardy." He turned back toward her and stared into her soul.

Growing up on the streets of London, Victoria had had her share of risk. His gallant thought of her safety made her heart melt. She didn't want to be in harms way, but she did want to help him.

"Just think about it, Anthony."

"I will," he promised.

"So, do we continue what I started with Hardy?" she asked quietly.

He breathed out a long sigh. "Yes."

"Good. Now, if Hardy discovers we both had breakfast in our room, he might become even more suspicious than he already is. I think we had best have breakfast downstairs and appear annoyed with each other."

He kissed her jaw and moved up to her ear. "I hate it when you're right."

"Perhaps we could sneak away after luncheon." She felt him smile against her cheek.

"That sounds slightly wicked, sweetheart."

"True. I am certain you must have never done anything wicked before."

He laughed. "Never. And the idea of suggesting we have sexual congress in the middle of the afternoon is horrifying. That should only be done after dark with all the candles snuffed and our nightclothes on."

Victoria giggled softly. "And definitely no more than once a month."

"Now you are jesting," he said as he pulled her closer so she could feel his erection jutting between them.

"Somerton," she said in a serious tone. "What makes you certain that there is a missive?"

He lay back against the bed and sighed. "I'm not. But until I know for certain, I must assume my information is correct."

"Who do you think the message is for?"

"I would rather not say just yet." He threw off the covers and picked up his trousers. "I shall ring for a bath."

"Thank you. Are you going out with the other men to cut down an evergreen today? Hannah said Lord Farleigh insists the tree be cut and installed in the house before the ball tomorrow night."

"If Hardy goes, so will I."

"Hannah asked me to help her with the decorations for the ball. She assumed I would have experience being the daughter of a squire." She pulled on her flannel nightgown to cover herself.

"Are you nervous?"

"A little. I have no experience decorating for a ball."

"Just pretend you are Jennette, Avis, or Elizabeth. Surely you have heard them discussing what must be done before they entertain?"

She had, but rarely had she added her ideas to the discussion. The ball tomorrow night would be the first she had ever attended. There would be more people attending from the local area. And there would be dancing. People would expect her to dance. She bit down on her lip in thought. Seeing the couples dancing the other night, she'd so wanted to join them.

"What is wrong?" he asked, walking toward her. "You look quiet pensive."

"It is nothing," she replied with a shake of her head.

"Something with the ball?"

"No, I shall be fine." She turned away and walked to the linen press. Perhaps she should feign a headache tomorrow night. But she could not do that because if Somerton needed her, she must be in attendance.

She would have to pretend her ankle was still bothering her and refuse all dances.

* * *

Anthony watched her reaction to the conversation about the ball and realized why she'd become so preoccupied. After eating a quick breakfast, Anthony sought out Hannah and explained that after mourning her husband for two years, Victoria felt apprehensive about dancing.

Hannah assured him he could have the music room uninterrupted while the men were on the hunt for a tree to place in the house. With that settled, he roamed the house searching for Nicholas. He finally found his friend in the conservatory with a book on his lap.

"Nicholas, I have been looking for you."

Nicholas looked up from his book as Anthony closed the door behind him. "Is there a problem?"

"No, I need a favor." Anthony took the seat across from him.

"You know I will do whatever I can. What do you need?" Nicholas closed his book and placed it on the table.

"I need to stay here this afternoon while the gentlemen go with Farleigh to cut down a tree. Can you keep an eye on Hardy if he decides to attend?"

"Of course. Why can't you go?"

"Victoria is worried about the ball tomorrow. She has never attended a ball and has never danced."

Nicholas smiled. "I would be happy to stay behind and teach her myself. I have been told by many women that I am a wonderful dancer."

"I am sure you are, however, *I* will teach her to dance."

"I do love the jealous tone of your voice."

"Go to the devil, Ancroft." He hated the thought that someone might see that he cared for Victoria. That could put her in danger. He couldn't let something happen to her because of this job.

"I'm quite sure I will, Somerton. But you may beat me there."

"Have no doubt about that," Anthony added. There was no saving his soul at this point in his life.

"I will follow Hardy," Nicholas said with a sigh. "Have you found anything yet?"

"No."

"I suppose mistakes can be made."

"Unfortunately, the people who give the information are usually as trustworthy as the criminals themselves," Anthony commented. "Have you decided what you will do after the party?"

"I believe I will travel for a short while. Get away from the cold of England in January. Then when I return, I will probably have to start my search for a bride. My father is rather upset that at the age of nine and twenty I haven't settled down and had a brood of boys for him."

"The curse of being a peer," Anthony said. "At some point, I will be in the same situation. Although, I do believe my father may be coming to terms with the idea of my not marrying."

Nicholas waved a hand at him. "You will marry, Somerton. But only for love."

"It's not love I'm looking for."

Nicholas eyed him carefully. "I have seen and heard the reactions of your attempts to gain acceptance back into Society. You want respectability."

"I seem to have lost that trait during the past ten years. It's been suggested that I marry to retrieve it."

Nicholas shrugged. "Respectability is overrated. Marry for love, Somerton."

"Says the man who loved his mistress until his father

paid her off, leaving said man with a young daughter to raise."

"That was a long time ago," Nicholas said with a grimace. "I heard about a woman in London. A matchmaker. It's said that she can find your true love. I may try her when I return from the Continent. Her name is Miss Reynard. I believe she may even be friends with my cousin, Elizabeth."

Wonderful, Anthony thought. Now Sophie would be after him to help Nicholas find a match. "Good luck with that. I believe I shall do as recommended and get my respectability back."

"Come along, Anne," Lady Farleigh said as Victoria walked down the hall.

Victoria had no idea what Hannah was up to this morning. Almost as soon as Victoria had finished breakfast, Hannah had insisted she join her. "Where are we going?"

"We have only an hour or two while the men are gone to refresh your memory on a few of the basic steps to a couple of dances."

They entered the room and Victoria looked over at Somerton who was lounging in a chair with a sardonic smile on his face. He'd told Lady Farleigh that she could not dance! "And why is Lord Somerton here?"

Lady Farleigh laughed. "To be your partner. And since you cannot dance without music, I will play the pianoforte while Lord Somerton dances with you."

"Very well," she said, waiting for Somerton to move. She had no idea if he was a good dancer or not. Then again, it hardly mattered as long as he could teach her a few dances.

"What shall we start with first, Somerton?"

"A waltz. I know it's your favorite, Hannah, so it's bound to be played more times tomorrow than any other music," Somerton replied. "Besides, with just the two of us, it will be easier to teach her that than a quadrille."

"And much more enjoyable," Hannah added with a smile. She paged through some music and said, "Any time you are ready, Somerton."

Victoria swallowed as he rose and walked over to her. He gave her a sardonic smile before holding out his arms. She took a step forward and clasped her hand in his. Feeling the heat of his bare hand on her back caused a tiny shiver to roll through her body. Seeing his smile widen, she knew he'd felt it too.

She attempted to pay attention as he gave her the brief instructions needed to perform the dance. Hannah started to play and he counted out the steps for Victoria.

"One, two, three," he said in his deep voice. She stepped on his boots. "Try it again."

Hannah started from the top of the song. After five attempts, Victoria stopped. "I will never get this."

He looked back at Hannah. "Would you give us two minutes alone, Hannah?"

"Is that all it takes you now, Somerton?" she replied with a seductive smile.

He arched one brow at her and shook his head.

"Very well," she said before walking across the wood floor. She closed the door behind her.

"Now look at me," Anthony said, staring down at Victoria. "A waltz is everything you love."

"What do you mean?"

He brought her back into his arms but closer this time. "It's scandalous to dance a waltz. You must stand in a man's arms with his hand on your back. It is almost seductive the way your body melts with his."

She stared up at the green tone of his eyes and paid no attention to anything else.

"With a waltz, body parts might actually touch, causing all sorts of inappropriate sensations." He pulled her even closer and they moved together without any music.

Her body heated from the close contact. She wanted more than a dance right now.

"You are dancing, sweetheart," he whispered.

"What?" her feet stopped moving. "I was not!"

His smile caused her heart to pound in her chest. "Yes, you were."

Just then, Hannah strolled back into the room. "It looks as if you two are getting along much better now."

Victoria backed away. "He was teaching me to dance, nothing else."

Hannah shrugged and returned to the pianoforte. "Start at the beginning. And this time, if you make a mistake, keep going."

Anthony pulled her back into his arms but not as close as before. "Ready?"

Victoria nodded. This time when the music started, she kept her eyes on him. They glided across the dance floor as if they had done this a hundred times.

"Much better," he said softly.

After practicing the dance for the better part of two hours, they heard the gentlemen return. Victoria's feet ached. She sat down on the sofa while Anthony left so Hardy didn't catch them together.

"So what are you two really about?" Hannah said as she walked to the sofa.

"What do you mean?"

"Somerton told me you hadn't danced in several

years because of mourning for your husband. You looked as if you had never danced a day in your life."

Embarrassment heated her cheeks. "I have never danced a waltz before, Hannah. It is a newer dance and is only just becoming accepted." At least she hoped that was a correct statement. She'd heard Jennette speak about how wonderful the dance was, but even her friend had told her that it was slightly wicked.

"Then why don't you show me the steps for a minuet. That is a much older dance and I am sure you must have danced it before."

Victoria looked away. She did not belong here or anywhere that involved Society. Even Hannah, a former prostitute and mistress was better at comporting herself in Society than she. If it weren't for the money, she would never have agreed to attend with him. Just keeping up the pretense of being a vicar's daughter became tiresome, but pretending to be a lady was impossible.

"I don't know how to dance the minuet either," she finally admitted. "I have never danced in public."

Hannah gave her a look that reminded Victoria of her own mother. "Anne, will you please tell me what is really going on?"

Victoria wanted to cry out that she wasn't Anne any longer. But deep inside her, she would always be the pickpocket. "I am not the daughter of a country squire."

"Are you Somerton's mistress?"

After last night, she assumed she was his mistress, at least for the rest of the week. "Yes," she admitted.

"Why the lie, especially to me?"

"Somerton didn't want anyone to know that I was not as educated as most of the women he associates with. He thought it best to make up an identity for me."

Hannah shook her head. "It makes no sense coming

from him. He, of all people, knows my background. He should have known that I would have accepted you no matter how you were raised. Unless . . ." Her voice trailed off and a faraway looked entered her eyes.

"Unless what?"

Hannah smiled. "Unless he made up the story to make you more acceptable to others in the *ton*. Widows are always taking lovers so for you to be with him is not the most scandalous of stories."

Victoria furrowed her brow. "I don't understand. Why would that matter to him?"

Hannah clasped Victoria's hands with hers. "Don't you understand? It means he intends to bring you to London and introduce you to Society. It means he will most likely ask for your hand!"

Hearing the excitement in Hannah's voice, Victoria wished she could feel the same enthusiasm. But she knew better. Somerton had not invented the story to introduce her to Society in town. Nor did he want to marry her. She was just his pretend, now real, mistress for the week.

Remembering Lord Ancroft's words about how Somerton did not keep mistresses, she knew once the week was over, so was their time together. A short-term mistress was all she would be to him.

And she would never be anything more.

After Hannah left the music room, Victoria wandered over to the window. It hadn't snowed in a day and now small patches of grass had started to show through the snow. She rested her forehead on the cold window as a shiver ran through her body. She missed her small house and the children.

But she also knew that once she returned to London, she would miss Somerton even more.

Chapter Eighteen

Anthony walked to the entranceway and almost laughed. Ten gentlemen attempting to bring a large fir tree into the house was almost comical. They finally pushed the tree through the door and stopped. He moved out of their way so they could maneuver the thing down to the ballroom.

"Is this not the most ridiculous thing you have ever seen?" Hannah asked him as she reached his position at the threshold of the salon.

"It is entertaining to watch."

"My husband is a madman. Why he insists on this foolish notion is beyond me. Last year the tree sat on the table. That was perfectly acceptable. But this monstrosity will overtake the room."

"He loves you," Anthony said feeling a quick stab of envy. He brushed aside the emotion. He didn't want love, only respectability again. "He only wants to make you happy and proud."

Hannah smiled and gave her husband a loving look. "That he does. Perhaps someday I shall be able to repay his generosity."

"I doubt he expects anything but your love in return."

Before Hannah turned her head away from him, he noticed the look of pain in her eyes. He wondered at her reaction. Maybe Hannah and Farleigh were not as in love as they appeared to be.

Love did not matter. It only caused heartache for one of the people involved. Love didn't help his mother when Father was having multiple affairs and even a child with another woman. Love was for fools and Anthony wasn't a fool.

He watched Victoria walking down the corridor. His heartbeat increased as she came closer. Maybe he was just a bit of a fool.

"Might I speak with you alone?"

Hearing the staid tone of her voice, he wondered if something was wrong. So much for the afternoon he had planned. A leisurely lovemaking and bath together. "Go to our room. I shall join you in a minute."

He watched her slim hips sway under the brown wool of her skirts.

"Did you say anything to her after I left?" he asked Hannah.

A slight blush darkened her cheeks. She quickly related the conversation in the music room.

"Damn," he muttered. "Now she is probably angry with me for letting you know about her dancing."

Hannah frowned at him. "She didn't seem angry. A little embarrassed but not mad."

"Well, she isn't about to take her anger out on you. She will reserve that honor for me."

"Good luck, then," Hannah said and then moved away.

With a sigh, Anthony walked up the steps to their room. Opening the door, he found Victoria staring out the window of the small salon.

"What is wrong, Victoria?"

She bit down on her lower lip. "Thank you," she whispered.

"What exactly are you thanking me for?"

She glanced down at the floor. "Teaching me to dance. You didn't have to do it. But it was a very kind thing—"

"I did not do it out of the kindness of my heart." Anthony wasn't even sure he had one. "You should know me better by now."

"Perhaps you didn't, but it was a thoughtful thing to do anyway."

"Maybe I had an ulterior motive," he suggested with a slight smile.

She looked up at him and returned the smile. "Oh?"

He stepped closer to her until he was only inches away from her. "You might want to thank me properly."

Closing the distance between them, she wrapped her arms around his neck. "Exactly how would I do that?" she whispered in his ear.

"Kissing me would be a perfect start." He waited to see if she would do as he suggested.

She gave him a sensual smile that almost made him forget about letting her control this situation. Her head tilted and moved nearer as her eyes closed. Tentatively, her lips touched his as if unsure how to proceed.

He resisted the urge to pull her closer, wanting her to learn that she could take the reins in lovemaking. Feeling her tongue touch his lips, he opened for her, deepening the kiss as his desire burned. She moaned softly when their tongues met.

He sensed the minute her shyness disappeared. She pressed herself closer to him, rubbing her hips against his hard cock. Moving her hands to his cravat, she untied it quickly. As his control slipped, he pulled off his jacket and waistcoat, eager to feel her naked skin on his.

He unfastened the buttons on her dress and slid it down to the floor. He made quick work of her undergarments as she tugged at his linen shirt. She pulled away slightly as she pushed his trousers down over his hips.

"Shouldn't we move to the bed?" she asked.

"No. I want you right here on the floor by the fireplace."

She frowned slightly, staring down at the carpet. "Won't that be uncomfortable?"

"Don't worry, I will be on the floor and you shall be on top of me." He pulled her back to him and kissed her again.

Victoria returned his kiss. He wanted her on top of him? A rush of excitement flowed through her veins. He moved his lips down her throat until he reached her nipple. As he drew it into the hot recesses of his mouth, she gasped. She grabbed his shoulders for support.

He dropped to his knees and kissed his way down her belly as his fingers slid between her folds. His lips quickly replaced his fingers. As his tongue slid across her nub, she thought her legs would give out on her. With nothing to reach for support, she tried to keep herself standing. Passion built to a steady crescendo and as his finger entered her, she let the climax wash over her until she collapsed against him.

With a laugh, he brought her down on top of him. She straddled his hips and sat up on him. Trailing her nails down his chest, she smiled at his little hiss.

"Now what?"

His smile set her heart pounding. "Do whatever you like."

"Oh, I like this," she said, bending over to swipe her tongue across his nipple.

"What else do you like?"

"There is just so much to like." She kissed her way across his chest and down his muscled stomach. Reaching his shaft, she wrapped her hand around it and slid her hand down. "Do you like that?"

He groaned in reply.

"What about this?" Gently, she circled the top of his cock with her tongue.

"Far too much," he whispered, clutching her hair.

"Then you must like this." She brought him fully into her mouth.

He bucked under her as he groaned. The sensual feel of him in her mouth made her moan. She felt powerful and in control as she slid him in and out.

Suddenly he dragged her back up on top of him. His eyes were almost completely green and filled with a burning desire.

"Ride me, Victoria." When she didn't reply or move, he added, "Slide me inside you and it's just like riding a horse."

Feeling his hardness at her opening, she glided down on him then stopped. With him fully inside her, she smiled down at him.

"I have never ridden a horse before."

He groaned and lifted her hips, showing her what she instinctively knew. She removed his hands from her hips and brought them to his sides. She wanted to be in control this time. She wanted to drive him mad with longing until he reached his peak.

Anthony watched her face as she rode him hard. He couldn't remember the last time he'd enjoyed making love with a woman as much as he did with her. She was sensual, playful, and definitely not shy. He wanted this to last for hours but the pull of desire was sending him quickly higher.

Her breathing became fast and shallow as she moaned in pleasure. He couldn't let go yet. He wanted to watch her face when she came, see the passion.

"Somerton," she moaned as she increased her tempo.

Watching her eyes close and her mouth open as she tightened around him did him in. He brought her hips down so he filled her completely and let go to the passion riding him. He couldn't ever remember feeling like this with a woman. Sex had always been just a physical release for him. He'd never wanted more.

He still didn't want more. But with Victoria, something was different.

And he wasn't certain he liked the feeling.

Victoria finally returned to the reality that she was lying on top of Somerton's hard body. His fingers splayed her hair across her back. Under her ear, she could hear the sound of his steady heartbeat. She didn't want to move. She didn't want this moment to end.

"If we don't get moving soon, we shall miss the luncheon," he said in a soft tone.

"Must we?"

"Hmm, I am afraid we must. I have a job to do."

She lifted her head and stared down at him with a smile. "Have I been distracting you today?"

He brought her lips down to his and kissed her tenderly. "Every day," he muttered.

"All right," she mumbled, crawling off him. "Do I have time for a bath?"

He glanced up at the clock on the small table. "No," he replied with a laugh. "And if we don't hurry, everyone will wonder why we were so late."

Victoria glanced around and noticed the time. With a gasp, she gathered her clothing and ran for the linen press. "I can't believe what time it is!"

Somerton followed behind her, dumped his clothes on a chair and poured water into a basin. As she pulled out her undergarments, he brought a cool cloth to her neck. She stilled as he moved the cloth down her chest, under her breasts and arms and lower to her folds. After washing her, he did the same to his body. As much as she wanted to wash him, she had to get dressed.

She pulled on her undergarments and then turned to him. "Will you please lace my stays?"

"Of course, my lady," he said, then nipped her shoulder.

She giggled. Once her stays were tied, she slipped the gown over her body.

"That is a perfect color on you," he said, staring at her pale blue silk gown.

"Thank you." She watched as he changed into his clothing for the afternoon. The urge to forget the luncheon overcame her as he pulled the linen shirt over his hard chest. She wanted to run her fingers through the smattering of fine hair covering his nipples.

"If you keep looking at me like that we will not make the luncheon," he said. "And as much as I would love to miss it, I believe Hardy would be suspicious if we both were gone."

She blinked as heat crossed her cheeks. She'd never been one to gawk at a man before, but with him, she could not seem to help herself. "I agree. We need to be at the luncheon."

She looked away from the temptation. "Does that mean you agree that we should continue our charade?"

"Yes. We shall attempt to make Hardy believe we are unhappy with each other."

"Very well."

When he finished dressing, they walked down to the dining room together. They entered the room to find Hardy staring at them from across the room.

"Someone does not look happy to see us together," Somerton whispered.

"No, he does not." Victoria glanced at the table to find her seat. Seeing her place card, she said, "He most likely won't be pleased with the seating arrangements either."

"And yet, you do not seem terribly distressed to be sitting near me again."

"Perhaps I should ignore you."

After taking their seats, Victoria did her best to pay no attention to the man next to her. But every intake of breath brought the redolence of sandalwood. Every movement he made caused her gaze to slide to him. She had thought that after making love with him her desire would be satisfied. The opposite seemed to be happening.

It was as if she could not get enough of him.

The consequences of her actions would most likely end up being heartache. Deep in her heart, she knew they were not meant to be together. There was far too big a difference in their positions. She was a thief. He was a viscount who would someday become an earl.

If she could only toughen her heart against him.

Once the luncheon ended, she met with Hannah to discuss where to place the decorations for the ball tomorrow night. Excitement filled her as she thought about attending her first ball. She entered the room and sighed.

Footmen stood on ladders attaching white festoons

to the ceiling. Lord Farleigh was in the corner of the room, directing more servants on how to tie the tree so it would not fall during the dancing. And Hannah was walking directly toward Victoria.

"Anne, come in and help me!" she said with a friendly smile. She took Victoria's arm and led her to the far end of the room. "I planned on gaming to be set up here, but I just don't think there is enough room!"

Victoria glanced around and then walked to a closed door, which led to a small salon. "Why don't you put the gaming room in here?"

"It's far too small."

"But wait," she said, walking to the end of the salon where another door was shut. "This one opens to the library. Why not set up the tables in both rooms?"

Hannah frowned as she walked through the rooms. "I do wonder if that will put those who want to gamble too far away from the others."

Victoria laughed. "Since it is mostly men who gamble, I think they would prefer it."

"You may be right." She glanced around the two rooms and smiled. "I think this will work."

Hannah linked arms with her. "Now, how are you and Somerton getting along? You both practically ignored each other during luncheon."

As much as Victoria would love to have a woman to confide in, she could not tell Hannah everything. "We are arguing more."

"I had heard that." Hannah sighed. "Somerton is a hard man, Anne. I do understand why it would be difficult to be his mistress."

"Yes," she murmured but was lost in thought. From whom did Hannah hear that she and Somerton had been arguing? Could Somerton have planted that seed?

"Well, not to worry," Hannah said. "I know just the thing to bring Somerton around."

"Oh?"

Hannah smiled. "You shall find out later."

Victoria continued assisting Hannah but could not get that ominous statement out of her mind.

Chapter Nineteen

Anthony waited for Victoria to finish having her hair put up by the maid before they walked down to dinner. His frustration with this assignment was growing with every day that passed. Having found no evidence that Hardy was associated with anyone the least bit suspicious, and no evidence of any notes handed to him, Anthony was starting to believe the information he'd received was incorrect.

Even without evidence, Anthony trusted his intuition. It had saved his life on numerous occasions. And his insight was screaming at him that Hardy was involved. Anthony had spent the afternoon secretly trailing Hardy who had done nothing more than speak with a few gentlemen and read in the library.

So why did Anthony feel there was something wrong?

It couldn't be jealousy over Victoria. She'd told him how disgusting Hardy was to her.

"How do I look?"

Anthony glanced up from his musing and stared at Victoria. With an emerald green and ivory striped silk gown, her hair up in a loose chignon, and a smile on her face, she looked like a perfect lady.

"Somerton?"

He blinked and smirked. "I apologize." He rose and walked to her. "I fear my thoughts may have been wondering how long it would take to get you out of that dress."

She laughed softly. "Already?"

"With you?" He pulled her close and kissed her neck, inhaling the sweet scent of lavender. "Always."

"I do believe you might be insatiable, my lord."

The comment struck him cold. He'd never found a woman he didn't tire of within a few days. It reminded him again about how he'd let his attraction to her distract him from his mission. That had to stop.

He pulled away. "We should go down now."

She frowned at his cold tone, but he didn't care. He had been letting her get too close and that had to stop. She was no different than any other self-serving woman. Once this job was completed, he would return her to her home. And never think of her again.

As they walked down the stairs, he wondered who she would sit next to tonight. He assumed it would be him. But as they walked into the dining room, he found out differently.

"Why am I next to Hardy again?" she whispered.

"I do not know."

"What am I supposed to do now?"

"You will sit next to him and attempt to glean some information from him," he replied harshly.

She turned and glared at him. "What is wrong tonight? Have I done something to anger you?"

"There is nothing wrong," he answered and then left her to find his own seat. Nothing wrong, he thought again. Everything was wrong.

Hannah sat in the chair next to him. "Are you all right this evening, Somerton? You looked a tad angry."

"I am fine," he bit out.

Hannah laughed softly. "Of course you are." She glanced down the table to where Victoria sat. "You do realize that Hardy wants her."

"He has made that abundantly clear."

"Yes, he does like his women thin with blond hair."

He looked over at her. "So, am I to assume you put her there to see if I would become jealous?"

She shook her head with a smile. "No, I sat her there because I *knew* you would be jealous."

"Why?"

"Because it's so interesting to watch. I have never seen or heard of you being jealous with any other woman." She sipped her wine. "You certainly were not with me."

"I am not jealous. I just don't trust Hardy or any other man here."

"Hardy is mostly harmless," she commented.

Anthony wondered at that. Glancing down the table, he noticed Hardy looking down the bodice of Victoria's dress. She looked dreadfully uncomfortable as she attempted to speak with him about something. Anthony's fist tightened around his knife.

He was not jealous.

Only bothered that Victoria had to put up with such a disgusting pig sitting next to her. That was all there was to it.

As dinner ended and the ladies retired to the salon for a poetry reading, Anthony sipped his brandy and eyed Hardy. After a few minutes, Hardy excused himself and departed the room. Anthony followed quickly behind him.

He slipped into the secretary's office when Hardy walked into the study. The same room Anthony had used to overhear Victoria and Hardy. Anthony prayed she would not be so foolish as to meet him again.

He waited in silence, hearing only the sound of Hardy walking around the room. Finally, the door closed again and he could barely hear the sound of a woman's voice.

"Tomorrow night at the ball," she said quietly. "And do not even think about bringing that whore with you when you leave."

Whore? Hardy hadn't brought anyone to the party.

"I will do as I wish. If she will leave the bastard and come with me, I will take her."

"He will kill you." The woman's voice sounded familiar but the plaster walls distorted her tone so he could not place it.

"Let him try."

"He is an extremely dangerous man," the woman stated. "He will kill you without a thought."

"Not if I kill him first."

Dammit! Were they talking about him? If Hardy was talking about killing him or anyone else, Anthony had to warn Victoria. She could not be alone with him again.

"Just get what you came for and return to London. Do exactly what the note says to do and nothing else. You will be paid when the job is completed."

Now, Anthony had no doubts that Hardy was involved. But who was the woman?

The door shut to the study. Anthony slowly opened the door and looked down the hall only to see a flash of silver silk. He ran down the hall but it was empty by the time he got there. Inhaling deeply, he walked to the salon where the women were waiting for the men.

He scanned the room and found five women wearing silver or light gray silk gowns.

Any one of them might be involved.

Victoria watched as Anthony glanced around the room. At first, she assumed he was looking for her. But he continued to stare at several of the ladies and didn't even glance in her direction. Finally, he walked toward her with a frown.

"I need to speak with you," he said, sitting on the sofa next to her.

"Where?"

"Follow me." He left the room with her and opened a door to a small room.

She looked around. "The butler's pantry?"

"I need a room that is private."

"What is this about?"

"Hardy is definitely involved." He wanted to pace but the room was far too confining.

"I thought you already knew that," she replied.

"There is also a woman involved." He explained the conversation that he'd overheard from the secretary's office. "Did you notice any of the women wearing silver silk that came in late after the break for brandy?"

"Many of the women did, Somerton. It is common for us to dash to the retiring room before we sit down again. Even I came back late."

He nodded slowly. "I understand."

"Thank you, though," she said softly.

"For what?" he asked with a deep frown marring his handsome face.

She stood on her toes and kissed his lips. "For trusting me."

"You weren't wearing silver silk," he replied in a harsh tone.

Victoria wondered why he seemed to be withdrawing from her again. She had first noticed his reaction in the bedroom. "Are you angry with me?"

"No." He turned toward the door. "I have a job to do that is all."

Was that his way of saying she was getting in the way of his mission?

He faced her again. "I will be next to you most of the night. Do not trust Hardy in any manner."

"Do you think he really might try to kill you?"

"I don't know. But the woman mentioned something about Hardy taking a woman along with him. They may have been speaking of you."

A sliver of fear rolled down her back. "You think he might try to kidnap me?"

"I don't know!" He pounded his fist on the cabinet. "I never should have brought you along with me."

He was worried about her. No one had ever worried about her before. She walked to him and wrapped her arms around his neck. Feeling him tense, she kissed him gently.

He pressed her close and deepened the kiss. As she slowly pulled back, she said, "You will keep me safe, Somerton."

"I can't make you any promises."

Certain he was talking about more than just her safety, she nodded. "I never asked for promises."

"We need to return before someone notices us missing."

"Very well."

They walked back into the salon as three of the ladies finished singing "The Holly and the Ivy." Victoria took a seat in the back and Somerton stood behind her. She wondered how Hardy was taking Somerton's protective act.

Sliding a glance toward Hardy, she saw the anger in his eyes. When he noticed her gaze, she looked away as if afraid to be caught eyeing him. Somerton's hand landed on her shoulder.

Whether that was for Hardy or herself, she did not know. Somerton's thumb rubbed the spot where her neck met her shoulder. She shivered. Desire flared from just that simple touch.

Finally, after yet another small group of people sang a different carol, Lady Farleigh announced that tea and lemonade were set out in the dining room.

"I will fetch you some tea," he said then walked out of the room.

Hardy immediately pounced. Sitting in the seat next to her, he said, "What is he about acting like your protector now that you want to leave him?"

"He may be more difficult to leave than I expected. Please be off before he returns."

"Come away with me, Anne," he whispered. "I'm leaving Wednesday morning. Meet me in the stables at eight."

"Go now," she begged. "I will let you know tomorrow if I can leave with you."

"Until tomorrow, then." He walked away just as Somerton returned with the tea.

Handing her a cup, he asked, "And how did that go?"

"How did you want it to go?" she asked and arched a brow at him.

"Did he proposition you again?"

She heard the slight tone of jealousy and smiled. "He asked me to go away with him."

"Indeed?"

"Apparently, he is leaving Wednesday morning."

"Good work, sweetheart."

She stifled a yawn. "I believe I shall retire now." Rising she looked down at him. "Will you be joining me?"

Watching the conflict on his face, she wondered why he would be unsure. Was he questioning their future? They had discussed no future arrangements because she knew there could be none. And why would he care? She had no illusions that this relationship would last longer than a week.

"Yes. I will join you."

Anthony pulled Victoria's naked body closer to him. An odd feeling of contentment filled him as they both recovered from another incredible climax. What was it about this slip of a woman that made him feel so odd? He couldn't remember the last time he felt this way. If he ever had.

He could not get enough of her. Yet, he knew he had to give her up in a few days. Maybe that was all there was to this obsession. He'd never had another woman with a time limit. He had to get his fill before he returned her to London.

Except, he had already made love with her more times than the majority of women in his life. He had never felt an ounce of remorse or regret with any of them. He was being foolish. Nothing had changed in him. He still believed women were only made for sex.

She rolled over and smiled at him in such a manner that his heart started to pound in his chest.

"I do believe we may have missed another lovely carol downstairs," she said.

"Shall we hurry back down?"

"No." She stretched her arm across his chest and

laid her head on his shoulder. "I believe I have retired for the night."

"Me, too." He held her tightly to him.

Gently caressing his arm, she asked, "What is your father like?"

"What?" Why would she want to know anything about that bastard?

"Your father? You told me he'd known about your mother being alive, but I was wondering what he is like as a person."

Anthony stared at the ceiling. "He was a hard man to live with, Victoria. His expectations of me were very high. I found it easier to leave his house than stay."

"How were his expectations high?" she asked then shifted up so she could look at him.

"He expected me to meet his standard for living. Which he told me included not cavorting with prostitutes, not having a mistress, finding a good respectable woman to marry and give him grandsons. Yet, he visited prostitutes and mistresses when he was married to my mother. She was a good respectable woman, and he couldn't stay away from other women."

"Is that why she left?"

"Yes. She found out that he'd had a child with an actress. My mother confronted him, and he admitted it without an ounce of guilt. He told her that he'd done his duty and given her a son and a daughter but his needs demanded an outlet."

She cupped his cheek. "Was she denying him his marital rights?"

"No. But he left her in Cheshire while he enjoyed the Season in London every year."

"I don't understand," she said, rubbing her thumb over his lips. "She was a countess. Why wouldn't he have brought her to town for the Season?"

"He was embarrassed by her," he admitted slowly. "She was from Wales. He married her out of a duty to both families. But he never loved her."

"And she loved him?"

"Very much so." He closed his eyes to keep her from seeing the pain there. "It almost killed her to leave him and her children. But she wanted revenge. She thought if she left he would chase after her and tell her how much he loved her. But he never did."

He opened his eyes to see Victoria brushing away a tear. He brought her to him and kissed her leisurely.

"That is the saddest story I think I've ever heard."

"Once she'd left, he did find her, but only to tell her that she could never return to the estate. He cut her off financially too."

"How did she survive?"

He looked away aware that he couldn't tell her the truth. "She found work. I met her quite by accident the same night you and I had sex."

"Yes, you told me that. But whatever happened to the other child?"

"My sister, Genna?"

"No, you said your father's mistress was an actress and she had a child . . ."

"What?"

She stared down at him with her bright blue eyes sparkling in the candlelight. Her finger traced his lips. "I cannot believe I never noticed it before."

"Noticed what?"

"The resemblance. You have the most perfect lips I have ever seen on a person."

She could not possibly know the truth. Sophie looked far more like his father than he did.

"It's Sophie, isn't it?"

"Of course not!" he almost shouted. How the bloody hell had she figured it out?

"You have the same lips. It makes so much sense now that I think about it. That is why you knew Sophie." She lay back against the pillows and laughed. "Her mother was an actress and her father an earl."

He leaned over her and stared down at her. "You cannot tell a soul about this. Not even Sophie!"

"I'm not a fool, Somerton. I know she receives money from your father to keep the secret."

He kissed her softly again. "I know you aren't a fool, Victoria."

"Good," she replied then kissed him back.

He pressed his growing erection against her. "Are we finished discussing my sister now?"

She rubbed her hip against his hard length. "I think we are."

Chapter Twenty

Victoria waited patiently while the lady's maid that Hannah had provided finished putting up her hair. Anthony sat in a chair brooding with a frown. Once the maid was finished and gone, Victoria asked the question that had been pressing on her mind for an hour.

"How am I to treat Hardy this morning?"

Anthony steepled his fingers in front of his mouth. "I think we have to set up Hardy perfectly."

"What do you mean?"

"We have discovered Hardy is definitely lusting after you. He may even want to take you away with him."

"So again, how do I treat him?"

He rose from the chair and walked over to her. "You play the hurt kitten while I play the dominating bastard. I want him to believe there is no chance that you will be able to leave with him. I want him to see me with you at every moment."

"Why?"

"Because if something happens and I do need you to pick his pocket, you will run to him. He will sympathize with you and want to protect you."

"You are a very conniving man," she said, drawing her finger across his jaw.

He caught her finger and kissed it, slowly drawing it into his warm mouth. Her breath caught.

"Not conniving," he finally said. He kissed the palm of her hand. "Just shrewd."

It was a fine line between conniving and shrewd, she thought. She turned out of his arms and checked the cheval mirror again. "I believe we should arrive at breakfast separately."

"I agree," he said tightly.

"What is wrong?"

"Nothing, just do not go into any room alone with him," he turned her back to face him. "Do you understand?"

His intense eyes burned into her. She rather liked his jealous streak. "I understand."

Victoria walked out of the room alone and stopped at the top step. With a breath for confidence, she moved down the stairs and made her way to the breakfast room. The room was set up with small round tables for intimate conversations over coffee and tea. Lady Farleigh had decorated the room with holly on the mantel and pine cuttings on each of the tables, which gave the room a fresh scent.

She noticed Hardy sitting at a table with Lord Brentwood. Hardy gazed at her with hunger in his brown eyes but only gave her a brief nod. Knowing a woman in her supposed circumstances would not sit with them, she walked toward the table where Ancroft sat drinking his morning tea.

"Good morning, Mrs. Smith," he said as she sat across from him.

"Good morning, Lord Ancroft."

"You and Somerton retired quite early last night.

We missed you," he said loud enough to get Hardy's attention.

"Yes, I was . . . feeling rather tired."

Nicholas gave her a quick smile. "And is Lord Somerton joining us for breakfast?"

The man seemed to know exactly how to handle this situation. "I would not care to know."

She slid a glance toward Hardy who seemed to be ignoring Lord Brentwood and listening intently to her conversation. A large firm hand patted her back.

"Good girl, Anne," Somerton said in a patronizing tone. He took the seat next to her. "It is nice to see you have decided to listen to me and sit with a man I trust."

"You're a pig," she hissed just loud enough that she knew Hardy would hear.

He grabbed her chin, forcing her to look at him. "Never say that in public again."

Knowing her back was turned toward Hardy, she stuck her tongue out at Somerton. He twitched as if attempting to contain a smile before letting her go. She ate breakfast with her head facing her plate, pretending to ignore the man next to her. Not that she could ever ignore the male scent of him.

She ate quickly and moved to stand. Somerton's large hand landed on her wrist.

"Where are you going?"

"Lady Farleigh asked for my assistance in the ballroom. With the decorations."

"Very well." He glanced down at his pocket watch. "I want you back in our room by one."

"Of course." She knew it was all a game, still there was something rather exciting about being dominated by him. And she didn't mind since he had no problems when she took control in their bed.

He released her hand with a quick wink. Glancing

back, she noticed Hardy had already left the room. She had no doubt that she would find him lurking in the hall waiting for her.

When she turned the corner toward the ballroom, he was there.

"Are you all right?" he asked with concern lining his voice. "I was worried about you last night."

"I was all right," she said but looked away from him as if trying to hide her true feelings.

"Did he take you again?"

Hearing the light ring of excitement to his voice, she replied, "Yes. The man is a pig."

"What did he do?"

She stopped walking and stared at the man. She could not believe the questions he asked of her. Did he want a detailed account of their lovemaking? "I would rather not speak of this."

"I am so sorry, Anne." He attempted to pull her into his arms, but she pushed away.

"Are you mad? If he catches us again, he will kill you!"

He leaned in closer to her. "But that is rather exciting, don't you think? The idea that he might walk in on us while we are making love."

"No, I would prefer to never see the man again. But until I return to London I can do nothing."

"How can you be certain things will be different in London?"

If this was in fact a truthful scenario, she had no idea how she could keep Somerton away. "I have friends who will let me stay with them until he finds another woman."

"I can handle Somerton," Hardy stated firmly.

"No, you cannot," she replied.

"I'll take you to London and find a house for you where you will be safe."

"I shall think about it, Mr. Hardy. I must meet Lady Farleigh now," she said then quickly walked away.

Anthony watched as Victoria walked from the bedroom to the salon wearing the red silk gown he'd bought for her. He'd known it would look beautiful on her with her pale skin and golden hair, but he never thought she would look like a seductress standing before him. How would he make it through the night watching Hardy when all he wanted to do was stare at her?

"Does it look all right?" she asked. "It feels a little tighter than when I tried it on before."

He smiled noticing that she had put on just a little much needed weight. The woman was still far too thin. "It looks perfect on you. Better than when you tried it on last time."

"Really? I have never worn a gown so low cut."

"And that is what is so absolutely perfect about it." He held out his arm for her. She wrapped her elbow around his and a shock of awareness ran up his arm.

"I am a little scared," she admitted while they walked down the steps.

"You shall do fine. You only have to dance with me tonight."

"I meant about this mess with Hardy," she whispered.

"There is nothing you have to do. If you see anyone deliver a message to Hardy, come get me. If you can't find me, then Ancroft."

She nodded and proceeded down the stairs, their arms linked together. A little tremor of apprehension rolled over his body. He just had to find the missive and get her out of here safely. But he kept getting these feelings about this job. He hated when that happened because it usually meant something was about to go terribly wrong.

As they entered the ballroom, Anthony smiled. Hannah had turned the room into a winter carnival. With white festoons covering the ceiling and fluffy white cotton around the edges of the floor. All the tables had fresh greens with red berries on them. But the centerpiece was the large fir tree in the corner near the musicians.

"Where are the candles for the tree?" he asked.

Victoria giggled. "Hannah convinced Farleigh not to put them on for the ball. She was terrified that a fire might break out."

"She is a sensible woman." He noticed the pained expression on Victoria's face. "And a sensible woman who loves her husband."

"I know," she murmured.

They walked along the edge of the dance floor. Victoria appeared spellbound by the dancers as they performed the steps of a quadrille. Seeing her rapt face, he wished he'd had time to teach her more dances.

Get your mind off her and back on the mission, he told himself. It didn't matter if she could only dance a waltz when this was the only time she would have the chance to dance. Once she returned home, she would be back to her routine with the orphans. No more balls or parties for her.

He forced his gaze off her and to the crowd. Nicholas sent him a quick nod and shrug from across the room. Where the bloody hell was Hardy?

Finally, he noticed Hardy walk into the room alone. He nodded to a few men and then his gaze went to Victoria. Lord Brentwood stopped in front of Hardy and engaged him in conversation. But Hardy looked around as Brentwood spoke, as if distracted and not interested in the discussion.

"Hardy keeps looking over at you," Anthony whispered in her ear.

"So I have noticed. He looks quite bored with whatever Lord Brentwood is speaking to him about."

"I agree. I do wonder if he's looking for someone, though."

"Perhaps he is," she said. "I will walk to the refreshment table. See if he continues to keep his eye on me."

As much as he wanted to watch her slim hips sway under the silk, he kept his gaze on Hardy. Brentwood finally walked away and Hardy continued to scan the room. Noticing Victoria not at Anthony's side, Hardy strolled toward the refreshment table.

Anthony stayed where he was when he noticed Nicholas walking toward the same table. He turned and watched as Nicholas quickly engaged Victoria in conversation. Within a moment, Victoria was back at his side with Nicholas, too.

"So, I am not to be left alone tonight, am I?" she asked with one brow raised.

He smiled back at her. "No."

"Well, I can see I am not needed here," Nicholas said and retreated.

"You don't trust me?" She sipped her wine slowly.

"I do trust you." He took her wineglass and stole a sip of the fruity liquid. "It's Hardy I don't trust."

"I can't help you retrieve a message if I can't be away from you and Lord Ancroft."

He loved the way her blue eyes sparkled when she became frustrated. "You are not here to retrieve a message. Only to pretend to be my mistress, remember?"

"Yes," she bit out. "I remember."

"Good. Now, dance with me."

"No, I can't dance and talk."

"But I am done discussing this," he said calmly.

"I am not." She crossed her arms over her chest. "If I cannot help you then why am I even here?"

There were just so many wrong answers to that question, he thought. And most of them revolved around sex. "I am not willing to risk your well-being. You will do nothing unless I specifically ask you."

She blinked and glanced away from him. He knew after hearing about her childhood that she needed to feel safe.

"Now, shall we dance?"

"If you think your toes will survive," she retorted but took his arm anyway.

"I will survive a little toe mashing."

They waited on the edge of the dance floor until the musicians were about to start a waltz. He pulled her close and they glided across the floor. As he danced, he continued to watch for Hardy and finally found him waltzing with Hannah. Knowing she had him occupied for a few moments, Anthony concentrated on dancing with Victoria.

"You really are a natural dancer," he said.

"Hardly. This is the only dance I know." She looked up at him and smiled. "But I am enjoying this dance immensely."

"Good. I would love to see you at all the balls, dancing until your feet hurt." *Damn.* That was the wrong thing to say. She could never attend any real balls of the *ton.* She was accepted at this one because Hannah liked to pretend she was a true lady. No one of social importance accepted invitations to any of the Farleighs' parties.

Of the peers in attendance, Bingham was most likely only here for some personal business with

Farleigh. Nicholas had been friends with Farleigh for years. Brentwood was a young viscount probably only here for the ladies. Although, he had spent a fair amount of time with Hardy. Perhaps there was something to that.

"Well, this is my one chance to dance at a ball," she finally said. "So I should take full advantage of it."

Expecting to hear a bit of sadness in her voice, he was surprised at the cheerful tone. "I'm sorry about what I said. I wasn't thinking."

She looked up at him and shook her head. "I am not a foolish girl with my head in the clouds. I know my lot in life and accepted it years ago. My life could have easily gone down a much more difficult path."

As they walked off the dance floor, he looked around for Hardy. "Do you see Hardy?"

"Over there," she said, pointing toward the refreshment table. "It looks like dancing with Hannah must have been hard work."

"Thank you." He led her toward the table but just as they reached it, the music stopped and Lord Farleigh announced that a full Christmas dinner would be served.

"Is that normal?" she asked him.

"It's not abnormal. Some hosts feel that a full dinner should be served to their guests. Since Hannah is still attempting to make an impression on some of the guests, I'm not surprised by it."

"What do we do about our current situation?"

"We need to keep him off guard, just in case."

She smiled up at him. "Indeed? I thought you didn't want me involved?"

"You are involved whether I like it or not."

"So what do we do now?" she asked as they entered the dining room.

"I do believe you should look angry with me," Anthony said softly in her ear. "Pretend I just said something dreadful to you."

Victoria turned on him with feigned anger. "I cannot believe you would say that to me!"

With an inward smile, she walked away from him. Immediately, Hardy moved toward her.

"Is everything all right?" he asked.

"The man is an animal," she replied. "I told him again that once we returned to London I would be seeking other accommodations. After all that has been settled, he just told me . . ."

"What did he tell you?"

She waved a hand at him. "Something completely inappropriate."

His eyes sparkled with eagerness. "Will you tell me after the dinner?"

"Perhaps," she said coyly. "It is not proper to discuss this in public."

The man was all but salivating! Seeing her place card, she realized Hannah seated Somerton next to her instead of Hardy.

"You do realize I will be forced to ignore you," she said to Somerton as she took her seat. "Perhaps if you hadn't forced me to learn how to dance, Hannah wouldn't have seated us together."

"But to see you on the dance floor was worth it. And of course, feel free to ignore me for the entire meal," he said after sitting next to her. "Do realize though, I can hardly accept responsibility for trying to teach you the social graces you need for this party."

She leaned in closer to him as a smug smile crossed his face. "Are you trying to get me angrier?" she hissed.

"Yes," he whispered. "The man is getting suspicious of our behavior. I think sitting us together is a good thing. Now look away and smile down at Hardy."

She did as he ordered and received a seductive smile in return. Shuddering in revulsion, she took a sip of her wine. She could do this. All she had to do was think of something Somerton might have said to her. Remembering her days in the brothel and the stories some of the ladies told her, she thought of something quickly.

She concentrated on her meal of roasted goose with potatoes. Soon this party would be over and she would have the money Somerton promised her. Then she could afford to buy enough food to give the children a Christmas dinner like this one. But it also meant her time with Somerton would be over.

During the meal, Somerton brushed his leg against her thigh and even skimmed his hand up her hip. The heat in her cheeks heightened with every movement. He leaned over to her, and she couldn't help but inhale the tantalizing aroma of his sandalwood soap. Her hands shook as she reached for her fork.

Hardy sent her sympathetic looks during the meal.

As she finished her plum pudding, Somerton leaned in closer to her. "I do not want you anywhere near that man right now. Seeing the way he is looking at you, I do not trust him."

She held her napkin up to her lips and whispered, "I understand. But the missive is the reason we are here. That is your job."

"Stay away from Hardy unless I tell you to get close to him."

Sensing Hardy's gaze on them, she stood up and glared at him. "I will do as I please. You do not own me."

She walked out of the room intent on returning to

the ballroom but needed just a moment to compose herself. She walked to the ladies retiring room for a moment of peace. As she strolled out of the room, she noticed Hardy in front of her. A footman stopped in front of him, and handed him a note. A note!

"Thank you, my good man," Hardy muttered as he placed the note in his waistcoat pocket. "Now I can leave this god awful party."

That was the missive Somerton needed. Seeing Hardy turn around, she realized there was no time to find Somerton.

Hardy turned and glanced back at her with a smile. He waited for her to reach his position.

"Mrs. Smith, I have been looking for you." He clutched her arm and dragged her into the nearest room, which happened to be Farleigh's study. "That must have been excruciating to sit next to him during the entire meal."

"You have no idea, Mr. Hardy." She strolled across the room eager to put some distance between them.

"You must call me Marcus," he said as he walked closer to her.

She backed up until she hit the edge of Farleigh's large cherry desk. He stalked her until his breath heated her cheeks. "So, do tell me what Somerton said to you. It has been driving me mad during the dinner."

How was she going to get out of this mess? She had to keep him talking. "You want to know what Somerton said to me?"

"Oh, yes." He skimmed his finger along the edge of the top of her dress.

Where was Somerton? Perhaps if she could keep Hardy talking he wouldn't want to do something else. Somerton had promised he would be watching her tonight. He must have noticed both she and Hardy were missing by now.

"He said he wanted to tie me to the bed and . . ." she let her voice trail off and forced a delicate shudder.

"What?" he pressed breathlessly. "What did he want to do to you?"

"He used a very coarse term."

"Tell me the word, Anne. Tell me the word." He pressed himself closer to her.

She could feel his erection growing. "I cannot say that word, Marcus. It's a dreadful word."

She skimmed her hand up his chest and tried to push him away. He kissed her jaw up to her ear.

"Say it," he ordered. "I want to hear that word come from your lips."

Trying to keep her stomach from emptying, she tried to think of some way to repulse him. "He said he wanted to . . . to . . ."

He grabbed her hands and lowered them to the desk. He pushed her down so she sat on the edge of the desk, and then he spread her legs apart. She trembled in fear as he pushed his hips against her. The hard bulge in his trousers rubbed against her.

Bile rose in her throat as she realized she had let this go too far. She should have listened to Somerton's warnings. Hardy's wet lips slithered down her neck to her collarbone.

"Tell me what Somerton wanted to do."

"I'll tell you what Somerton wants to do," said a deep voice from behind Hardy.

Chapter Twenty-One

Fury as hot as white lightning struck Anthony with the sight of Victoria pinned down by Hardy. He strode across the room with Nicholas on his heels. Grabbing Hardy by the cravat, he pinned him to the desk.

"I should kill you for what you were trying to do to her."

"Somerton, take Mrs. Smith back to your room," Nicholas said calmly.

"No," Hardy gurgled. "She doesn't want him any longer. She already told him that."

Anthony tightened the grip on the man's cravat until his eyes bulged. "She is mine. Do you understand that?"

Hardy nodded slightly.

"If you come near her again, I will kill you," he said in a menacing tone. He quickly pinched the note while Hardy was too busy trying to breathe to notice.

Hardy nodded again.

Anthony released the bastard and turned his anger on Victoria. "Go up to our room and do not move until I get up there."

She stood there staring at him.

"Now."

She pressed her lips together and nodded. He tried to ignore the tears he saw in her eyes. He could not let her tears affect him. He had a job to do. As she walked out of the room, he turned back to Hardy.

"Never touch her. Never talk to her." He took a step closer until Hardy backed up again. "In fact, do not even look at her."

He walked to the door as Nicholas stayed behind as planned. Nicholas reached Hardy and grabbed him by the lapels of his jacket. Now Hardy would never know which of the three had taken the note.

As he reached the door, he heard Nicholas berate Hardy.

"You are ten kinds of fool. I told you he was a jealous man and to stay away from her."

Now to have a little talk with the woman who couldn't seem to listen to him. He made a quick arrangement with Hannah then walked up the stairs slowly to give her time to worry about what he would say. He opened the door to find her staring out the window at the falling snow.

"Just say it," she said not even looking back at him.

"Say what?"

"Tell me I was a fool to go into the room alone with Hardy. I was mad to take such a chance. I should have let you handle everything."

He walked closer to her and then pulled the pins out of her hair. She looked at him with curiosity.

"What if I told you that almost everything you did was perfect?"

"What?"

He combed his fingers through her silky hair. "The only thing you did wrong was not tell me your plan.

Luckily, I already had an idea that you would attempt something, so Nicholas and I were prepared."

"I—I . . . How could you have known what I was going to do?"

He smiled down at her bemused face. "Because I know you, Victoria. You and I are very much alike. And I would have done the same thing in your situation."

"You're not angry with me?"

"No."

"But how? How did you know? I just happened upon Hardy and noticed that a footman gave him a note."

He smiled at her. "I was right behind you. I saw the same thing."

Her face fell. "But I wasn't able to get the note. So it was all for naught."

He pulled a note out of his waistcoat. "This one?"

Her eyes widened. "How did you get that?"

He leaned in closer to her and smiled against her neck. "You are not the only one who can pick pockets."

"Is this really the note, Somerton?"

"Yes. I already read it and it confirms the location where an attempt will be made on the prince's life."

"What now?"

He glanced out and knew they could not leave. "There is nothing we can do until morning. Hopefully, the snow won't continue too long, and we will get back to London tomorrow."

"We cannot leave now?"

"Are you in that big a hurry to get away from me?"

She shook her head and bit down on her lip. "No. I fear Hardy will discover the note missing and come after us. A little distance would increase our odds."

"Not in the dark and snow. Hardy would not dare

try anything at Farleigh's home. Besides, Nicholas promised to keep his eye on Hardy for the rest of the evening so there is nothing we can do until morning." He walked to the bureau and pulled out a loaded pistol. He placed it on the nightstand. Just in case.

Victoria gasped. "Do you think you will have to use that?"

"I hope not. But I won't take a chance."

A knock on the door sounded and she started.

"Everything is all right, Victoria." Anthony walked to the door to let in the footman. They brought in a very large copper tub, which he would have to thank Hannah for later, steaming buckets of water. After the servant left, he locked the door behind them and looked at her with a smile.

"Your bath, my lady."

"I took one this morning. Though not in a tub that big."

He took her hand and turned her around. As he unbuttoned her gown, he said, "I want the stench of that man off you."

"Very well," she replied as she waited for him to finish with the stays. She spun around and let her shift drop to the floor. "Will you be joining me? That tub is big enough for the both of us."

Exactly the offer he wanted. "In a few moments. Get in the tub and I will wash you."

Her blue eyes darkened to the color of sapphires. He wanted to buy her sapphires and rubies to wear around her neck. He wanted to see her dressed in nothing but the finest silks and satins. She slipped into the warm water while he stripped off his jacket.

He rolled up his sleeves and knelt behind the tub. "Give me your soap."

She handed him the lavender soap. He quickly

rubbed it between his hands to lather. After dropping the soap, he brought his soapy hands to her neck, where that bastard had been kissing her.

"What are you doing?" she whispered in a shaky voice.

"Removing all traces of Hardy from you."

"Why?"

He cupped water in his hands and rinsed the lather off her neck. "Because you belong to me," he whispered in her ear. "Now tell me what it is that I wanted to do to you."

"How did you hear any of that?"

"Nicholas and I were in the secretary's office. You can hear almost everything in there. Now I heard something about me wanting to tie you to the bed. What was I supposed to do after that?"

She whispered the word in his ear.

"Now where did a lady like you hear such a word? Hmm, it makes me wonder what other interesting things you might know of from working in a brothel."

He soaped up his hands and slid them down her chest to her rose-colored nipples.

"I don't think Hardy touched me there," she said with a laugh.

"Good, because I would have to kill him if he did."

"Were you really jealous, Anthony? Or was that feigned for Hardy's benefit?"

He glided his hands down her belly until he reached the soft curly hair between her legs. Her question stopped him. Bending his neck, he nipped her shoulder with his teeth. He was getting in far too deep with her. No other woman had ever affected him as she had. But he'd promised her honesty where he could.

"Yes. I wanted to rip the man apart with my bare

hands. Quite honestly, if Nicholas hadn't been there to stop me, I probably would have."

She glanced back at him with a slow smile. "Are you ever going to join me in here?"

"Oh damn," he whispered, then stood up and quickly removed the rest of his clothing. As he entered the other end of the tub, water swished over the sides.

Victoria giggled when his feet slid up her thighs. She had never imagined taking a bath with a man could be both sensual and slightly amusing. His feet continued to propel through the water until they reached her ribs. He brought his feet across her chest and rubbed his toes against her nipples.

He smiled and her heartbeat increased. Moving his feet again, he locked them behind her back and pushed her toward him.

"What are you doing?"

"Hmm, I was thinking you might be far more comfortable on top of me."

"You can't mean to make love here in the water?" she squeaked.

He pulled her up the length of his chest until her hips were on top of his and she hovered above his hard cock. "It's not much different than the last time."

"But water will go everywhere!" She felt his erection at her opening and suddenly did not care how much water spilled. Moving slightly, she opened for him. As he filled her, she stared at his eyes and knew she was lost. No matter how much she knew this was a mistake, she was falling in love with him.

Watching his face fill with desire as he slid in and out of her was almost her undoing. She wanted to wake up in the morning to his stubble covered face. She wanted to sleep against his chest at night and know she was safe from harm. He thrust deeper into her, causing her passion to rise further until she shook with the ecstasy that he brought her.

He grabbed her hips and ground them down on his shaft. His head rolled back against the tub as he spread his seed inside of her. And she knew without a doubt that she had lost her fight.

She loved him.

And she was doomed to love a man she could never have as a husband.

Anthony had dozed in the carriage on the return trip to London. After spending most of the night awake and waiting for Hardy to burst in their room, he had received no sleep. He looked outside and noticed the carriage driving very slowly through the freshly fallen snow. He was certain they would not make it back to town before nightfall.

He looked over at Victoria who was gazing out the window. "Victoria, we will have to stop for the night."

She nodded. "I assumed we would." Looking over at him with worry clouding her eyes, she asked, "Do you think anyone followed us?"

While he didn't wish to frighten her, she would want the truth. "I would be completely surprised if they didn't."

She bit down on her lip and nodded. "Will I be safe when I get to London?"

"Yes. Hardy and whoever else is involved will assume I took the note, not you." He prayed that was true. The only way to ensure her safety was to get the note to Ainsworth as quickly as possible.

"Thank you for your honesty."

They arrived in St. Albans by three. As they walked into the King's Mistress Inn, he noted Nicholas climbing

down from his carriage and strolling into the Black
Swan Inn across the road. Their original plan had been
for Nicholas to go north but the weather made that
impossible. Instead, they decided to take separate inns
and see if anyone from the party joined them.

Anthony looked at the bed longingly. He needed just
a little more sleep so he could manage to stay awake
tonight.

"Victoria, have you ever fired a pistol?"

She turned away from the blazing fire, pale with
fear. "No," she whispered. "Do I need to?"

"Hopefully not. But for me to stay awake tonight, I
need to sleep for an hour or two."

She nodded her head slowly. "So I need to stay on
watch while you sleep."

"Exactly. If anyone comes through that door without knocking, you must shoot them." Anthony hated
asking this of her. He knew of very few women who
could manage such a thing. But if any woman could,
it was Victoria.

"I can do it."

He brought the loaded pistol to the table by the
fireplace. "Sit in this seat so you're facing the door."

She gave him a shaky smile. "Go sleep. I shall be
fine and protect us both."

"Do not let me sleep more than two hours."

"Very well."

Anthony blew out a breath. He'd never trusted a
woman with his life before today, and wasn't certain he
would even be able to sleep. Walking slowly to the bed,
he tossed off his jacket, waistcoat, and cravat. After
pulling off his boots, he glanced over at her once
more. She sat straight in the chair with her hand inches
away from the pistol.

Her concentration almost made him smile. He

doubted anyone would attempt something in the middle of the day at a crowded inn. Sinking down into the bed, he closed his eyes.

Victoria only took her eyes off the door to glance at Somerton's sleeping form. The poor man looked completely exhausted from watching over them last night. As the first hour passed with only the occasional sound of footsteps walking by their room, she let her tense muscles relax slightly.

She struggled not to let her thoughts focus on what tomorrow would bring. But no matter how hard she tried, every time she glanced over at him, the thoughts returned. Her emotions swelled knowing tonight was their last night together.

A part of her wanted to tell him how she felt. But the sensible side of her understood that it would not matter. Somerton was not the type of man who fell in love. After the lies and secrets he'd been subjected to from his mother and father, she doubted he even knew how to love.

If only she had more time with him. Perhaps she could help him understand how love heals deep wounds. The love of the children in her care helped her so much. He deserved love, too.

But it would never be her love that would help him.

She could only hope that maybe someday he would find a wife who could give him enough love. Although, she understood he wanted respectability and wondered if a woman who married just to please her father could ever come to love her husband. And appreciate his good and bad points.

A low groan from the bed made her smile. She had

planned to give him five more minutes before waking him. Obviously, he did not need a clock.

"I thought I said two hours," he grumbled.

"You have five more minutes," she replied.

He rubbed his face with his hands and slowly sat up. "I take it there were no problems."

"No."

He tossed the covers off him and walked toward her. "Then why do you look as if you've been crying?"

She wiped her face. How could she not have realized that tears had been streaming down her cheeks as she thought about him? "I guess I was a little frightened."

He pulled her up out of the chair and into his strong arms. "You could have wakened me."

Shaking her head, she said, "No. You needed your sleep."

"Everything will be all right, Victoria." He cupped her cheeks and kissed her softly. "I will protect you."

But he couldn't protect her from the heartache that would hurt her so desperately tomorrow. No one could prevent that from happening.

"Put the pistol in your reticule," he said. "That way if we need a weapon during dinner, we have one."

Victoria did as he ordered and they left for the dining room. They ate a quick meal of cider and meat pies. She noticed the way Somerton constantly scanned the room. From what she could see, there was no one here from the party. He finished dinner and rose.

"Stay here for a moment. I need to speak with the innkeeper."

Victoria finished her meat pie and cider. Somerton returned and sat back down.

"Well?" she asked.

"Only three other people have arrived to stay the

night. Now that it's dark, it's highly unlikely many other people will come. The innkeeper pointed out the newer people. None of them were at the party."

Victoria breathed a small sigh of relief but knew Ancroft was across the street and someone might be there.

A soft knock finally rapped on their door at ten that evening. Anthony walked to the door, opened it barely a crack and then let Nicholas inside.

"What did you discover?" Anthony asked as soon as Nicholas had taken a seat by the fire.

"That it's damned cold outside." Nicholas looked abashed when Victoria cleared her throat. "I apologize, Miss Seaton."

"Was Hardy there?" she asked and then joined the men closer to the fire.

"No."

"Did you see anyone you recognized?" Anthony pressed.

"Only Lady Farleigh."

"Lady Farleigh? Why the devil was she at the inn when there were still two more days to her party?" Anthony stood and paced by the fire.

"She received a note this morning that her sister, Mrs. Hatfield, is very ill. They don't expect her to last the week. Lady Farleigh was distraught when she entered the inn with her maid."

Anthony nodded. He'd met Mrs. Hatfield several times and she had never been in the best of health. "Poor Hannah. I know she loves her sister."

"So what do we do now?" Victoria asked.

"We go back to town and let Ainsworth handle this," Anthony said with a shrug.

"Good night, then," Nicholas said and left the room.

While Victoria slept, Anthony paced the room again. Something felt wrong. Not just the slight twinge Anthony usually had when something wasn't right. He had missed something on this case. Of course, he had no one but himself to blame. He had let Victoria preoccupy his brain and other parts of him during the entire mission.

Once he returned her to her home on Maddox Street, he could get her out of his mind. He sank into the chair by the fireplace and raked his fingers through his hair. Just bringing her home would never get her out of his mind. He had to figure out what to do.

Marriage was out of the question. With her background, he would only sink lower in the eyes of Society if her secret became public. A part of him did not care. But another part knew he had an obligation to marry an upstanding woman who could give him heirs.

He stared over at her asleep on the bed. He knew she still held secrets from him just as he did with her. Perhaps that alone was telling. If they couldn't be perfectly honest with each other then perhaps they were not meant to be anything but lovers. Not that he would ever be able to tell even his wife the truth about his mother.

That scandal could never get out.

His mother was right. He needed a respectable woman. Perhaps Victoria would agree to become his mistress until he married. He'd made the decision long ago that he would never keep a mistress once he married. After seeing what that situation did to his mother, he couldn't do the same thing to his wife.

Looking over at Victoria, he knew she would never agree to become his mistress. She had the responsibilities of the orphans she cared for. Once they arrived in London, their time together would be done.

Knowing tonight might be his last night with her, he slowly stripped off his clothing. He wanted to make love to her, watch her face as she reached her passion. Love her one last time.

Chapter Twenty-Two

Victoria awoke to a strong hand on her breast and warm lips on her neck. His thumb stroked her nipple until it rose up for him. She moaned softly as he moved his lips to her ear and gently pulled her lobe into his mouth.

She rolled over on her back and gazed at Anthony's intense face. The look on his face made her quiver with desire. His gaze followed her neck down to her breasts and lower still.

"Anth—"

He cut off her question with a kiss that stole her breath. His tongue slashed hers with passion and heat. Rolling on top of her, he moved his mouth to cover her nipple with moist heat. She arched and moaned as he suckled her deeply.

She never wanted this to end. The sensation of him being on top of her, his mouth on her. He slid his tongue down her belly until he reached her folds. When his mouth touched her there, she was lost. Her desire doubled as he slipped a finger into her wetness.

She gripped the sheets when she felt the passionate sensations building deeper inside her. He wasn't going to stop, and she could no longer control the feelings. Closing her eyes, she shattered from the upheaval he caused in her.

Lying back on the bed, her breathing shallow and fast, she opened her eyes to see him smiling down at her. But before he could enter her, she wrestled him over on his back. He arched an eyebrow at her but said nothing.

Kissing him, she tasted herself on his tongue. Tonight she wanted to taste him and give him as much pleasure as he had given her. She slid her hand up his erection as she brought his nipple into her mouth. Hearing the groan from him, she grew bolder, letting her fingers caress him from top to bottom. She continued her downward path with her mouth, across his chest and to the muscles of his stomach. He clenched his muscles when her mouth found its intended target.

Bringing her mouth down on him excited her even more. She slid him in and out, loving the sensation of his hard shaft against her tongue. His moan of pleasure sent moist heat to her folds.

With a groan, he moved her off him and rolled her onto her back. He filled her completely. He thrust into her over and over until the waves of pleasure washed over her again. He stilled his actions and followed her over the peak of desire.

Victoria rolled off him and turned away from him. Her breath caught in her throat when she realized why their lovemaking felt more intense. It wasn't just that she loved him.

It was their last time together.

Tomorrow, she would return home and back to the routine of caring for the children. He would return to his home and probably start his search for a wife.

A respectable woman.

Something she would never be.

But she was strong and no matter what, she would not cry in front of him. She'd had no expectation of marriage. The simple reality was she was not the type of woman a peer married. She was the type of woman a peer kept as a mistress.

He turned on his side and pulled her close to him. Wrapping his arm around her, he said nothing. They both knew this was their last night. They both knew nothing more would ever come of their relationship.

After an unbearable ride back to London, Anthony watched as Victoria stepped down from the carriage. He fisted his hands in frustration. She looked back at him when she reached the door to her home. She gave him a forced smile then walked inside.

He moved to chase after her, but restrained himself. Tomorrow he would return with the money he owed her for the job and to pick up his sister's necklace.

"Where would you like to go, sir?" the driver asked.

"White's."

"Yes, sir."

He would send a note to Ainsworth to meet him there. Then after his meeting, he planned to get completely and utterly drunk. There had to be a way to numb his heartache. Somehow, he had to forget her.

He walked into White's a few minutes later and found a quiet table in a corner. After sending the note to Ainsworth, he glanced around the room glad to see no one he cared to speak with today.

Ainsworth arrived in his typical fashion, quietly slipping into the seat across from him. And getting straight to the point. "Did you find the missive?"

"Yes." He slid it across the table and watched Ainsworth's white brows furrow.

Ainsworth looked up. "Did you see who gave him the note?"

"A footman in service for the Farleigh's. I don't believe he had anything to do with it. There is a woman involved but I am not sure how. Personally, I believe the note may have come from Lord Brentwood."

Ainsworth took a long draught of whisky. "Brentwood? Why?"

"None of this makes any sense to me, Ainsworth. The only person at the party high enough for a succession possibility was Lord Ancroft. I can personally vouch for Ancroft."

"Are you certain about Ancroft?"

"I have known him since Eton and would bet my life on it."

"So was he assisting you at the party?"

Anthony knew Ainsworth wouldn't like the answer. "Yes. He helped me keep an eye on Hardy."

Ainsworth leaned forward and whispered harshly, "You let a possible suspect assist you?"

"I trust him with my life." Anthony picked up the whisky bottle and poured a large glass for himself.

"You are getting sloppy, boy. Do you think I don't know that you brought a woman with you, too?"

Damn. He should have known Ainsworth would have another man there. "There was no other way I could attend that party. Lord Farleigh has always been jealous of Hannah and I. So I brought a woman who pretended to be my mistress."

"Pretended, my arse." Ainsworth chortled.

"Who was your other man?"

"Brentwood."

"What?"

"And as you say, I trust Brentwood with my life." Ainsworth picked up his glass and sipped. "He arrived in London an hour ago after following Hardy from the party."

That at least explained all the conversations Brentwood was attempting to have with Hardy. Conversations that Anthony should have been having if he hadn't been so obsessed with Victoria.

Anthony shook his head. None of this made any sense. "Now what?"

"Hardy will be arrested. This would have gone much better if we knew who gave him the note. Now we shall have to coerce the information out of Hardy."

"Do you want me to continue?" Anthony felt responsible for not doing as thorough of a job as he usually did for Ainsworth.

"I might need to call on you again." Ainsworth put up his hand to stop Anthony from interrupting him. "Only to complete this job. Then I know you are finished."

"Thank you."

"I kept you longer than most of my peers because you have been one of the best. But I understand you have responsibilities to your family. A wife to find. And children to have. You're not my first peer, Somerton. I know how long I usually have with them, and I should never have kept you this long."

Anthony nodded. Until Brentwood's name was mentioned, Anthony had no idea that Ainsworth had several peers working for him. It made sense. A titled gentleman could go places many others could not. Ainsworth patted him on the shoulder and left.

One drink had not even started to numb Anthony's heart so he poured another glass and sipped it slowly.

When he reached for the bottle to refill his glass a fourth time, Lord Selby sat down across from him.

"You look like hell, Somerton."

Bloody hell. Now he had Selby here to once again tell him how wonderful married life was. "Go away, Selby."

Selby only laughed. "I've known you for years. And yet, I don't ever remember seeing you look so miserable. Nor have I ever seen you foxed."

"I am not foxed." He knew it would take much more alcohol to get him there.

"Perhaps not yet." Selby picked up the bottle and poured a glass for himself. "But you are at least halfway there."

"Go home to your wife."

"I would love to but she is visiting with her Spinster Club friends at my sister's house."

Anthony closed his eyes against the pain of knowing exactly where Victoria was then. "Since three of the five women are married, perhaps it is time to rename the club."

Selby laughed. "I suppose since I named them the Spinster Club, I should be the one to rename them. Hmm, perhaps 'The Ladies of Scandal' or 'The Scandalous Ladies' Club'."

"I don't believe all five have had a scandal," Anthony reasoned.

"Well, there is my wife. Yes, she qualifies. My sister, there is another one. Lady Elizabeth is the newest member of the group. That leaves the Misses Seaton and Reynard. Miss Reynard reads peoples futures and is the illegitimate daughter of an unnamed earl. So she just makes the qualifications for the club. The only person who doesn't seem to fit in with these scandalous ladies is Miss Seaton. But if she continues to associate with the other ladies, it's bound to happen."

If he only knew, thought Anthony. Between being a pickpocket and going away with him as his mistress, Victoria would be the president of the club.

"So now, back to you. What fine lady has you drinking at the early hour of five in the afternoon?" Selby asked, then helped himself to more whisky.

"No lady has done this to me nor will a lady ever do this to me." Anthony slammed down his glass on the table.

"I would have said the same thing two years ago. And I never would have believed that Avis Copley would be the woman to bring me down." Selby shrugged and then laughed. "But it was damned worth it."

Anthony's hand gripped his glass so tightly he thought it might break.

"Tell me, Somerton. Did Miss Reynard match you with someone?"

"Bloody hell," he mumbled then rose from his seat. That explained why she wouldn't give him Victoria's name. Sophie always said the timing had to be perfect or things would not work out. "I am going to kill her."

Selby laughed. "I knew you had that look. I had a feeling about you and Miss Reynard."

"What the bloody hell are you talking about, Selby?"

"You and Miss Reynard. I've seen the looks you two give each other. And I've seen you sneaking out of rooms at the same time."

"Go to the devil, Selby."

Anthony stormed out of White's and took a hackney to see his half sister. He pounded on the door until her butler finally answered.

"Good evening, Lord Somerton."

He pushed past the butler. "Where is she?"

"She is out, my lord."

Dammit! Selby had told him the ladies were at Lady Blackburn's home. "I shall wait for her."

He walked down the hall to the small parlor she kept for meeting her clients. A footman entered behind him and moved to light a fire.

"Bring me some whisky and a glass," he ordered. Each moment that passed, his anger and frustration grew. Selby had best be wrong. But as time passed, Anthony started to believe this was Sophie's doing.

After an hour of drinking more whisky and waiting, he heard the front door open. A low murmur of voices echoed down the hall until the soft click of her heels rang out on the marble floor. He crossed his arms over his chest as she entered the room.

"I heard I have company at this late hour." She sat down on the sofa and stared at him. "What do you want, Anthony?"

"Did you match us?"

She gave him a sardonic smile. "I don't do the matching. I just know whether or not the couple belongs together."

His anger at her vague answer rose. "Did you?" he shouted.

A footman ran down the hall to the room. "Is everything all right, ma'am?"

"There are no problems here. I can handle Lord Somerton, Wills. Now shut the door behind you."

"Yes, ma'am." The door closed firmly behind the young man.

"Anthony, if you fell in love with her it is probably because you put yourself in a situation that would have anyone thinking about sex and love. Yet you believe I matched you two? According to you, I have no powers."

Hearing the words he'd spoken in anger to her when she was trying to match Lady Elizabeth only increased his ire. There were times he wanted to hate his half sister. Times when he wanted to blame her for what happened between his mother and father. But he knew it wasn't her fault, only theirs.

He looked over at her and noticed a touch of sadness in her gray eyes. "She and I both know it's not meant to be. We are from completely different backgrounds."

"If you love her, it shouldn't matter." Sophie brushed a tear from her cheek. "Look at Elizabeth."

He shook his head. "No, the old duke never publicly denied Elizabeth was his daughter. So in the eyes of the *ton,* she was the duke's daughter. This situation is entirely different. And you know it."

"She needs you, Anthony." Sophie paused. "And you need her."

"I won't ruin Genna's chances for a good match. She deserves that after growing up without a mother." He had to get out of here. He rose to leave the room but Sophie's words stuck in his head. "Besides, I would only hurt her."

"You already have. You need her, Anthony."

"I cannot," he said, pounding a fist on the door.

"She might just save you," Sophie whispered.

Anthony spun around and looked at his half sister again. "Save me from what?"

"Yourself."

Victoria finally arrived back home at six. The children were still excited by her return and they wouldn't leave her alone. Especially Bronwyn. Victoria promised Bronwyn they would read together after all the other children were in bed.

But first, Victoria had to catch up on what had been happening. Christopher and Katherine, the two youngest children had been taken to an aunt's house while she was gone.

"Maggie, are you certain this woman was their aunt?"

"Yes, and she said she would be happy to meet with you upon your return. It took her a fortnight to hear about the fire and then another month to discover what happened to the children. But Christopher recognized her."

"Very well. I will send her a letter requesting a meeting in the morning."

A knock sounded on the front door. Cautiously, Victoria looked out and then sighed when she noticed Sophie there. Opening the door, she said, "What are you doing here?"

"I think you know."

"Come on in. Are you here to take one of my children too?"

Sophie frowned. "What are you talking about?"

Victoria explained about the two children leaving her as they waited for Maggie to bring them tea. "So what brings you out on such a cold night?"

"I could tell when we were at Jennette's home that you were not looking well. What happened?"

"Is there any sense in lying to you?"

"Not really."

"I went away with Lord Somerton," Victoria started. "It's not as you think. He asked me to pretend to be his mistress to help him with a job he had to perform."

"But it became more than that, did it not?" Sophie pried.

"Yes." Victoria sipped her tea. "I really am not comfortable talking about this to you."

"Nonsense," Sophie said, waving a hand in dismissal.

"I have heard this all before from Avis and Jennette and Elizabeth."

"True, but they weren't talking about your brother, were they?"

For the first time in the seven years Victoria had known Sophie, she appeared speechless. She stared at the fire with her mouth agape. "He told you that?"

"No. I figured it out when he told me about his parents' marriage."

Sophie blinked and looked at her with the same intensity that Somerton always had. It was now so apparent to Victoria that they were siblings.

"He told you about his parents? About his mother?"

"Not everything about his mother, but enough. Why does that surprise you?" She was confused by Sophie's questions. Her friends had always told her that their husbands were completely honest with them. Why would lovers be any different?

"He has never told anyone about his mother. I knew because of my abilities. He has never even told his sister about her."

Victoria understood why. "He doesn't want to hurt her. He thinks it best that she believe her mother died."

"I just cannot believe this," Sophie muttered.

"Why are you so shocked by this?" They had been lovers and lovers told each other secrets that others might not know.

"Because my brother confides in no one. Almost everything I have learned about him is because of my abilities. He tells no one anything. *Ever.*" Sophie shook her head.

Victoria shrugged. "It wasn't easy to get the man to talk but eventually he did."

"How did you two get along? The man has a quick temper."

"I only saw that once," she said, remembering the afternoon he almost took her in anger. "Mostly, he was a gentleman and treated me extremely well."

"Somerton a gentleman, now that is an oxymoron."

"I found him quite pleasant." She sounded like she was speaking of the weather and not the man she had fallen in love with.

"Do you love him, Victoria?" Sophie asked in a soft tone.

"I do," she answered as tears welled in her eyes. "But it does not matter. Nothing can come of it."

"I must be off," Sophie said with a secret smile. "I have some work to do for a client."

"At this hour?"

"Yes. She is quite demanding."

Sophie walked out of Victoria's house and stopped at the bottom step. The fact that Somerton had confided in Victoria was incredible and wonderful. He was a hard man to love. And yet, Sophie had always known that Victoria was perfect for him. Victoria had been able to break through his icy heart, so Sophie was convinced they would have a great love for each other.

She was still a little shocked by the confidences Somerton had told Victoria. Sophie knew from what she'd heard about him that he never gave away personal information to a woman he'd only known for a few days. Sophie clutched the railing. They were exactly what the other needed.

Somehow, she had to find a way to get them together.

Chapter Twenty-Three

Anthony knocked on the door of Victoria's home the next morning. He glanced over at his mother's house and prayed she was not awake yet to see him entering Victoria's home. The door squeaked open and Victoria stood in the entranceway wearing a serviceable, gray wool day gown.

She looked exactly like a woman whose sole purpose was to help orphans. And nothing like the seductress who had gone away with him.

"Do you not have a footman to answer the door for you?"

She rolled her eyes. "Oh yes, twenty of them and ten maids and of course, my butler."

He couldn't miss the sarcasm in her voice. "I apologize."

"Come in before someone sees you standing on my doorstep," she said, opening the door wider for him to enter.

He walked inside and removed his coat and hat. She took them and placed the items on a hook. The house held a warm feeling and the aroma of baked bread filled the air. Children's voices sounded from upstairs.

"What are the children doing?" he asked, curious about what she did all day.

"The older ones are working on their studies while the younger ones play."

She walked along the worn wood floor to a small study. "I have been quite busy today and haven't retrieved the necklace yet."

"I understand. I cannot imagine what it must take to get eight children dressed, fed, and doing schoolwork in the morning."

"Only six children now."

Hearing her voice catch, he said, "What happened while we were gone, Victoria?"

"An aunt of the two newest children came and collected them." She looked away from him.

He came up from behind and dragged her against his chest, wrapping his arms around her. "Is it not best that the children are with family?"

"Of course. But . . ."

"Shh," he said, then turned her in his arms. A part of him wondered if she cried only for the loss of the children.

She looked up at him with watery blue eyes. "I am sorry. I don't normally cry like this."

"I suspect this has been a difficult two days."

She nodded and stared at the button on his waistcoat. "I should get your necklace now. Would you like to wait here while I get it?"

"No, I will go with you." Now that she was near again, the idea of her leaving even for a moment troubled him.

"It is in my bedchamber."

"I will follow you." The thought of going into her

bedroom sent all sorts of lecherous thoughts into his head. But with a handful of children roaming the house he doubted anything he wanted to do would happen.

"You still don't trust me, do you?" she asked.

"Yes, I do. But I am a wicked man who can't resist the idea of entering a woman's bedroom."

She laughed softly. "You are definitely a wicked man."

He followed her up the stairs, watching her slim hips sway and his thoughts turned erotic. The sound of children's laughter floating down from the second floor cooled him off.

"This way," she said. "My bedroom is on the first floor."

The small room was neat but bare. One small bed, a clothes press and nightstand were the only furniture.

She opened the clothes press and reached for a box on the bottom. Bringing it to the bed, she opened the box and gasped.

"Oh, my God!"

"What is the matter?" He looked in the box and noticed a few children's drawings and other small things.

"It's not here!"

Suspicion crawled up his back. "Oh?"

She looked up at him wide eyed. "I left the necklace in the box. With the crest on the pendant, I could not pawn it. I swear, Somerton. It was in the box."

"You told me you wouldn't be foolish enough to store the pendant at your house," he reminded her. His anger rose higher with every second.

"Of course, I said that." She looked at him frantically. "I didn't want you ravaging my home in front of the children."

Seeing the look on her face, he believed her. "Very well. Who had access to your room while you were gone?"

She shrugged. "I don't lock my room so any of the children or Maggie or that woman you hired, Mrs. Trumble."

"Did anyone know you had the necklace?"

"Only Maggie." She rustled through the box again. "Maggie would not have taken it. She has worked with me for the past eight years."

The door flung open and a young girl came running in. "Miss Torie, I forgot to show you . . ." Her high-pitched voice trailed off as she noticed him. "Who are you?"

Anthony looked at the girl and grabbed the bedpost. His mind raced and his fingers wrapped around the small locket he always kept with him. It wasn't possible. She couldn't be. Victoria would have told him.

"Bronwyn, that is a very rude question. This is Lord Somerton who came for," Victoria laughed softly then went to the girl and the pendant around her neck, "this."

"But I found it in the box of things with my name on it so I thought it was for me."

"No," Anthony whispered. Not only did she look just like Genna, she sounded like his sister at that age, too.

"I am sorry, Bronwyn." Victoria removed the necklace from the girl. "I was keeping it for Lord Somerton while he was away. It is far too valuable for a young girl."

While Victoria spoke Anthony's mind raced with questions. "How old is she?" he finally managed.

"Nine."

His grip tightened on the bedpost as his world spun around him. Except for with Victoria, he'd always been a careful man with regards to bastard children.

But ten years ago, like this past week, the thought hadn't even occurred to him.

"Miss Torie," Bronwyn said and then started to tremble. "He's the man."

"What man?"

"The one from my dreams. The one who tries to take me away."

Victoria patted the girl on the head. "He is not the man. Bronwyn, I think you should leave Lord Somerton and I alone."

"Yes, Miss Torie."

Anthony stared at her as she raced out of the room and closed the door. He couldn't take his gaze off the door as his anger grew. Finally, he turned toward Victoria. "Why didn't you tell me?"

Victoria frowned. "Tell you what? I had no idea Bronwyn had the pendant."

Fury rose over him. "I am not talking about the goddamned necklace. How could you have kept her secret from me? Especially after the past two weeks?"

She stared at him with confusion and pain. "I have no idea what you are talking about."

He pulled the locket from his pocket and opened it. The miniature of his sister had been painted at the age of ten. He handed it to her.

"How did you get a miniature of her?" Her hands shook as she looked down at it. "How?"

"That is my sister Genevra, or Genna as everyone calls her. Painted when she was ten."

"You're wrong. It's Bronwyn. It looks exactly like her!"

"Why didn't you tell me I had a daughter, Victoria?" He grabbed her shoulders and gave her a little shake. "I had a right to know about her!"

Comprehension finally dawned on her face. "Oh, my God, you think she is *our* daughter."

"Of course I do. Who else's would she be?" he shouted.

Victoria sank to the bed. Bronwyn was certainly not *her* daughter, then . . . "Oh God," she cried. *"You and she!"*

It all made sense now. Lady Whitely told her to stay away from Somerton. That he didn't respect women and would only hurt her. Lady Whitely never wanted Somerton to find out about their daughter.

He had lied to Victoria, telling her that she was the first woman he'd been with. Lady Whitely gave birth seven months after that night. And Bronwyn had been a very healthy baby, not premature.

He lied to her.

Again.

"Get out," she whispered. "I never want to see you again. Get out of my house!"

He grabbed the necklace and stormed to the door. "I will be back tomorrow for my daughter."

Victoria's heart turned cold. She had already lost two children this week. She would not lose another. "You will not take her from me."

"Even if I have to bring this to the regent himself. Do you honestly think he will let a child of mine languish in a home for orphans?"

"Don't you ever step foot in my house again!" she yelled and then threw a pillow at him. She clutched her stomach as he slammed the door behind him.

Tears streamed down her cheeks as she collapsed on the bed. She couldn't lose Bronwyn. She hated to admit that she had favorites, but Bronwyn had been her first baby. When she agreed to take in some of

the other ladies' 'accidents,' she loved them too. But
Bronwyn always had a special place in her heart.

She could not lose her.

Losing Bronwyn also meant losing everything:
the house, the other children, her life. Without Lady
Whitely's support, Victoria knew she could not keep
this house. The children would have to be sent to other
homes. Maggie would have to find another position.

And Victoria would have absolutely nothing. She
would be out on the streets. She might even be forced
into working at a brothel. Only this time, she doubted
she would be cleaning the rooms.

With steeled determination, Victoria sat up and
wiped her tears. She refused to become a prostitute.
There had to be a way to fix this problem.

The first thing to do was speak with Lady Whitely.
Perhaps she could convince Somerton not to take the
child. But seeing his reaction today, she doubted even
Lady Whitely could change his mind.

Still, she had to try, even if it meant admitting to
Lady Whitely that she had slept with Somerton.

Anthony stormed out of Victoria's home. He'd
never felt so betrayed in his life. With fat snowflakes
falling from the sky, he looked around and realized
there was only one person he could talk to, the one
person who had warned him against her in the first
place. He should have listened to his mother for once.

He opened the door to the brothel and stepped
into a world that didn't sleep. At eleven in the morning, there were already two men sitting in the parlor
leering at the women. Without a word, he trudged up
the steps to his mother's room.

Knocking softly, he waited for permission to enter.

During the evening hours, he could safely walk into her room unless stopped by one of the girls. But not during the morning when a client might still be inside.

"Come in," she said in a testy tone.

He walked in to find her already dressed for the day. "Sounds as if you are having a wonderful day, too."

She rolled her eyes. "That blasted girl Maryanne has agreed to become Sourwood's mistress."

"Is that all?" He walked to the window and stared down at the street. "I just discovered I have a daughter."

His mother had the nerve to laugh. "Only one?"

He turned his head and leveled her with an icy glare. "You know I have always been careful. You taught me that."

"True, but there were a few years that we didn't speak to each other. Can I assume you might have been less cautious then?"

"Only once." And the past week. For all he knew Victoria could be carrying his child right now. He picked up a glass from the table and hurled it at the fireplace. "Dammit!"

"Ah yes, that first time with the girl on the street. Surely, that can't be the one. You didn't even know her name."

He remained stony silent.

"*She* told you, didn't she?"

"Yes, Sophie knew the girl's name." He returned his gaze to the window and watched a black coach pull up in front of Victoria's home.

"And as a matter of fact, you know of her, too."

She made a face at him. "I do? The only women I know who have children out of marriage are the girls here." She wandered the room with a frown. "I hadn't thought that maybe one of them had been with you before."

"It wasn't one of your girls." He banged his fist against the window frame. "It was Miss Seaton."

"Victoria?" she whispered. "But that's not possible."

He spun around with his hands on his hips. "Indeed? Then why does the oldest girl in her home look exactly like Genna? And I mean exactly like her at that age!"

"Oh, God," she whispered. His mother's face turned ashen.

"What is wrong?"

"I never wanted to tell anyone this. I cannot believe I have to tell you." She clenched the back of a chair for support.

"Tell me what? Did you already know Bronwyn was my child?"

His mother closed her eyes and for the first time in the years he had known her, a tear fell down her cheek. "Bronwyn is not your daughter, Anthony."

"Is that what she told you?" he demanded.

"Victoria had no need to tell me about Bronwyn." She inhaled a short breath. "Bronwyn is your sister."

"Goddammit! Why didn't you tell me I had another half sister before now? You know it wouldn't have mattered to me!"

"I know, Anthony. It wasn't you I was protecting her from." She came around the blue chair and sat down. "Sit down."

"I really do not wish to sit right now."

"If you wish to hear my story, then sit."

He blew out a breath of frustration and sat across from her. "All right. It's not that difficult to figure out how I arrived with another sister, but I would like to know how Victoria came to care for her."

"Very well, we shall start with that. About twelve years ago, I was shopping for a new bonnet. On the way into the milliners, a slip of a girl bumped into me. I quickly realized she had picked my reticule."

Victoria had never told him how she ended up at the brothel, but now it made perfect sense. "You were the woman who let her clean rooms."

She tilted her head and looked at him. "And how did you come to learn that?"

Heat crossed his cheeks. "I think you can hazard a guess."

"Dammit, Anthony. I told you to leave her alone." His mother sighed. "As I was saying, she came here to clean rooms. I told her that if she wanted to work upstairs, she could. Then two years later, I discovered I was with child. I couldn't lose this child as I had you and Genna. One night, Victoria came home dreadfully upset because she'd given her innocence to someone."

She cast him a cold stare. "I decided that night that I would buy a home and set Victoria up to care for my child. That way if she'd gotten with child, she would have a place to raise her child, too. We decided on a new identity for her. I taught her to read and write and comport herself amongst higher quality people. I wanted my daughter raised properly."

"You saved her life," he mumbled.

"She saved me from losing another child." She looked over at him. "While I can't raise her, at least she is only next door. If I want to see her, I can. Now how exactly did you come to meet Victoria?"

He explained how they had come to meet each other after his first arrival at the brothel. Then he told her about the rest of the story. A slice of guilt cut into him when he thought about the way he'd treated Victoria this morning.

"So was she your mistress in truth or only pretend?" his mother finally asked.

"I would prefer not to answer that question."

"Then I believe I have my answer." She shook her head and stared at her green silk skirts. "Tell me something, were you furious when you saw Bronwyn because you found out you had a bastard? Or because you thought she had kept it from you?"

"The latter. If I had a child, I would do everything in my power to raise the child myself." Just as Nicholas had done with his daughter. Anthony respected Nicholas for his decision, especially after seeing what Sophie went through due to their father.

"Are you in love with her?"

He knew the answer but refused to answer the question. "It does not matter."

She pressed her lips together and looked up to the ceiling. "Yes, it truly does matter, Anthony. If your father had loved me, honestly loved me, my life would have been very different."

"Do you regret your decision?"

"Some days," she answered slowly. "I made a choice. It might not have been the best decision I could have made, but it was *my* decision."

"Tell me about Bronwyn," he said, wanting to know more about his newest sister.

"Victoria has done an excellent job with her. I couldn't have asked for a better woman to raise her."

"I should have realized by her name that she wasn't Victoria's child. You named her after your mother." Anthony owed Victoria a huge apology. And once he finished speaking with his mother, he would go to her. But there was something bothering him about all this mess.

"Mother, I don't understand how Bronwyn can look so much like Genna. I mean it's uncanny. And yet, Genna has more of Father's darker looks than your fairer appearance."

Her cheeks turned red. "I never said Bronwyn was your half sister."

"Oh bloody hell, you let him f—"

"Do not say that word in front of me," she ordered. "Your father has visited here a few times in the past eighteen years."

"You have no reason to be with him."

"He is still my husband, Anthony. As such, if he chooses to demand his husbandly rights, I cannot refuse."

He watched his mother's face go completely red. "You don't want to refuse him, do you? Oh hell, you still love him."

She shrugged. "Only slightly. I will admit I enjoy the time he spends with me. But I like it even more when he leaves. Your father and I are volatile together, which while enjoyable in bed is not the best recipe for marriage."

Anthony stood and returned to the window. "Does he know about Bronwyn?"

"No," she replied. "If I had told him then he would have brought her to his home with Genna. Then I never would have seen my daughter again. I lost one daughter, I will not lose another."

He could not fault her. The burning sensation that ate at him when he thought he had lost nine years of his daughter's life could not compare to the reality that she faced every day. And while most people would condemn her for leaving her husband, he knew she'd felt betrayed by the man she loved.

"I still do not understand how you can let him into your bedroom after what he put you through."

"Can you honestly tell me if you were to marry today, you could forget about Victoria? Would you still think about the things you did together? Still dream about how she felt? How she kissed?"

"I would prefer not to discuss this with my mother," he said harshly.

"But yet you are interrogating me on my private life."

"Touché," he replied. "It does not matter. I will find a wife and be faithful to her."

"And yet in your dreams, you will only see Victoria," his mother whispered.

"Stop," he ordered. "You are the person who told me marriage to a respectable woman would solve my problems."

"That was before you fell in love."

"I never said I was in love," he retorted.

His mother laughed. "You don't have to say a word, Anthony. Since you arrived in my room, you have looked over at her house so many times I lost count."

Anthony closed his eyes and rested his head on the window frame. "A carriage pulled up and I was just curious who was calling on her."

"And did you recognize the coach?"

"It looks like Lady Farleigh." His brows furrowed. How did Hannah know Victoria's identity? She'd wanted no one to learn her real name.

"Oh, I saw her sister three days ago," his mother said offhandedly.

"Lady Farleigh's sister? Lily Hatfield?"

"Yes, she was at the drapers. She was thrilled because her new doctor finally decided she needed to eat more meat even though she does not care for it. Once she started, her fatigue disappeared, and she has been in much improved health."

Anthony swallowed and stared at the coach. Nicholas had told him that Hannah relayed to him that her sister was dying and that's why she was at the inn and on her way to London.

"Anthony, whatever is the matter?"

He looked down once more and noticed Hannah clutching Victoria's arm and all but pushing her into the carriage. Oh hell, Hannah was Hardy's accomplice.

"Victoria's being kidnapped."

Chapter Twenty-Four

Victoria attempted to twist out of Hannah's grip but the woman was stronger than she appeared. Knowing Victoria had no one to help her out of this mess, she aimed for Hannah's toes. Stomping her heel down on the woman's foot only led to a fierce elbow jab to Victoria's ribs.

"You little bitch, just get in the carriage before I kill you right here," Hannah rasped.

"Then do it," Victoria taunted. "But then you won't have whatever it is you're looking for, will you?"

Victoria could only assume they wanted the note Somerton had taken from Hardy. The door to the carriage opened and Hardy stared down at her with a gleam in his eyes.

"Maybe all we want is you," he replied.

Terror struck her when Hardy grabbed her arm and yanked her into the carriage. "Let me go," she screamed, praying someone would hear her.

She fell onto the floor of the carriage. Hannah kicked her legs out of the way and sat down. The coach rolled away from the only home Victoria had ever truly loved. Only the children knew what had happened. Maggie had gone to the butcher's to buy some beef for a stew and Victoria doubted the scullery maid had heard anything.

She scrambled to the seat across from Hardy. No matter how scared she truly became, she could not let them see her fright. Thankfully, she had remembered to snatch her reticule before Hannah could drag her out of the house. Somerton had never removed his pistol from it. Now, she had a pistol loaded with one shot, but two people were in the coach.

Hannah might be unarmed, but Victoria couldn't take that chance. The woman had threatened to kill Victoria in front of her own home. Hardy most likely had a pistol and the driver might too. At some point, there was a possibility that she could be left alone with just one of them. She had to concentrate on that thought.

"Would one of you tell me what this is all about?" she finally asked.

Hannah shook her head slightly. "We will discuss this in private."

"When?"

"When we get where we are going," Hardy said in a rough voice.

Hannah glared at him. "Don't yell at her. This is all your fault, you spineless bastard. If you could have kept your mind on the goal and not *her*, this would never have happened."

"I can't help myself," Hardy said hoarsely. "Everyone knows I like my women small and blond. She even has blue eyes. Just thinking about her sitting here in the same carriage is getting me hard."

"You are an utter pig," Hannah replied. "Once again, you are thinking with that head," she pointed to the bulge in his trousers, "instead of your brain."

Victoria went silent and tried to look out the slit
in the window covering. Seeing what appeared to be
buildings, she assumed they had not left town. After
numerous turns, the carriage rolled to a stop.

Hardy turned his attention on her. "You will walk
out of this carriage and up those stairs like a lady. Not
that you are one, but you can pretend once more,
can't you? When we get inside, you will say nothing
to anyone or I will shoot you right there."

"Where are we?" she asked, glancing up at the large
home.

Hannah smiled. "You really don't need to concern
yourself over where we are."

"Why not?"

"Your only concern should be what we plan to do
with you," Hardy said with a sneer.

Victoria swallowed down her fear. She would figure
a way out. She had to because the only other choice
would be death.

They walked inside the magnificent home after
the butler opened the door for them.

"Good afternoon, Lady Farleigh, Mr. Hardy." He
waited for an introduction.

"This is a new one for His Grace."

His Grace? Which duke could they be speaking of?

The butler pursed his lips but nodded. "Very well,
then. Take her up to his other room."

A new slice of fear cut down her back as they escorted her up the stairs. Tossing a door open, they
walked into a room with a large bed in the middle and
a long table to the side.

"Tie her to the bedpost to start," Hannah ordered
Hardy.

Hardy shoved Victoria up against one of the posts
and tied her hands tightly behind her back. He

grabbed the reticule and tossed it on the bed. The ropes cut into her skin as she tried to twist out of them.

"Don't bother," Hannah said with a laugh. "Hardy used to be a sailor so he knows how to tie a knot."

"What is this about, Hannah?" Victoria demanded. "I should at least know where I am and why!"

"I think you know exactly why you are here."

Pain struck her cheek where Hannah hit her. "I don't know why I am here," she cried out.

"Where is the note you picked from Hardy?" Hannah's hot breath stung Victoria's cheek.

"I did not take any note from Hardy," she said.

"Of course you did," he said. "Luckily, the first one was only a letter to my mother."

Seeing the look of shock she couldn't hide, he continued, "Did you think I was stupid? I had already checked the study when you returned and put the letter by the chair."

"I never did that," she cried.

"Do you think we are fools?" Hannah walked past her. "Now where is it?"

"I do not have any note."

Hannah laughed coarsely. "I never thought you had it. I want to know who you gave it to, Somerton or Ancroft?"

She could not tell them. There was no doubt in her mind that they would kill Somerton. But if she didn't they would kill her.

"Neither," she replied. *Think, Victoria! Think!* Who else might want that missive? "Your husband wanted it, Lady Farleigh. He wanted to know what you were about, sneaking around with Hardy."

"Liar," she said and slapped Victoria even harder than before. "Farleigh knows nothing about this. I

278   *Christie Kelley*

guess we will wait for Maldon to get the information out of you. He will have you talking in no time."

"The Duke of Maldon?" she whispered. She had heard of his depraved ways from some of the women next door.

Hardy walked closer to Hannah. "Can't I have her just once before the duke? I promise, he'll never know. I will take her arse."

Hannah slapped Hardy. "No one uses her until His Grace says they can."

Victoria swallowed down the lump of fear in her throat. They planned to rape her to get the information. And even if she gave them Somerton's name, she was certain they would still do the same. For the first time since Hannah stormed into her home, a sense of hopelessness invaded her.

Hardy finally left after an hour of suggestive taunts meant only to scare her. Hannah sat in a small chair near the fireplace.

"Hannah, why are you doing this?"

Hannah turned her gaze from the fireplace to Victoria. "You of all people should understand."

"But I don't."

"When Farleigh married me, he lost his reputation. The *ton* believed he was a fool for marrying his mistress, especially since I was a former prostitute. I love my husband and want only the best for him. When Maldon reigns, I will be the leader of the *haute ton* because of my friendship with him. People will look to me for social acceptance."

"And if your plan fails?" she asked softly, not wanting to get Hannah upset, only help her see the reality of the situation.

"But it will not fail. You did not stop us."

"Then why do you need the note?"

SCANDAL OF THE SEASON

"We don't need the note, you fool. Hardy read it. Now we just need to tie up all the loose ends."

"And that would be me?"

"Yes—and whoever else read that note."

Victoria was still confused on one thing. "What does Hardy get out of this?"

Hannah cackled. "A title. Maybe even a duchy. What man wouldn't love that?"

Victoria could think of no way to stop them now. She had to keep Somerton's name out of this but wondered how she could if they threatened her with rape. If they discovered Somerton's name, they would find the note and kill him.

She could not let that happen.

Anthony raced down the stairs of the brothel, dodging a man attempting to take one of the ladies up the steps. He had to get outside and save her. As he ran out the door, he noticed the plain black carriage turn the corner to George Street. He climbed up on his phaeton and urged the horse on.

Most of the delivery carts were gone by now so his only impediments were the pedestrians and carriages headed out for a day of shopping. When he turned the corner to George Street, he scanned the road for the carriage. Most of the coaches looked similar.

Desperate for some sign of which way they had gone, he continued down George Street and then continued to Hanover Square. He stopped at Farleigh's home in the square only to find the footman had not seen Lady Farleigh since they left the house in November for their estate.

They must have gone to Hardy's house. Dammit. He had to find her before it was too late. The ride to

Hardy's modest house seemed interminable. Carts and wagons slowed him down and a sense of dread permeated the air around him.

A footman opened the door to Hardy's house. "Good afternoon."

"Get out of my way, man," Anthony said hoarsely. "Where is your master?"

"Mr. Hardy left the house a week ago and has not returned."

If Hannah and Hardy had not returned to their homes, where the hell were they staying? Not trusting the young man, Anthony searched the lower level and raced up the steps. Hearing the heavy feet of two footmen following him, Anthony headed to the bedrooms. Every room he searched came up empty.

The footmen caught him as he left Hardy's bedroom. After dragging him down the stairs, they thrust him out the door and slammed it behind him. Anthony tumbled down the three brick steps.

"What do you think you are doing?"

Anthony stumbled to his feet, ignoring the sting of the cuts on his hands and knees. He looked up to see Brentwood staring down at him.

"Hardy and Lady Farleigh took Victoria," he mumbled and then headed for his phaeton. He had no idea where to look next but he could not give up.

"Who the bloody hell is Victoria? And didn't Ainsworth tell you that you were done with this case?"

"Victoria is Mrs. Smith. The lady with me at Farleigh's party."

"Oh hell," Brentwood said. "How is Lord Farleigh connected to this mess?"

Anthony stopped and looked around. "I have no idea. He is too far removed from the line of succession. Why would he care who became king?"

"Maybe he is not involved?" Brentwood offered. "Lady Farleigh may be doing this for her own benefit."

Anthony pounded his fist on the edge of the phaeton startling the horse. "Lady Farleigh has never been accepted by the *ton*."

"Oh hell," Brentwood said again. "But if she is in close with the next king then her station would greatly improve. The *ton* would have to accept her."

"Exactly." Anthony walked to his horse to calm her down. "So who else is involved? There is someone much higher in rank who is in control."

"I don't know," Brentwood admitted with a shrug. "What are we missing?"

"I don't know but I have to find Victoria before they hurt her."

"Let me help you, Somerton. Ainsworth said you were the best, and I could learn from you."

Anthony stared at the younger man and nodded. "Very well, then. We need to go to Miss Reynard's home."

"The matchmaker?"

"Yes."

"Ma'am, you have two visitors," Hendricks announced.

Sophie looked up from her book and frowned. She had no clients scheduled until tomorrow and her friends had all claimed to be busy today. But a sense of trepidation had been with her all day.

"Who is it?"

"Lord Somerton and Lord Brentwood, ma'am."

Why would Somerton have brought Brentwood here? The hair on the back of her neck prickled. "Send them in and bring us tea, please."

"Yes, miss."

Within a moment, she heard the hard booted footfall of her half brother followed by a lighter step. As soon as Somerton entered the room, she knew Victoria was in trouble.

"Oh Lord," Sophie said, seeing the pain in his eyes. "What happened?"

Brentwood stared at them as Somerton explained what he'd seen this morning. Sophie looked at her brother not wanting to tell him of the dread she'd felt since this morning.

"Do you have anything of hers on you?" she asked.

"Why?"

"Because while you two are emotionally connected, I still need something from her to help her. Just your emotions are not enough right now."

He pulled out a hairpin from his waistcoat and gave it to her.

"Thank you." She held the pin in her hand and clasped his hand with hers. Closing her eyes, she waited for the slight dizziness that always accompanied the sight.

"She is in a very large home. Elegant."

"Where, Sophie?" Somerton pressed. "I need to know where."

"Shh." Sophie concentrated on the image in her mind. "The house is in Mayfair. The word duke keeps coming to me but I don't know why."

The image slowly faded. "I'm sorry, Somerton. That's all I could see."

"How the bloody hell does she do that?" Brentwood muttered.

"Miss Reynard, this is Lord Brentwood. He does some occasional work for Mr. Ainsworth," Somerton said.

"So I expect I will see you from time to time when you need assistance?"

Brentwood's mouth gaped. "You mean this is where you get the information no one else is able to find?" he said to Somerton.

"Only sometimes." He turned to Sophie. "Thank you."

"I'm sorry I couldn't see more, Somerton."

"I know," he said in a resigned voice. "Is she all right?"

"I cannot tell. Do you know who the duke is?"

Somerton sank into a seat and raked his fingers through his short hair. "No. It might be any duke. Or it might mean a street with the word duke in it."

"Wait," Sophie said, slowly walking around the room. "You said Lady Farleigh is involved. I think I might know who the duke is."

Somerton turned his head toward her. "How?"

"Lady Farleigh used to visit me before she became the countess. She was involved with another man who only came to see her at the brothel. She desperately wanted him to offer her a position as mistress but he never did. Still, they parted on friendly terms when Farleigh made her an offer."

"Who is it, Sophie?"

"The Duke of Maldon," she whispered. "I think that is where she is. Oh God, you have to find her. The stories of what he did to Lady Farleigh were dreadful."

"If he treated her so horribly, why would she have wanted him as a protector?" Brentwood asked.

"In money and position, a duke trumps an earl," Somerton answered. "We have to get out of here."

"Anthony, wait," Sophie cried out as he reached for the door. She didn't even care that she'd called him by his Christian name in front of Brentwood. "His Grace is a dangerous man. He looks innocuous but he is not."

"Thank you, Sophie."

"Bring her home safely."

"I will do my best."

"And Somerton," she paused as her emotions took control, "watch out for your own safety. I should hate to see something dreadful happen to you."

"I understand, Sophie."

Sophie watched the two men leave but the sense of dread would not leave with them. She had a feeling something terrible was going to happen but had no way to stop it.

Chapter Twenty-Five

After three hours of standing, tied to a bedpost, Victoria felt as if her knees would give out. The late afternoon sun was slowly fading into the horizon and long shadows filled the chilly room. Once Hardy and Hannah realized Victoria wasn't about to tell them where the missive was, they left the room. While she preferred being alone to their company, she could not stop trembling.

Not knowing what was going to happen terrified her completely. And worse, no one would ever find her here. No one would suspect the duke was associated with this plot. Even if someone notified Somerton of her kidnapping, she wasn't certain he would look for her. After his behavior toward her today, she was not sure she wanted him to.

The fact that he didn't believe her hurt worse than any pain inflicted upon her. She was a fool for falling in love with him. And yet, the time with him had been the best of her life. What apparently would be a short life.

The door opened and the Duke of Maldon traipsed into the room followed by Hannah and Hardy. Maldon stood straight and walked briskly. While he had a head of white hair, he hardly appeared to be a feeble old man. He came closer until his foul breath wafted in front of her nose.

She turned her head away from the odor. Maldon grabbed her chin and forced it back, so she had no choice but to look at him.

"Now, how much pain am I going to have to inflict upon you before you give me the name of the man who has the missive?"

"You plan to rape me anyway so why should I tell you who I worked for?"

His smile turned evil. "Again, it depends on how much pain you enjoy, Miss Seaton." He held out his hand and Hannah placed a whip in it.

Victoria shivered in fear. She had heard stories from the prostitutes about men who wanted to whip them for pleasure. One or two of the women didn't mind it but most hated it because of the pain. But she didn't believe Maldon wanted pleasure out of this, only pain. Her pain.

"So again, Miss Seaton, who is your contact?"

Trying to delay the pain, she attempted to change the subject. "How did you find out who I was?"

Maldon laughed. "Lady Farleigh followed you back to London. Did you and Somerton think you were being sneaky?"

"No, but why didn't you follow Ancroft?"

"We had another follow him." He put his lips on her neck and bit down until she screamed. "You will be such an easy one to get information from."

He went behind her and untied her hands. Before she could move, Hardy was there holding her.

"Turn the bitch around," Maldon said. He retied her wrists to the post that she now faced.

"Please don't hurt me." She hated herself for begging with these bastards.

"Tell me, was it Somerton or Ancroft?"

When she didn't answer, the cold steel of a knife sliced through the back of her dress. Maldon tore the back off the dress, then cut her stays and shift. With the cool air hitting her back, she knew what would happen next. Still, when the end of the whip hit her, she cried out in agony.

Nothing had ever hurt that badly.

"Do you like that," Maldon said, grabbing her breasts. "My these are small. I much prefer large-breasted women like Lady Farleigh. But Mr. Hardy here, well he spent quite a lot of time on ships so you will remind him of all the boys he's had. He does like to fuck in the arse, but you were Somerton's whore so I would guess he tried that with you, too."

He squeezed her breasts until she cried out again. "Last chance to stop the pain. Who?" He moved back to ready the whip again.

"Oh, God no," she screamed as the lash struck her again.

It didn't matter how much this hurt. She would not give Somerton's name to them. She couldn't be responsible for his death.

"Who?" Maldon yelled then let the whip hit her back again.

Victoria jerked back from the pain. She clutched the bedpost as tears streamed down her face.

"Why were you there?" Maldon asked, holding the whip in the air again.

This she could answer. "I was only there to pretend to be Somerton's mistress. It was the only way he could get into the party because Lord Farleigh is jealous of him."

She slid a glance back to Hannah whose cheeks turned red.

"Were you there to entice Hardy?" he asked, still waving the whip in the air.

"No. Yes. I don't know," she cried. "Somerton and Ancroft wanted me to be able to get close to Hardy if they needed me to pick his pocket."

"Damn easy job when everyone knows he likes thin, young blondes, man or woman."

She went cold. Everyone knew he liked thin young blondes. No wonder Somerton said she was perfect for this job. He used her as bait. "That bastard!"

"Oh, you didn't know that, did you?" he said with a wicked laugh.

White-hot pain licked her back again. She clung to the post and blinked her eyes trying not to faint from the torture. "Please," she begged. "Please stop."

"Then tell me the name," Maldon shouted.

Maldon stepped behind her and rubbed his erection against her. "I think she is ready for me, Hannah."

"No," Victoria cried out. "Please don't do this to me."

He walked toward Lady Farleigh. "Get me ready, Hannah."

Hannah stripped off his jacket and waistcoat. She smiled over at Victoria and said, "Wait until you see the size of this man's cock. You shall be impressed."

Hardy moved closer to her. "And when he's done, I'll have my fun."

Hardy sliced the remains of her tattered clothing off until she was naked in front of everyone. Shame forced tears down her cheeks.

"Make her look at this, Hardy," Hannah said.

Hardy forced her head toward them. Hannah was pulling down the old duke's pantaloons until his cock sprang forth. She stroked the long length of him, until Maldon closed his eyes.

"Maybe he'll stick that large pole up your arse and get you ready for me," Hardy said with a gleam in his eyes.

"Untie her, Hardy. I'm almost ready for her."

Hardy untied her wrists but held them tightly in his large grip. She heard Maldon walking back toward her.

"Last chance to save yourself, Miss Seaton." He cracked the whip across her back again then held it high. "Who has the note?"

"I don't know," she yelled. "I do not know."

The whip struck her down once more. Her back felt as if it were on fire. There was no saving her now.

The sound of footsteps racing down the hall sounded and before anyone could react, the door hurled open. Victoria almost fainted at the sight of Somerton rushing through the door with a pistol in each hand.

Anthony took in the room and pain exploded in his head at the sight of Victoria, naked and exposed to everyone in the room. God only knew what they might have already done to her.

Hardy released Victoria who fell face down on the bed. He reached for his pistol.

"You bastards!" Anthony shouted. Seeing a clear shot of Hardy, Anthony fired his pistol. Hardy fell to the floor screaming.

Victoria yanked the coverlet off the bed to hide her nakedness. Anthony turned his attention on the old naked duke who now had a pistol aimed at Anthony.

"So who will die first, Somerton?" Maldon taunted.

"You will pay for what you have done to Miss Seaton." Anthony slid a glance to Victoria who seemed to be fumbling with the coverlet.

"If you kill me you shall hang for murdering a duke. My servants will protect me."

"And you shall hang for treason, Your Grace." Anthony was certain they had no idea that both Ainsworth and Brentwood were following behind him.

"No one else knows I am involved in this. Those Hanoverian kings should never have been allowed to rule this country. And I intend to make sure they are all eliminated and a new ruling house is formed."

Anthony's finger trembled slightly on the trigger of the pistol. He wanted to kill the man right now but had promised Ainsworth justice would prevail.

"But I do think your whore should watch you die as I'm fucking her."

"No," Victoria screamed as Maldon's pistol fired. She held the small pistol that Anthony had given her and fired at Maldon.

Lady Farleigh shrieked as Maldon sank to the floor. She glared up at Victoria and pulled another pistol from her pocket. Anthony, felled to the floor from Maldon's shot, scrambled to reach Victoria. Smoke filled the room as Lady Farleigh aimed at Victoria and fired.

Victoria screamed and fell to the bed. Anthony raced for the bed as Ainsworth and Brentwood ran into the room.

"Damn," Brentwood mumbled. "It looks like a battle scene in here."

Anthony pulled the coverlet off Victoria's shoulder and gaped at the wound. The shot Maldon fired at him had only scraped his shoulder. But Lady Farleigh's shot had been almost perfectly aimed. He felt the backside of Victoria's shoulder praying for an exit wound.

Feeling blood, he felt a sense of relief. As he moved her slightly to check on the exit wound, he realized how wrong he'd been. Nausea threatened to overcome him at the sight of the whip marks.

"Hell, Ainsworth, call the surgeon now," he ordered.

"Home," Victoria mumbled. "I want to go home."

"Shh," Anthony murmured to her. "Save your strength."

He stared at her as tears filled his eyes. He had never seen anyone so pale. Pressing a piece of linen from the pillow to her wound, he prayed as he never had in his life.

"Somerton, I don't want to die here. Take me home."

He looked up at the ceiling and pressed his lips together. He could not deny her the only thing she'd truly ever asked of him. "Brentwood, help me with her and send the surgeon to her home."

As he picked her up in his arms, she fainted again. He could only hope it was from the pain and not loss of blood already. Brentwood helped him get her into Ainsworth's carriage.

"Somerton," Brentwood said then stopped. "I'm dreadfully sorry."

"She will be all right." Even as he said the words, he knew it was likely a lie.

The ride to her home was a nightmare for him. She came in and out of consciousness, moaning in pain. Anthony held her tight in his arms as tears burned down his cheeks. He never should have gotten her involved in this mess.

She blinked her eyes open for a moment and smiled at him. "You saved me," she whispered.

"Why, Victoria?" he said hoarsely. "Why didn't you tell them my name?"

"I love you," she whispered. "They would have killed you." She fainted again.

She loved him? That was why she didn't give up his name. Tears burned down his cheeks as he stared at her. He had treated her like every other woman, expecting her to hurt him.

But she hadn't.

She had put her own life at risk for him out of love. Love! Until he met her, he had never had an idea about love. But now? Now he understood how much he loved her. How his life would never be the same without her. How his life would never be better without her.

Her pain was his fault. He would never forgive himself for bringing her on this mission. As his own shoulder throbbed, he knew it was nothing compared to the pain of being whipped and shot.

The carriage stopped in front of her house on Maddox Street. The driver opened the door and helped Anthony out with her still in his arms.

"Open the door, then go next door and tell Lady Whitely that Somerton needs her over here now." He stared at the driver. "Do not accept a no answer for *any* reason. I don't care if you have to drag her off a man."

The driver's shocked expression finally wore off. "Yes, my lord."

Anthony kicked at the door to Victoria's home until a middle-aged woman opened it. "The surgeon is on his way. Boil water and get fresh linens up to her bedroom as fast as you can."

"Oh my, what happened?"

"She was shot." And he didn't want to think about the other possibilities of what might have happened. He walked slowly up the stairs to avoid causing her any further pain.

She blinked her eyes open as he placed her on her bed. "Thank you for bringing me home, Somerton."

"Don't talk, Victoria. The surgeon will be here soon and get that ball out of you."

"Please don't leave me," she whispered. "I'm so afraid."

"I won't leave you, I promise."

She nodded but tears fell from her eyes. "I told Lady Farleigh it was bad luck to bring the holly in before Christmas Eve."

"What?"

She only shook her head.

He bent over and kissed the tears off her face. "I'm so sorry," he murmured. "This is all my fault."

"Oh Lord," his mother's voice sounded from the door. "What happened to her?"

"She was shot."

"By who?"

He shook his head. "It's a very long story but Lady Farleigh shot her."

"I told you to leave her alone, Anthony." His mother came over to the bed and sat on the edge. Gently, she pushed back gold strands from Victoria's forehead. Anthony barely remembered how she used to do that to him as a child.

The older woman entered the room with a gasp. "Lady Whitely!"

"Maggie, she needs cool fresh water for her brow. Go get it now. If you need ice go next door and tell them I sent you."

Maggie ran out of the room.

Victoria blinked her eyes open again. "Lady Whitely?"

"Shh, dear. You will be all right. The surgeon is coming. Just remember all you have to live for, the children, your home, your friends . . . Anthony."

Tears fell down the sides of her cheeks. "He hates me," she said as if she didn't know he was in the room. "H—he thinks Bronwyn is our child."

"Hush, I corrected him on his misunderstanding," his mother said in a soothing tone.

Maggie rushed back into the room. "The surgeon's here, ma'am."

"Everyone get off that bed," he ordered. "My name is Mr. Michaels."

The doctor walked over to the bed and examined the wound. Victoria howled as he probed the wound, and it took every ounce of effort for Anthony not to kick the man out. He stood by the bed with his hands fisted tightly.

"The ball is in deep but luckily it is in muscle." He looked around the room at the people gathered. "Lady Whitely, I need your assistance. The rest of you need to leave the room."

"I am not going anywhere," Anthony stated.

"Perhaps it would be best if you let the surgeon do his work without you glaring at him every time she moans," his mother suggested softly.

"I will not leave her. I promised her."

She nodded in understanding. "Mr. Michaels, Lord Somerton will stay."

The surgeon pulled out his tools but shook his head. "Very well, but I did warn you."

The man set to work on the wound as Anthony clasped Victoria's hand in his. "Be brave, Victoria," he murmured. But as she groaned in pain and clutched his hand tighter, he wondered how brave she could be.

"Don't worry, my lord, the ladies usually faint before I get too far into the process."

Was that really supposed to make him feel better? Victoria moaned again and tried to twist away.

"Don't just sit there, man. Hold her down," Mr. Michaels ordered. "I can't have her move when I go in for the ball."

Anthony placed a hand on her chest and shoulder to hold her still. The surgeon took out something from his bag that looked like long tweezers. Anthony glanced away unable to watch the woman he loved going through such pain. He had been shot one time where the ball didn't exit and the pain had been unbearable.

As the surgeon placed the object into the wound, Victoria screamed and tried to move. Anthony held on to her so the man could work.

"Look at me, Victoria," he said softly. "Just look at me."

She did as he suggested but he wondered if she could see through the tears. Her eyes widened slightly. "I love you," she whispered and fainted again.

"There, it's so much better when they just give in and faint," Mr. Michaels commented. "And here we are." He pulled out the ball and handed it to Anthony.

He wanted to throw the damned thing across the room. Instead, he placed the bloodied object on the bed. He watched as the doctor poured a little whisky into the wound and then stitched it up.

"She was also whipped," he said once the surgeon had finished dressing the wound.

Mr. Michaels rolled her over onto her side and cleaned the wounds on her back. "Who did this to her?"

"It doesn't matter. Two are dead and the other will hang for this and other crimes."

"Good," the surgeon mumbled. He finished and laid her gently back against the pillows. "You need your wound cleaned, too."

"Will she live?" he asked, not sure if he wanted to hear the answer.

Mr. Michaels cleared his throat and cleaned Anthony's wound. "If she survives the night, she has a chance. She lost a good deal of blood. But if the wound becomes septic, she might not make it."

"What can I do?"

The surgeon covered Anthony's shoulder and shook his head. "Pray."

Chapter Twenty-Six

Anthony prayed all night as Victoria slipped in and out of consciousness. Even when she was awake, she did not appear to notice him sitting by her bed holding her hand. He made every deal he could think of with God just to allow her to live. He promised he would be a much better person. He wouldn't drink to excess. He would even consider returning to church.

By morning, he was exhausted and she seemed no better. He touched her forehead and found no trace of fever. His mother slipped back into the room and put a hand on his good shoulder.

"How is she?"

"About the same. She wakes but doesn't seem to realize where she is or that I am even here."

"But she is still alive, Anthony."

He nodded, afraid to voice his concerns that she still might not make it. He knew it could take a few days before the fever set in. And once it did, her chance of survival dropped considerably.

God, but he hated the Christmas season. This was just one more example of how bad things always seemed to happen to him in December.

"You need to rest. Go next door and sleep in my room. No one will disturb you."

"I can't, Mother."

She blinked quickly as if trying to combat tears. "Anthony, you were shot, too. You could succumb to a fever just as easily as Victoria. Please just go sleep for two or three hours. I promise if anything changes, I will call for you."

He knew she was right but couldn't stand to be so far away. "I will think about it."

"Please, Anthony."

"I cannot be so far away from her."

"Lord Somerton," Maggie said from the door, "my room is directly above this one. You are welcome to go up there and sleep."

"There," his mother said. "Now go get some rest before I send for a doctor to give you some laudanum."

"Very well, but if she awakens I want to know about it."

"I will send someone to you."

Anthony looked back at Victoria's pale figure once more before taking his mother's advice. Maggie led him to an even smaller room. She left and he removed his boots.

Before he could lie on the bed, the door squeaked open and his muscles tensed. Victoria could not have taken a turn already. Bronwyn peered around the door.

"Come in, Bronwyn."

"Why are you here, Lord Somerton?" she asked with only a slight hesitation.

"Miss Seaton was hurt. I brought her back here to recover her strength." He swallowed down the lump in his throat. "Why are you here?"

"Are you going to take me away from her?" She walked into the room and stood by the end of the bed.

"Why would I do that?"

"Because I keep dreaming that a man who looks like you is going to take me away."

Anthony closed his eyes. She was dreaming. He understood all too well what that meant. Sophie had told him many times that her abilities were not just from her mother. Sophie had taught him to listen to his intuition and trust it. While Genna had never spoken about any of this, he had a feeling Bronwyn shared some of the same abilities.

He also didn't know how to reply to her. If Victoria did not live, he would ask his mother if he could care for Bronwyn. If Victoria did recover and agreed to marry him, again, he would request that his sister live with them.

"I will not take you away from here unless you decide you wish to go with me."

"Are you my father?"

He was so damned tired of the lies. "No, Bronwyn." He looked directly at the little girl. "I am your brother."

"Oh," she gasped. "I didn't know I had a brother."

"I didn't know I had another sister until today."

Tentatively, she walked closer to him. "What do I call you?"

"Tony."

She smiled up at him shyly. "It's nice to meet you, Tony."

"Yes, it is." He patted the bed. "Come sit with me for a few minutes."

She sat down on the bed next to him. "Are you really a lord?"

"Yes, I am a viscount and someday will be an earl."

"Does that make me a lady?" she asked.

He blew out a long breath. He had no idea how to answer that question. She was the legitimate daughter of an earl. However, since everyone believed her mother was dead, she could not be considered legitimate. What a confusing mess, he thought.

"I am really not certain," he finally said.

She stared down at her hands. "Oh. I so want to be a lady."

He tilted her chin upward. "Being a lady is more than just being born to a peer. Take Miss Seaton, she is more of a lady than many of the women in the *ton*."

"Miss Bronwyn," Maggie called from the door. "You must leave Lord Somerton alone so he can sleep."

"We shall talk again, soon," Anthony said with a smile to the young girl.

As Bronwyn left, he lay on the bed his head spinning. So many things were about to change for him. He only prayed Victoria would be there with him to see them.

By late afternoon, Victoria moaned from the throbbing eating at her shoulder and back. She blinked her eyes briefly but the sunlight was too bright for her to keep them open. The quick look had told her so much. Lady Whitely sat in a chair next to her bed. Maggie was wringing her hands together.

And Somerton was nowhere in the room.

He had promised he wouldn't leave her.

She fought against the pain, knowing if Lady Whitely saw her discomfiture, she would give her more laudanum. Victoria hated the taste and the way it made her feel. She would rather feel the pain than the strange sensations of the opium.

But Lady Whitely noticed her slight movements. "Victoria, I know you are awake but wonder why you hide it."

Victoria slowly opened her eyes. Thankfully, the sun had hidden behind a cloud, darkening the room enough for her.

"Should I get him?" Maggie said from the doorway.

"No, he hasn't slept all night." Lady Whitely moved to get a bottle from her nightstand.

"No," Victoria moaned looking at the bottle.

"Shh," Lady Whitely said in a motherly tone. "Right now, you need to sleep and let your body heal. The laudanum will help you do that."

"No," she groaned again, but Lady Whitely was able to get some down her throat. "Somerton . . ."

"Anthony is sleeping in Maggie's room. He has been with you all night but will make himself sick if he doesn't sleep." Lady Whitely replaced a cool cloth on Victoria's forehead. "We all want you to rest and recover."

Victoria had so many questions but her mind whirled from the laudanum.

Several hours later, Anthony felt slightly revived and returned to Victoria's room. As soon as he entered, he noticed his mother hovering over Victoria and Maggie running from the room.

"What is wrong?" he demanded.

His mother looked back at him and said, "She has a very slight fever. I sent Maggie to get ice and water."

He sat on the bed and held Victoria's warm hand. "How long ago?"

"She woke two hours ago, and I gave her more laudanum to make her sleep. She wasn't warm then."

Hearing the sound of footsteps, he expected to see Maggie returning with ice. Instead, Sophie stood at the doorway covering her mouth with her hand.

"Sophie," he whispered.

"Anthony, what happened?" She raced to his side and stared down at Victoria.

"She was shot." His gaze returned to Victoria's pale face. "Now a fever has set in. I'm sorry. I should have sent a note to you."

"I kept waiting for a message from you. The sense of dread I felt continued to grow until I had to find out what happened."

"Sophie," his mother whispered as if testing the name.

Anthony blew out a breath as the women looked at each other. "It is her, Mother."

"Oh," was all his mother was able to say.

"Lady Whitely," Sophie said with a quick curtsy. "It is a pleasure to meet you."

His mother nodded and examined her with a critical eye. "You look very much like your father, young lady."

"Thank you." Sophie looked away as if uncomfortable meeting his mother.

"I don't blame you, Sophie." His mother looked directly at her. "I never did."

"Thank you, Lady Whitely."

Maggie entered the room with a bucket of ice and water. Lady Whitely grabbed the bucket from her and dipped the warm cloth into the water.

"Let me see the wound," Sophie said to Lady Whitely. "I know a little about healing herbs and might be able to help."

"You do?" Anthony asked.

She smiled at him. "You do not know everything about me, Anthony." Lady Whitely moved so Sophie could look at the wound. Sophie slowly removed the dressing and stared at the surgeon's work.

Anthony clutched Victoria's hand tighter as he saw the irritated abrasion.

"This actually looks all right," Sophie said with a frown. "I do not understand why this would give her a fever."

"Her back," he and his mother said at the same time.

"What happened to her back?" Sophie demanded as she gently rolled Victoria onto her side.

"She was whipped," Anthony replied.

"I should never have told you her name." Sophie looked under the dressing and shook her head. "This one does not look good. I need someone to get a message to the Ladies Selby, Blackburn, and Kendal."

"I will do it." Lady Whitely opened the nightstand and pulled out paper and pen. "What do you need me to say?"

"Tell them I need them to go to my house and get my healing book and herbs in my study. Avis will know where they are. Then I need them all here to help out."

"We are managing just fine without all the extra fuss," Anthony said.

"Indeed?" Sophie said roughly. "Then why is her back starting to fester? With their help, everyone will get a chance to rest and get a chance to care for her."

"I will send a footman to Lady Selby's house," his mother said, then left the room.

"What happened, Somerton?" Sophie demanded.

He explained everything that had happened regarding Victoria's kidnapping. "What am I going to do, Sophie?"

She squeezed his shoulder. "I don't know," she whispered.

He stared down at Victoria's pale face. Seeing her like this was killing him. "They can't lose her, Sophie. Not now. Not right before Christmas."

"I'll do everything I can."

"You don't understand," he whispered. "All she wanted to do was give the children a nice Christmas. They can't lose her now." He paused as his breath caught in his throat. "I can't lose her now."

He glanced back at his half sister and noticed the tears running down her cheeks. Brushing his own tears aside, he rose and embraced Sophie. "Please save her," he whispered.

"I'll do my best."

Within an hour, the three ladies Anthony had helped Sophie match were congregating in Victoria's entranceway. Thankfully, none had come up the stairs to see her just yet. He refused to leave her bedside. Instead, he kept changing the cloth on her forehead to help keep her cool.

Hearing the murmur of women's voices, he knew they were coming.

"What exactly happened?" Lady Selby asked.

"Victoria was whipped and shot," Sophie replied in a quiet tone.

"Who would do such a thing?" Lady Blackburn demanded.

Anthony smiled slightly. Lady Jennette Blackburn was as demanding as her brother Selby. They entered the room and all three women groaned.

"So now we know who shot her," Jennette remarked.

He turned at her with an icy glare. "Why would you assume I did this to her?"

The Duchess of Kendal walked up to him, and said, "I most certainly do not think you did this, Lord Somerton. But why are you here?"

"He saved her life," Sophie said with a touch of pride in her voice.

"Sophie," Anthony said roughly. "Enough of this nonsense. What can you do to help her?"

"Avis, I need you to organize a schedule for when you all can be here to help her." Sophie paged through her book of herbs. "Here is what I need."

Anthony glanced over as Sophie mixed a variety of herbs and water into a poultice. "Your Grace, will you help me turn her onto her side?"

Elizabeth glanced back at him with a little frown. "Lord Somerton, it really isn't appropriate for you to be helping with her. She doesn't even have a night-rail on."

"Elizabeth, do as he says," Sophie said in a commanding voice.

Elizabeth walked over and helped roll Victoria onto her side. Anthony tensed when she moaned again.

"Don't worry, Somerton," Sophie said as she applied the poultice. "It still may take a few days, but this will help."

She leaned closer to his ear and whispered, "I promise."

He looked over at his sister and wanted to hug her for all her assistance. But he knew she did not want anyone else to learn about their relationship.

Avis, Jennette, and Elizabeth left the room to organize their schedules and make certain Maggie was keeping the children under control. Once they left the room, Anthony gave his sister a hug.

"Is your mother returning?" Sophie asked.

"Not until morning unless we need her. I also thought with the ladies downstairs it might be best if she left."

"True, but at some point she will wish to check on

Victoria," Sophie said, pulling away. "She cares very
deeply for Victoria."

"Is there anything you don't know?"

Sophie looked away pensively. "Unfortunately, there
are many things I don't know." She walked to her
herbs and packed things up again.

"I believe it might be best to just say she is a concerned neighbor," he said.

"Elizabeth will know who she is, Anthony."

"But they don't need to know everything," he retorted.

"Some day it might come out."

"And some day your secret might be revealed, too."

Sophie nodded with a sigh. "I realize that."

Sophie walked back down the stairs and found her
friends in Victoria's study discussing the timing of
their visits. With Avis and Jennette nursing their
babies, they had limited time to spend here. As soon
as she entered the room, their questions started.

"What exactly happened, Sophie?" Avis asked.

"Why is Somerton upstairs with her . . . alone!" Elizabeth said.

"Victoria was kidnapped after she helped Somerton
with a small job. It took longer than expected to find
her captors. By the time he arrived, she had been
whipped." Sophie glanced down at the floor. "We
don't know if anything else happened to her."

"Oh, no," Jennette whispered.

"When Somerton arrived, he shot one of the men
but another shot him. Victoria fired at that man and
killed him."

"Then how did she end up hurt?" Avis asked.

Unsure what to say regarding Lady Farleigh, Sophie

decided to be vague. "There was a woman in the room who shot Victoria. Somerton rushed her back here. He and Lady Whitely have been helping her."

"Lady Whitely?" Elizabeth said. "She owns the brothel next door!"

"Yes. But she is a very compassionate lady. You all should treat her with respect."

They all murmured their consent.

"But he shouldn't still be upstairs with her when she is wearing nothing," Elizabeth said again. "It will ruin her."

Sophie stared at Elizabeth. "It would not be the first time he has seen her naked."

All three women slapped their hands over their mouths. Avis was the first to recover.

"Victoria? With a man?"

"Were any of you any different?" Sophie said knowingly.

"Well, no," Jennette sputtered. "But she always was the voice of reason. Telling us it was sinful to lie with a man without marriage."

"And yet, it did not stop you, did it?"

All three women giggled and shook their heads.

"Victoria and Somerton," Elizabeth whispered with a grin. "Do you think he loves her?"

"Did you not see the fierce look on his face?" Avis replied. "That is a rake in love."

Chapter Twenty-Seven

After two more days of watching Victoria's fever continue, Anthony thought he might go mad. By the fourth day, her fever had increased. She fought delirium and dreams that he couldn't understand and wasn't sure he wanted to. Based on what he'd heard, Mrs. Perkins was not a pleasant woman when Victoria returned home with nothing to pawn.

The few things he heard about his mother made him happier. At least there, Victoria was safe and warm. Anthony replaced the cloth on her forehead with a cooler one.

Sophie entered the room, glanced at Victoria and bit her lip. "Her fever still hasn't broken?"

"No." He wanted to rail at his sister. She had promised him that Victoria would be all right. But now, Victoria looked paler than before and had barely eaten anything in days.

"Did she drink the broth?"

"Maggie did her best." He closed his eyes for a moment. "She was so thin to start with, Sophie."

"She will put weight on once she recovers." She

stopped him before he said the words on his mind. "Do not even think it, Anthony. She will survive this."

He prayed his sister was right.

"Will you be all right if I leave for a few minutes? I want to go through my herb book and see if there is anything else I can try. I shall only be downstairs."

"Go. It's quiet in here." While he had been here most of the time, he always made sure he was here at night. Since Sophie had no husband to return to, she stayed the night with him. The room and entire house had a different feel to it. Eerily quiet with the children in bed.

Soon after Sophie left, the delirium started again. Only this time, he was the subject of her dreams.

"Somerton," she whispered. "More secrets, more lies."

"Shh, Victoria," he said, wiping her brow again with the cold water.

"I can't love him," she mumbled. "Wrong."

His eyes started to water. "No, Victoria. It's right."

"I'm all wrong. Liar. Thief."

"I don't care about that." He picked her hand up to his mouth and kissed her hand. He stopped and kissed it again. Her hand felt warmer than before. Then he felt her brow and noticed she seemed even hotter.

"Sophie!" he shouted.

He heard the soft footfalls of her quick step. "What is it?"

"Her fever is getting worse."

"Ice," Sophie muttered. "We need to ice her down completely."

They had waited to try this method to see if her fever would break on its own. Neither was sure this would work. But Sophie had convinced him to try it if her fever worsened.

"Maggie," he shouted and then waited for her to arrive.

"Yes, my lord."

"Go to Lady Whitely and ask her for as much ice as she has."

Maggie's face went pallid. "Yes, my lord."

"I will go get some more blankets," Sophie said hesitantly. "Anthony, I have no idea if this will work."

"I know. Just get the blankets."

Victoria writhed on the bed as her delirium returned worse than the last time. Anthony went back to the bed and stared down at the woman he loved more than he ever thought possible.

"You will not die," he ordered.

She moaned softly.

"Do you hear me, Victoria? You are not to die." He clasped her hot hand in his. "I just couldn't bare it," he whispered.

Within minutes, his mother returned with Sophie and Maggie. Sophie put a blanket over Victoria and placed chopped ice chips all over her.

"How long do we wait?" he asked his sister.

"Five to ten minutes."

Sophie paced the room as the minutes ticked away while Anthony sat at Victoria's bedside. Every minute or two, he would touch her forehead for any sign of a reduction in her fever. After ten minutes, they removed the ice. Victoria shivered and groaned.

"I cannot tell if this helped," Sophie admitted with tears in her eyes. She covered her mouth with her trembling hand. "I've tried everything I know. I'm sorry."

Anthony closed his eyes against the pain of knowing there was nothing left to do for her. The other women slowly left the room as if understanding he needed to be alone with Victoria. Returning to his chair, he fought the exhaustion tempting him to sleep. After an hour of fighting, he closed his eyes for a moment but prayed she would not pass while he slept for a few minutes.

Victoria slowly blinked her eyes open. The room was dim with only the light from the fireplace and one candle. Her lips cracked when she smiled seeing Somerton sleeping in the chair next to her.

Very little of the past few days remained in her mind. She remembered being shot but only hazy things after that. She knew Somerton had been here and Sophie, too. Victoria frowned but she was certain Lady Whitely had been in the room a few times. She moved her left arm slightly but groaned in pain.

"Victoria." Somerton immediately awoke and stared down at her. "Are you still delirious?"

"I don't think so." Her voice sounded raspy to her ears. She tried to smile again but her lips were so cracked they hurt.

He felt her forehead and grinned. "Your fever is down."

"How long have I been here? I cannot remember how many days it has been."

"Five very long days."

"Have you been here the entire time?"

Moving to her bedside, he held her hand in his strong hand. "Almost. I did take a few chances to sleep in Maggie's bed."

"I get shot and you take to another woman's bed?" she joked, trying not to laugh because of the pain.

"You know I'm a rake," he replied with a laugh. He leaned in closer and said, "But not that much of a rake."

"Thank you," she whispered.

"For what?"

"Saving me. Bringing me home." She blinked back the tears. "Staying with me."

"It was my fault that this happened." He clasped her hand with his strong calloused hand and brought it to his lips. "I should never have offered you money to come with me. I knew you needed money or you never would have attempted to pick a pocket at Avis's party."

"I was so ashamed of what I did."

He smiled against her hand. "And you couldn't even pawn the necklace."

"No."

"Oh, Victoria," he said. "Did Hardy or Maldon do anything else to you?"

Seeing the worry on his face, she squeezed his hand. "No. But if you hadn't arrived . . ." She couldn't think about what they would have done to her.

"Shh," he whispered. "You don't have to say anything more. You should have given Maldon my name."

"They still would have raped and then killed me." She looked at the pained expression on his face and wished she could take that agony away. "What happened to Lady Farleigh?"

"I have not heard yet."

"Have you left this house at all since you brought me here?"

He shook his head. "I couldn't take the chance that something would happen while I was gone."

Her heart pounded against her chest. She wanted to tell him how much she loved him but there were still so many secrets and lies between them.

"Did you order me not to die?" she asked softly.

His cheeks reddened. "I believe I did."

She smiled at him. "Thank you."

The sound of soft footsteps forced her to look to

the doorway. Sophie and Lady Whitely stood at the threshold with their mouths agape.

"She's awake!" Sophie said then came running to the bed. She placed her hand on Victoria's forehead and smiled. "She's still a little warm but so much cooler than before."

"Thank you for helping me," Victoria said to Sophie.

Lady Whitely walked to the end of the bed and gave her a look filled with love. Victoria's lower lip trembled. Lady Whitely had saved her life twelve years ago, and Victoria had never really appreciated all that the woman had done for her.

Lady Whitely could have turned her over to the authorities for picking some loose coins out of her pocket. She could have left Victoria out on the street. Instead, Lady Whitely had taken Victoria in and had given her a room and food to eat. Without Lady Whitely, Victoria would probably be a prostitute or worse, already hanged for picking pockets.

And even if Bronwyn was Somerton's daughter with the lady, she still deserved Victoria's thanks.

"Thank you, Lady Whitely."

Lady Whitely moved to Sophie's position on the bed. She pushed back the hairs on Victoria's forehead. "I did very little, dear."

"You know all that you have done for me. And I have never properly thanked you."

Lady Whitely glanced over at Anthony and then back to Victoria. "Hush, you have done an amazing thing for me."

There was so much she wanted to say to each person, but her eyes wouldn't cooperate and quickly she was back to sleep.

* * *

Anthony left Victoria asleep with Avis watching over her and walked downstairs for breakfast. He felt lighter than he had in days. As he passed a mirror, he stopped and looked at himself. He hadn't shaved in five days, had only washed up at a basin and had barely eaten enough to keep a child alive.

"You look like hell," he said to the mirror in the hall.

"You really do," his mother said with a smile as she walked down the steps. "Why don't you go next door and ring for a bath in my room? Get a good meal while you're there, too."

"I think I will take you up on your hospitality."

"But the girls cost extra," she said with a grin.

"I don't think I will need any of them again."

"Somehow, I had a feeling you would say that."

Anthony walked next door and spoke to a footman about having clothes brought over from his home. After a large breakfast of coddled eggs and ham, not only did clothes arrive but also his valet. Huntley shaved him and drew a hot bath.

Anthony tore off his clothes and tossed them to Huntley.

"They have blood stains on them." Huntley grimaced. "And after all this time, I doubt the stains will come out."

"I believe you can burn those. After five days of wear, I really don't want to ever wear them again."

He slipped into the hot bath feeling better than he had in days. The steamy water relaxed his tense and cramped muscles. After cleaning off a few days of grime, he leaned his head back and closed his eyes.

Everything would be all right now. Once Victoria recovered completely, they would marry. Her friends would help her become accepted in the *ton*. At some point, she would be with child and give him a beautiful son or daughter of his own.

And he would teach her to dance all the dances. He wanted her to dance until her feet ached.

Hearing the door shut, he assumed Huntley had left to get him something.

"What are you doing bathing in Lady Whitely's room?"

Anthony blew out a breath and opened his eyes to see his father staring at him. "I am enjoying a nice hot bath. Whatever are *you* doing here?"

"Do not talk to me like that," his father ordered. "I suppose you had to bathe after being with one of those ladies downstairs. Where is she?"

He ignored the comment regarding the ladies downstairs. "She is next door with Miss Seaton."

"The orphan lady?" His father roamed the room as if it was his own. "Why would she be over there?"

"Miss Seaton was badly injured so she was assisting her." Anthony grabbed a towel hanging over a chair, stood and wrapped it around himself. "Where is my valet?"

"He walked out as I came in."

"But again, why are you here?"

"What I do with my time is my business," his father said. "And where have you been? Your sister is worried about you."

He wanted to ask which one, but he could not betray his mother. "I have been busy. Tell Genna I will call on her in a few days."

"But where have you been?" His father stopped his pacing and stared at him. "Whoring and gambling, I presume?"

"I have been next door helping Miss Seaton, too."

He grabbed his drawers and trousers and put them on. "In fact, I need to return."

"What happened to Miss Seaton that has everyone assisting her?"

Anthony knew there was no point in denying what happened. The story was bound to get out. "She was shot."

"How are you involved?" His father continued his pacing. "Never mind, I am quite certain I do not wish to know."

Anthony continued to dress, eager to finish and leave this room. "Actually Father, I saved Miss Seaton. Not that you would likely believe it, but I did."

"By the by, I spoke with Coddington and he would be agreeable to a marriage."

His hand stopped on the button of his waistcoat. "Marriage? To whom?"

"His daughter Susan, of course."

His mother had mentioned her name before he left for Farleigh's. His mother must have talked to his father about this. Anger flared within him. "I am not marrying Susan Coddington."

"Yes, you are." His father stopped and crossed his arms over his chest. "I have waited long enough for you to sow your oats. You are twenty-eight and it is time to marry and produce an heir."

Anthony continued to button his waistcoat. "Oh, I have every intention of marrying."

"Good, then. I will send a note to Coddington stating that you will call on him in the morning."

"I am marrying Miss Seaton," he retorted, tying his cravat. He grabbed his jacket and pulled it on.

"You shall do no such thing." His father's white brows furrowed deeply. "I forbid it."

Anthony laughed. "Forbid it, then. It will not change a thing. I am marrying Miss Seaton."

"Anthony, think about what you are saying. The woman is the daughter of a vicar. She is not a member of Society. She will never be accepted, nor will she help you regain your respectability."

"Her dearest friends are Lady Selby, Lady Blackburn, and the Duchess of Kendal. I am quite certain they can assist in her acceptance amongst the *ton*."

"What if there is a scandal in her past?"

"What if there is a scandal in my past?" Anthony retorted, staring at his father. "One that no one knows about."

His father tightened his jaw. "You are a viscount and will be earl some day, so all can be forgiven. Not true for the daughter of a vicar."

"Leave it be, Father. I have already decided on my wife."

Chapter Twenty-Eight

Victoria awoke a few hours later to the sound of whispered arguing outside her bedroom. Straining, she finally realized it was Somerton and Lady Whitely. And their argument revolved around marriage.

"How could you tell him who I should marry?" Somerton asked.

"I was trying to help you."

"It wasn't your place to do so. I never said I wanted to marry her." His voice while quiet was harsh with anger.

"Shh, you shall wake Victoria."

Hearing footsteps, Victoria pretended to sleep. She forced her breathing to remain calm even though her heart raced. The footsteps retreated, and she listened further. She had to know what this was about.

"She is still asleep," Lady Whitely stated.

"I won't marry that girl," Somerton said in a harsh whisper. "I won't."

"I had a feeling you would not. But I went to him before all this happened."

"But why did you go to him in the first place?"

"I thought he might convince you it was the right thing to do," Lady Whitely replied.

"He is the last person I would listen to after all the lies."

Victoria wondered who this "he" was and why Somerton would not listen to him. She heard what sounded like Somerton's heavy footsteps walking away from Lady Whitely. Why did this surprise her?

Victoria blinked back the tears of heartache. She had known he would not marry her. But hearing him say so hurt her deeply. She had never had false expectations. They were from completely different worlds. Still, her heart ached.

She loved him more than she ever thought she could. When he walked into that room in Maldon's house, she had been certain he did it out of love for her. Now, she had no idea why he had followed her. Duty, perhaps.

Responsibility. He'd told her that he felt guilty for dragging her into this case. All she had been was a responsibility to him. Now that she was on the mend, he could go about his business and forget about her.

But she would never forget him.

Sophie walked in so quietly that Victoria did not hear her until she neared the bed. "Why are you crying, Victoria? Are you in pain?"

Yes! But Sophie wouldn't have any herbs to mend her broken heart. "No, I—I . . ."

"What happened, Victoria?" Sophie sat on the edge of the bed.

"Oh, Sophie, I thought after all this that maybe there was a chance that he loved me. That maybe he would even ask for my hand." Victoria brushed aside a tear. "But I'm just a foolish woman. We are from completely different backgrounds."

"Victoria, when you were in the confusion of your fever, Somerton only left your side when we forced him to. I have never seen a man so devoted to a woman. He loves you."

Victoria looked up at the white ceiling. "Perhaps, but not enough to marry me. And I never expected marriage so I don't even know why I'm upset."

Sophie smiled down at her. "Because you love him. And you want to spend the rest of your life with him."

"Sophie, I love him so much it hurts."

"Why do you think he doesn't want to marry you?" Sophie said, fussing with the blankets.

"I heard him speaking with Lady Whitely. He said he would not marry me." She lowered her voice to a whisper. "I think Lady Whitely is in love with him."

"What?" Sophie frowned. "That makes no sense. I will speak with him."

Victoria grabbed her hand. "Please, do not talk to him about this. The matter is between him and me. Not you. I know you love to see your matches work out, but this one isn't meant to be. I will say good-bye to him and let him go."

"Should I send him up, then?"

"Yes. I suppose I should get this over with now."

Sophie walked down the stairs feeling as if she were in a daze. Perhaps Victoria had been delirious and heard the conversation incorrectly. It didn't matter how it happened, Somerton was going to fix this situation now. Sophie walked into the study and found him pacing the room.

"What is wrong?" he asked as soon as she entered.

"I was about to ask you that same question. You look as if you have received some terrible news."

He threw his hands into the air. "It is my parents, of course." He walked over to the door and closed it. "Do you know that my father visits my mother?"

"Visits as in . . . ?"

"Yes!"

Sophie giggled. "Well, by law they are still married. So . . ."

"That's the same excuse she tried to use. She told me she was allowing him his husbandly rights." He stopped in front of her. "Husbandly rights! She lets him into her room. She lets him into her bed!"

"Anthony, maybe they still have some feelings for each other."

"Oh yes, lust. And they talk to each other about Genna and I." He released a low growl and started pacing again.

"Sit down. You are making me insane with all the walking back and forth." She waited for him to sit before continuing, "Just because your parents don't have the relationship you wanted them to have doesn't mean it is wrong. Perhaps they just cannot live together."

"That was her explanation."

"So maybe that is the truth for them. After your father spread the rumor that she had died, he would have no choice but to keep their affair a secret. She cannot come back from the dead."

"Why not, she did for me."

A knock sounded and Maggie poked her head into the room. "I'm sorry to disturb you but there is someone here to see Lord Somerton."

"Me? No one knows I'm here."

"She says she's your sister, my lord."

"Genna? Send her in." Somerton looked at Sophie, and said, "Would you like to meet your sister?"

Sophie swallowed down a lump in her throat. She had wanted to meet Genna for as long as she had known Somerton. No words would come out of her mouth so she nodded.

"I should have introduced you both a long time ago," he said.

"Please do not introduce me as your sister. It would only cause her pain."

He tilted his head. "Very well, then."

Genna entered the room, took one look at Somerton and ran into his arms. "Tony! I have been worried sick about you."

"Genna, I apologize. I should have sent you a note."

Genna turned her head toward Sophie and gasped. "I am sorry I didn't realize you had company in here. Are you Miss Seaton?"

"No, I am Sophie Reynard."

"The matchmaker!" She turned back to Somerton. "Is that what you have been doing? Trying to find a woman?"

"No, I found her," he replied with a genuine smile.

Genna's eyes widened. "You mean . . . Miss Reynard?"

"No," they both said at the same time.

"How did you find out I was here, Genna?"

"When Father arrived home a short while ago, I told him again how worried I was about you. He mentioned that you were here helping Miss Seaton."

"Father told you I was here."

"Yes."

Sophie stared at her younger sister with such a yearning in her heart. She'd never had a sister to share things with, talk with, or shop with.

"Did Miss Reynard match you with someone?" Genna asked eagerly.

Somerton looked over at Sophie. "I am not entirely certain."

"He might have had a little help. But he didn't need much. He's known for ten years who he was searching for."

"Well who is she?" Genna said. "I want to meet her."

"I suppose she might not mind too much. But she has been very sick so she is not herself. Perhaps just a quick introduction." Somerton started to lead Genna out of the room.

"Somerton, I wouldn't advise introducing them just yet." Sophie walked closer and whispered, "She is under some mistaken assumptions that you need to correct. Once that is done, I believe introducing your sister would be an excellent idea."

"What assumptions?"

"Something about Lady Whitely being in love with you," she said with a little grin.

A feminine laugh sounded from the doorway. "How did she come up with that idea?"

Sophie turned at the sound of Lady Whitely's laugh. "I am not certain. But one of you needs to set her mind to rights."

"I will talk to her," Anthony said, then looked at both Lady Whitely and Genna. He blinked and glanced over at Sophie.

"Excuse me, I know I am being slightly rude, but have we met?" Genna asked Lady Whitely.

Anthony groaned inwardly at the question. He was sick of the lies and secrets his family kept. But he had promised his mother not to speak of her being alive to Genna. As he watched the array of emotions cross his mother's face, he just didn't care any longer.

"Genna, this is—"

"Lady Whitely," his mother interrupted in a harsh tone. "I live next door to Miss Seaton."

"Oh." Genna's dark brow furrowed. "I must be mistaken then. I am Genna, Lord Somerton's sister."

"I know," she whispered then covered her mouth.

"How would you know?" Genna abruptly asked.

"I have been friends with Lord Somerton for many years." His mother looked away.

Genna continued to stare at her mother. "Tony, did you ever notice how much she looks like that portrait of our mother? The one that hangs in Father's study. It's remarkable."

Anthony stared at his mother. Her eyes filled with tears. "Tell her," he said to her. "Do it or I will."

"Perhaps, I should leave," Sophie said quietly. "I do not belong here."

"Indeed?" Anthony said. "It seems to me you belong here just as much as I do. In fact, perhaps we should call Bronwyn into the room, too."

"Anthony!" his mother exclaimed. "Do not do this to me . . . and her."

"I am sick of the lies. *Tell her.*"

"Genna, sit down on the sofa and we shall have a little talk," his mother said gently.

"What is going on?" Genna looked between them all.

His mother closed her eyes. "Tell her, Anthony," his mother whispered. "I just don't think I can do it. I still remember the look on your face when you discovered the truth. And how you reacted."

"Sit down, Genna." Anthony went to the sofa and took his sister's hand. "Lady Whitely does indeed look like the portrait of Mother. That's because she is our mother."

Genna's face turned pale and for a moment, he thought she might faint.

"No," she whispered, shaking her head in denial. "Mother is dead. She died when I was only two."

"I did not die, Genna," his mother replied softly. "Your father told you that because I left him. He wanted everyone to think I had died."

"No," she said louder this time. Then she turned to him. "When did you find out?"

Anthony closed his eyes against the painful memories. "Ten years ago."

"And you never told me?"

"You were only ten years old. How could I explain what had happened to such a young girl? After I started to visit Mother, she asked me not to tell you."

"I cannot believe this," Genna said. "And why did you infer that Miss Reynard should be part of this."

His mother sat down on the other side of Genna. "Genna, your father was having various affairs with widows in addition to the mistresses he kept. When I discovered your father had another daughter from one of his mistresses, I was furious. That was when I left him."

Genna looked at him with confusion.

"Sophie is that daughter," Anthony said.

Genna stared over at Sophie. "You're my half sister?"

Sophie nodded. "I am."

"And who is Bronwyn? Another half sister?"

"No," his mother answered slowly. "She is your sister. And no, Anthony did not know about this until a few days ago. No one knew, especially not your father."

Genna put a hand to her forehead. "I do not understand any of this."

"Anthony and Sophie, please leave us to talk about all this," his mother requested. "And someone bring

Bronwyn in. I believe you are right, Anthony. The time for secrets is done."

Anthony walked upstairs to speak with Victoria while Sophie brought Bronwyn down to her mother. A sense of relief filled him now that his sister knew the truth. He hoped she would sympathize with their mother's position better than he had when he had discovered her.

Now he just had to tell Victoria everything.

He walked into the room and found her sitting up in bed. Her cheeks were pink but not with fever for the first time in days.

"How are you?" he asked as he took the chair by her bed.

"Well," she answered, staring down at the blue coverlet.

"Did you eat?"

"Yes."

"What is wrong, Victoria? You are not a woman who gives one word answers."

"All right." She looked away from the coverlet to the fireplace. "I wanted to thank you for all that you have done for me the past few days."

"Then why are you looking at anything but me?"

"Somerton, please, this is hard enough without your comments."

He crossed his arms over his chest. There was more to this than just her believing Lady Whitely was in love with him. "Very well, continue."

She closed her eyes. "You have been here too long. People will start to talk. I think it might be best if you return to your home this afternoon."

"Indeed? So you would like me to leave and not return?"

"Yes."

How could he have been so stupid? He never apologized for their argument about Bronwyn. "Is this about my getting angry with you about Bronwyn? I can explain."

"There is no need. I can only imagine how difficult it must have been to discover you have a daughter. If I had known she was yours, I would have told you."

"Even if Lady Whitely told you not to? Even if you would have lost everything if I had ascertained the truth?" He had to know the answer to his questions. Even if they were not relevant.

"Yes. If there is a parent who can take care of their child, then I believe it is in the best interest of the child to be with that person."

Anthony tilted his head and looked at her. "I would agree. But if that is the case, why did you not request that Lady Whitely care for her daughter?"

She rolled her eyes. "That is entirely different."

"How so?"

"Lady Whitely could not raise a daughter in a brothel. It was in Bronwyn's best interest to be raised here."

"And did you ever question Lady Whitely about the father?"

"No," she said, finally looking at him. "I just assumed he was some man who paid for her services, and she would not know which man it was."

"Ah," Anthony said with a smile. "That makes sense. So now that you have determined I am her father, I should make arrangements to bring her to my home."

Victoria attempted to blink back tears but one

slipped down her cheek. "Yes," she said. "I suppose that is the correct thing to do."

"I see." Anthony stood and started to walk closer to her bed. "Suppose I tell you I am not Bronwyn's father?"

"We both know you are. That is why you were so angry with me. You thought I had kept that from you."

"True, but only because I assumed she must be mine based on age and looks. Considering I met Lady Whitely on the night you and I had sex at the church, and didn't meet with her again for a year, I had assumed Bronwyn must be our daughter."

"But that is not true," Victoria cried. "You had sex with Lady Whitely and it must have happened two months before we ever met. Bronwyn was born seven months after we had relations the first time."

"Yes, your first time." He walked back to the bed and leaned over her only inches from her face. "And my first time too."

Her breathing turned shallow as he hovered over her. "You are lying."

"I am not. You were the first woman I was ever with. You were the only woman I wanted to be with that night."

"Then how—"

He cut her off with a soft kiss. God, he'd missed her kisses. "Bronwyn is my sister."

Chapter Twenty-Nine

"Bronwyn is what?" Victoria asked breathless from his kiss.

"She is my sister."

Victoria frowned at him as he sat on the bed next to her. Perhaps the accident did something to her mind. Because if Bronwyn was his sister then either his father had had sex with Lady Whitely or . . .

"Oh, my God," she said, staring at him. For the first time she noticed how much his smile reminded her of Lady Whitely. He'd told her that he'd met his 'dead' mother that night ten years ago. And Ancroft had mentioned they had gone to Lady Whitely's. "How? Is she really your mother?"

He walked to the door and closed it so this went no further. "Yes."

She had no idea what to say to him. Suddenly so much about the man made sense. His lack of respect for women, his lack of trust especially with women, his reaction at the church that night. Her heart quickly ached for him.

"How did you find out? You told me that you had discovered she was alive that night ten years ago."

Somerton walked back to the bed, sat down, and clutched her hand. "Nicholas and Lord Kesgrave took me gambling for my eighteenth birthday. Then they figured they should introduce me to the pleasures of the flesh. They brought me to the house next door. When Lady Whitely walked into the room, we could only stare at each other."

She could not imagine how hurt he must have been to find out his dead mother owned a brothel. Squeezing his hand, she felt a tear fall down her cheek. "Oh Anthony, I'm so sorry you had to find out that way."

"As you can imagine, I was in shock. I pilfered a bottle of brandy and ended up at St. Georges where I took a young woman's innocence."

"But how?" she mumbled. "How could she have opened a brothel?"

He told her about how his mother had left the children and his father's response. But that still did not explain everything.

"I still don't understand. How could she afford to open a brothel? She would have needed money. And you told me your father gave her nothing."

Somerton grimaced. "Believe it or not, before she owned the brothel, the original owner found my mother on the street, attempting to prostitute herself. According to my mother, she never would have made a penny on the street. The owner brought my mother in and immediately realized how intelligent my mother was. Mrs. Lee taught my mother the business and sold it to her four years later."

"Just like your mother brought me into her house," Victoria whispered.

"Yes."

Wincing from the pain, she moved her hand to stroke his cheek. Finally hearing the truth from him made her love him even more. But she had to stop loving him. This didn't change what she heard in the hall this morning.

Slowly, she drew her hand back. "Anthony, thank you for telling me the truth. I will never tell a soul that she is your mother."

"What else is wrong, Victoria?"

"Nothing," she said with a catch to her voice.

"Then why do you look as if you might cry?" He brought his hand to her cheek.

She let her head rest into the warm strength of his hand. "I am not about to cry."

At least not until he was out of the room. Then she wouldn't be able to stop her tears.

"Look at me, Victoria."

She blinked and looked up into his warm hazel eyes. She couldn't look away even if she'd wanted to.

"I love you," he whispered. "When you were shot I thought I would never be able to tell you how much you have changed my life. For the better."

"Please, don't." She could not bear to hear his words of love and know that they could not be together.

"Don't what? Tell you how much I love you? Tell you that I almost died watching you fight for your life, and I was unable to help you?"

"Stop!" She turned away from his hand and let her head rest on the pillow. "Stop torturing me. I cannot be your mistress."

"I don't want a mistress, Victoria. I want a wife."

"But you don't want me."

He took her chin and forced her to look at him again. "You are the only woman I have ever wanted to marry."

"You told Lady Whitely that you didn't want to marry me. I heard you this morning right outside my room."

He laughed softly. "You need to stop eavesdropping on conversations. You tend to get things all wrong."

"What are you talking about?"

"My mother had been discussing who she thought would make me a proper respectable wife with my father. They both agreed that Miss Coddington was just the thing to set my reputation right. I told my mother this morning that I would never marry that girl."

"Oh," she whispered, ashamed of listening in on their conversation.

"My mother knows that I love you. Sophie knows. And I can pretty much guarantee that your friends know, too. I might have been a bit difficult when they asked me to leave the room a few times."

"You, difficult?" She smiled. "I cannot imagine that."

He tilted his head back and laughed.

"So everyone knew that you loved me, except me?" She laughed softly. "Do you know how much I love you?"

"You saved my life by shooting a duke. You wouldn't give up my name when whipped." He smirked at her and her heart raced. "I think I have a feeling."

"Your birthday is tomorrow and Christmas two days after that."

"So it is," he commented, wondering why she brought up that topic.

"I haven't bought you anything for either," she whispered.

He smiled down at her. "Seeing you up and awake is the best present you could give me. And if you want to give me something then give me your consent to become my wife."

"Very well," she said with a watery smile. "I will

marry you, Anthony." She bit down on her lower lip in thought.

"I know that look," he said.

"What do we do about the orphans? I cannot desert them."

"Why would you need to? Most women of the *ton* do charity work. This is yours. You can hire someone to help Maggie with the children." He paused and looked down at their joined hands. "But do you think we might be able to have Bronwyn come live with us?"

"What do you think your mother would say?"

"I think that as long as she can visit us, the idea would please her."

"I would be honored to have her visit us. Although, there may be talk."

"I do not care if there is talk. People can say she is our child, my child, it doesn't matter. All that matters is we are together and my sister is with her family."

Her heart swelled with emotions but still she had questions. "What about your wish to gain your respectability back? Marrying me will not help your situation. In fact, if anyone ever discovered my past then you would be ruined."

"A wise man told me that respectability was overrated. He also told me I would marry for love."

She tilted her head. "Who said that?"

"Nicholas."

"A very wise man."

Anthony watched the turn of emotions on her face and knew she still was worried. And honestly, after his encounter with Lady Farleigh, he had a few doubts. "Are you worried about the fact getting out or what might happen to your social status?"

She laughed softly. "What social status? My only

concern is the effect it might have on you. You wanted your respectability back."

"Well, there is something we could do. But I will warn you that it is rash and possibly foolish."

"What is your idea?"

"We let the scandal out. We leak the gossip that you are really Anne Smith before we marry. I cannot marry Victoria Seaton anyway. It wouldn't be a legal marriage."

Her blue eyes widened. "That would be scandalous indeed."

"I do believe if we discuss this with our friends they will support us."

She truly liked the idea but hesitated remembering his words only a few weeks ago. "And if they decide their wives should not be around a woman with a background like mine?"

He should never have put the thought in her head that her friends' husbands would never allow them to see her if the scandal of her background came out. Most of the men would not care as long as Victoria married him. And nothing would stop those ladies from visiting Victoria. They all knew from experience that scandals only last until another one replaces it.

"I believe your friends would never listen to their husbands in regards to you."

"They are all a little headstrong," she said with a giggle.

"A little? After seeing how they attempted to bully me the past few days, I'm starting to feel sorry for their husbands."

Victoria giggled and then winced from the pain. "Do you really think this scandal idea might work?"

He smiled at her. "We would be the scandal of the season. At least the Christmas season. I'm quite certain

once the Season arrives, we will be old news and some
new scandal will have taken our place."

"It is a rather wicked idea," she said. "And I rather
like it . . . and you."

He brought her hand up to his mouth. "And I
rather love you."

Epilogue

Christmas Day, 1817

Anthony watched as Maggie took all the children out of the parlor for their beds. He and Victoria kissed them all good night before they left. He could not remember a Christmas he'd enjoyed more. Victoria had asked him sweetly if he would accompany Maggie and the children to church in the morning. Afraid she might insist on attending if he didn't, he agreed. Surprisingly, he'd found the message of the Christmas service encouraging. He'd returned to Victoria's home with a lighter heart.

After a large goose dinner, they let the children open their presents. In addition to the small tokens Victoria had bought for them, he brought a toy for each child.

Now, he leaned back against the worn chair in her parlor and smiled. Their friends had joined them here since Victoria was still recovering from her injuries. Thankfully, she was now eating better and had some color to her.

Lady Farleigh had been arrested and was being interrogated as she awaited her trial and certain conviction, as well as probable hanging for attempted murder along with her other crimes.

The gossips had already started their tongues wagging on the subject. But knowing they risked a cut by the Duchess of Kendal, many kept their opinions to themselves. Already, a new version of the gossip was starting to emerge, with a little help from Ainsworth.

"Victoria, everyone wants to know if it's true that you helped save prinny from assassination?" Elizabeth asked.

Victoria blushed and looked over at him. "I might have assisted with it, but Somerton was the true hero."

"Still, the gossips have suddenly stopped talking about your childhood of thievery," Avis remarked with a salute of her wine glass toward him.

"Everyone is also saying that for your actions you will be ennobled so we will have to start calling you Lady Seaton now," said Jeannette.

"Just in time for a wedding," Anthony said, looking down at Victoria.

They had decided to marry on New Years Eve. It was supposed to have been his sister's wedding day. But Genna had decided she could not marry Lindal after all. She needed time to come to terms with the discovery of her mother.

His eagerness to have Victoria in his own home grew with every day. He wanted to spoil her, give her everything she'd been denied as a child.

"I just wish Sophie could be here for the wedding," Victoria mused.

Jennette leaned forward. "Did anyone else find it strange that she suddenly decided to travel? It seemed very odd to me."

Most murmured their agreement. But Anthony did not find it terribly odd.

"I think she may have realized her fatal flaw," Anthony said quietly.

"What do you mean?" Selby said, and then sipped his wine.

"She matched every one of us. Now, all her friends are married and several have children. She has no one."

Victoria smiled broadly. "Then perhaps it's time the matchmaker became matched."

Don't miss any of these passionate
romances from Christie Kelley . . .

EVERY NIGHT I'M YOURS

A woman who wants to know what she's been missing . . . A man perfectly suited to train her . . . Christie Kelley weaves a scintillating novel of one rapturous night of ecstasy . . .

A WOMAN YEARNING FOR A TASTE OF THE FORBIDDEN . . .

At twenty-six, aspiring novelist Avis Copley intends to wear spinsterhood as a badge of honor. But when she discovers a volume of erotica that ignites a searing fire within her, Avis realizes just how much she doesn't know about the actual pleasures of the flesh. Determined to learn more, she devises a daring plan . . .

A MAN READY TO TEACH HER MUCH, MUCH MORE . . .

Avis chooses Emory Billingsworth, a fellow novelist—not to mention a beautiful specimen of manhood—to instruct her in carnal pleasure. But when the brash earl of Selby, Banning Talbot, a man she has known for years, unearths Avis' true intentions, he claims she's made a dangerously bad choice. Volunteering his services for one wicked night of reckless, abandoned passion, Banning promises he will satisfy *all* of her deepest longings. Yet Banning cannot begin to imagine the effect his willful, voluptuous, and very eager student will have on him—or how far an innocent lesson in desire can go. . .

"Sometimes becoming a fallen woman isn't as easy as it sounds. Oh! My!"
—Kasey Michaels, *New York Times* bestselling author

"Her appealing characters, sexual tension, and charming story will enchant readers."
—*Romantic Times*

EVERY TIME WE KISS

GUILT KEPT THEM APART . . .

It's been five years since Lady Jennette Selby's fiancé died. Each courting season since has been filled with suitors eager to win her affection. But Jennette's guilt has prompted her to swear off marriage. For her secrets are as dark as she is beautiful, and the accidental death of her fiancé was tainted by a forbidden attraction . . .

PASSION BROUGHT THEM TOGETHER . . .

Matthew Harris, the new earl of Blackburn, has been scorned by the *ton* for unintentionally killing Lady Jennette's fiancé. Forced to sell his estates and abandon his tenants if he does not marry a wealthy, respectable woman, Matthew turns to Lady Jennette to help him find a suitable wife. But sharing such close quarters only re-ignites an all-consuming desire neither can resist—even as every shadow of the past threatens to tear them apart . . .

"Rollicking, sexy . . . you'll enjoy this one!"
—Kat Martin

"Kelley knows how to bring a great depth of emotion into a romance."
—*Romantic Times*

"With *Every Time We Kiss*, Christie Kelley has penned an original and enjoyable Regency romance between two complicated, passionate characters."
—*Romance Junkies*

SOMETHING SCANDALOUS

HER SHOCKING PAST . . .

Raised as the youngest daughter of the Duke of Kendal, Elizabeth learns a devastating truth on his deathbed: he wasn't her father at all. And because the Duke had no sons, his title and fortune must go to his only male heir: a distant cousin who left England for America long ago. Anticipating the man's imminent occupation of her home, Elizabeth anxiously searches for her mother's diary, and the secret of her paternity . . .

HER UNEXPECTED FUTURE . . .

Arriving in London with his seven siblings, William Atherton intends to sell everything and return to his beloved Virginia farm, and his fiancée, as quickly as possible. But as Elizabeth shows William an England he never knew, and graciously introduces his siblings to London society, it becomes clear the two are meant for each other. Soon, Elizabeth finds herself determined to seduce the man who can save not only her family name but her heart . . .

Christie Kelley was born and raised in upstate New York. After seventeen years working for financial institutions in software development, she started writing her first book. She currently writes regency historicals for Zebra. Christie now lives in Maryland with her husband and two sons. Come visit her on the web at www.christiekelley.com.